Kingdoms Fall

The Cerulean Queendom

Tegan Abbott

Kingdoms Fall
The Cerulean Queendom
Copyright © 2023 by Tegan Abbott
ISBN: 978-0-6457635-1-5

For Jonathan.

CONTENTS

Life is a permanent cycle of ruin and rebirth.

CHAPTER 1

UNEQUAL EXCHANGE

Syriel

Syriel had chosen a simple purple dress that was far more comfortable than any She'ehlarah fashion.

"You don't think it's too simple, do you?" she asked her husband.

"No," Tenro replied with a smile. "You look like my beautiful foreign queen."

"But should I look foreign?" she asked.

"I think you should look like yourself above all else. I also think that you should spend less time worrying about insulting our culture and keep hold of your own," he said.

Syriel smiled. She couldn't convey her feelings about her connection to her culture to him precisely, so she knew better than to try. It was complicated at best. She did love her culture, but often it was as strange to her as his culture.

"Besides, our parents' agreement for us to wed was as much about us learning about each other's colonies," Tenro said.

Syriel nodded, although she thought she might have been the worst choice in that case.

"I'm ready," she said.

"Don't be nervous. I'll do most of the talking if you want," Tenro said.

"Thank you," Syriel said, taking his hand.

Tenro nodded and then led her out of their room to the council meeting chamber. It was a short walk, but even with Tenro's hand in hers, Syriel worried. Her thoughts circled about how she wasn't a shining example of a Yurelle, but an outcast.

Tenro entered the open door, and the guard on the other side closed it behind them. Six She'ehlarah stood within the room, their quiet chatter silenced in a moment. They all bowed when their king and queen were present.

"You're all early," Tenro said.

"We were most excited to meet our first ruling queen. I am Natai, advocate for the people," a dignified but simply dressed female said.

Her aesthetic immediately comforted Syriel about her clothing choice, but there was something incredibly comforting about her in general. Syriel nodded as Natai and each of the other council members introduced themselves.

"Good morning. I am Shara, High Priest. It is an extraordinary pleasure," Shara said.

She wore simple clothing, typical of priests. She too had a comforting presence. She looked older than the others in the room; Syriel presumed she was 7 or 8 seasons. Her shoulders sunk from the weight of age, but only slightly; most people of her age carried themselves a lot worse than her.

"I am Craime, the economist," said a middle-aged male who wore the finest clothing in the room. Syriel was curious about this; she'd have thought someone in his position would want to dress more simply.

"I am Alina, the archivist. I work with Aspects and the great plant," another woman said. She spoke slowly and looked at Syriel, unblinking. Syriel's first thought was that she was worried that Syriel didn't appreciate the great plant.

"If you wouldn't mind, I'd like to ask you about the Aspects a bit later, if that's all right," Syriel said.

When Syriel said this, the mood in the room changed instantly. Syriel glanced at Tenro, who smiled at her. There was silence for a moment. When the shock settled, Alina spoke again.

"It would be my honour to answer your questions," Alina said.

"To all within this room, I am Hye, the spy master of the She'ehlarah," Hye said. He dressed simply and stood out in the room of significant She'ehlarah. It was likely the only room where he would stand out.

"Shall we be seated, then?" Tenro asked.

The council said or nodded their agreement as Tenro guided Syriel to a seat at the head of the table that he pulled out for her. She sat, and he then sat in the chair beside her. When they were both seated, the council too seated themselves.

"First of all, I'd like to speak on behalf of the people of the She'ehlarah and share their delight, but also, their concern about our first ruling queen—but also for the only foreign monarch in any realm, ever. It's as intriguing as it is concerning, since this is entirely new territory," Natai said.

"I can sympathise on all points I am as concerned about the change in history for the arrangement that was made when I ..." Syriel wanted to say Zona's name, but she felt that same guilt from before.

It was probable that his death was because of their marriage, and if she had married him when she was supposed to, he might be alive today.

"I think these are important things to say, as we create history. Caution should be advised in the first choices, that's true. But we shouldn't hold our king and queen accountable for the plans of King Amer and Grand Chancellor Olianna," Hye said.

"Thank you, Hye. Becoming king and getting married was never a path I imagined for myself, especially given who I lost to be here. We will do the best we can to honour my uncle's ruling," Tenro said.

Syriel reached for Tenro's hand under the table to find his hand waiting for hers. This pleasantly surprised her, and she let slip an accidental smile.

"I'd like to focus on what we can specifically do for the kingdom," Tenro said.

With Hye's help, Tenro had taken control of the room in an instant. She'd seen her mother turn the conversation in a room, but with so many people in the Senate, it wasn't possible to do what Tenro just had. She now understood what was said about the power of a king. It was an incredible moment to realise she had that same power, though still limited by social hang-ups.

"Aspect Sirathen has died," Alina said.

"That's disturbing," Tenro said.

Syriel furrowed her brow. When she did, Tenro leaned in to her.

"He's too young, so something must have gone wrong," Tenro said.

"Any known reason why?" Hye said.

"None; there was nothing wrong with the soil or water. He wasn't old enough to die. We asked Cthessa, but none of her Aspects answered us clearly, so she likely doesn't know. We're going to keep looking into it," Alina said.

"Thank you. Please tell me the moment you find anything," Tenro said.

Alina nodded. "Yes, sire."

"It was a good year of trade until we reduced trade with the Iewen. We haven't spent much on the Eclosure, and I would recommend spending more on the celebration. With losing our prince, it was a hard year, not just for us in the castle, but for the people too," Craime said.

"Thank you, Craime, it's easy to forget that we suffer together. I think that's a fantastic idea. How much were you thinking?" Tenro asked.

Syriel listened to the meeting with great care. She wasn't confident enough to speak on a topic. She also wanted to let her presence become less confronting first.

She liked the way the direct and assertive way the She'ehlarah spoke in the council room. Senators had to mind their public image far more carefully; it became a whole different game. The power each of these council members had was based on their skill, not their seat. And they had no games to play, no front to keep. They simply held their own responsibly and spoke openly on topic.

Fiare

A well-dressed elegant purple-haired beauty sat at her desk, dutifully reading reports. Her skin was adorned with purple swirls and dots that showed that she was a descendant of house Dairsen. It wasn't only her markings that showed her legacy. She wore the finest silk of the She'ehlarah, and even seated, she showed the incredible confidence of a princess.

A knock at the door of her study interrupted her morning reading.

She heard the voice of her father on the other side of the door. "Fiare, do you have a moment?"

"Always, Father," she said warmly.

The door opened and she smiled welcomingly and placed her report and quill down to give her father her full attention. With sunken shoulders and a sleepless face, he looked burdened.

"Father, are you unwell?" Fiare asked, standing.

"No," Amer said, gesturing for her to be seated.

She did as she was suggested to do as he took a seat.

"It is the responsibility of a king and a father to do what is right for his kingdom before his children, but I have always tried to do both," Amer said.

"Father, just tell me," Fiare said gently, her face crinkling with concern ever so slightly.

"King Methis asked for a child agreement with you," Amer said, shifting in his chair. "I declined it, as we know he murdered your brother. I had to be careful and give him a good reason. I asked Grand Chancellor Olianna for you to be placed in Malarmha, and she accepted."

Fiare's mouth opened as she stared at her father in disbelief. He'd always done everything he could to protect her and the kingdom. She felt the burden of such a choice on her heart the moment she heard it, but she also understood and nodded.

Amer stared at her in silence for a time. He was pale; the guilt was thick between them in the air and curled her antennae.

She always tried to be composed and appropriate, but after losing her brother, the memory was too recent. She felt tears streak down her cheeks, but she still smiled through the pain.

"Thank you, Father," she said in almost a whisper.

"I'm so sorry, Fiare," Amer said. He stood, closed the distance between them and hugged her where she sat.

"It was the best choice," she said over his shoulder.

Losing her brother had weakened her, but moving away from her family would break her entirely. She was a Dairsen, and she would do what was needed of her, like a true She'ehlarah royal.

"The last thing I want is you distant from me," Amer said, stepping back.

"I know," she said gently.

She wiped the tears from her face and looked at her father with the great respect that he was due to him. He had always served his kingdom. Despite her devotion, she had been a problem for him her whole life, as princesses should be promised.

"Females can rule in Malarmha. Perhaps I can fulfil our legacy after all," she said.

"The clean god has been cruel to you," Amer said.

"But at least the wild god is kind, thank you for telling me yourself. I should start packing. What should I leave behind?" Fiare said, standing.

"You should have left right after the wedding, but I couldn't ask you then," Amer said.

"Well," Fiare said, looking at the door.

Amer nodded and seemed to understand what she was asking, and he thus obliged her and left.

Fiare waited a moment and then again sat in her study chair. She put her hand to her mouth and tried to keep from screaming aloud. Tears pushed out of her eyes too fast for her to wipe them from her face.

She had to be strong. She'ehlarah princesses were otherworldly strong.

Remin

A whole day of work the day before had resulted in Remin planning out the area of his home. He stood in the middle of a single layer of mud bricks, then looked to what he hoped would be enough mud bricks to complete his new home.

It was so much darker here than at the top of the tree. It wasn't the distance that stopped the light, though; it was the branches above. But most of all, it was the tree they'd been exiled from. Living in the shadow of the great tree wasn't a metaphor; it was a truth of Remin's new reality. It was cruel and left him feeling a deep bitterness.

When the strained rays of light gently touched the rainforest floor, Remin got to work. He applied a thick layer of mud to the layer of bricks he'd already placed and then layered dry bricks atop it. Around and around he went. He kept his hands working and focused his mind on his task as he worked. If he couldn't think, the rot of his new reality couldn't wound him.

After a while, the bricks were too tall for him to place, so he piled some other bricks to stand on as he continued. His small house was completely surrounded before sunset. He stopped the exhausting labour to look at his work.

For the last level, he used some sticks and branches to hold the thatch roof. He'd secure the branches with another layer of mud later; for now, he had walls and a roof. It was poorly built, even looking at the houses around his. But it was his.

"You'll have to finish it later by painting the walls with mud again. And finish the roof," Gerathen said.

Remin turned to see the stranger who'd helped him build the house standing behind him.

"Tonight, I sleep in my own home," Remin announced proudly.

"A house you built alone," Gerathen said.

Remin nodded and smiled at Gerathen for a time. Gerathen's smile echoed his own. He was an exile, too, and he knew what it felt like to build his own house.

"Thank you for your help. I would have had no idea how to build a home without you," Remin said.

"That's why it's part of our law that someone has to help. We all come from different legacies. And no one in Daltay builds like this. No one is born up there knowing how to do this." Gerathen motioned around him as he said this. "You should be really proud. You're an outlier now, like the rest of us," Gerathen added.

Remin looked at Gerathen directly. With the king's blood in his veins, it seemed so strange to be called such. It was like a dream. At first it had been a nightmare, but now his whole life was a passing thought: what if he wasn't a king? Remin found that he didn't hate the answer. He didn't like it, but at least he didn't have to exile anyone anymore.

"It's getting late. No doubt you want to rest," Gerathen said.

Remin nodded.

"I'm exhausted," he confessed.

"Rest well earned," Gerathen said, tapping Remin gently on the shoulder.

Remin looked back at his house.

"Now you get to sit in your home and imagine how to improve it. And who you want to visit you," Gerathen said.

Remin smiled. He thought about the only visitor he wanted. Kyra had to have been murdered by Methis, or maybe she died when they murdered him. Remin shook the thoughts from his tired mind.

"Thank you again. I'll repay this to you and the next person who…" His words trailed off when he realised he was waiting for the next exile.

Gerathen nodded and mercifully walked off without replying. Thoughts were tricky. Remin would just have to keep busy. Always.

Kyra

Kyra stared uncomfortably at a small plant in the corner of the room. The petals of the bloom were opening. It was a simple pink flower, the tiny petals curling more and more each day. Every reference to the passage of time was an inescapably horrible reminder of her future. It was the lack thereof that was most terrifying.

"Kyra, are you listening?"

Kyra looked up at her tutor. She blinked a few times and then, knowing the lesson from listening before, she looked at the words on the wall behind her tutor. She saw enough to realise the topic hadn't changed. She'd noticed that usually, most of her theoretical tutors couldn't easily trip her up.

"We're still don't entirely know our origin, though the ancient Feularah narrowed it down to a winged subclass of insect *pterygota*. Although not all in this subclass can fly, we ... most of us clearly can," Kyra said confidently.

Her tutor widened his eyes and nodded. "Good," he said, uncrossing his arms. "What are some of the commonalities between us and such a creature?"

"Wings ..." Kyra began.

A knock on the door interrupted them. Kyra breathed a sigh, as time had saved her from her inattentiveness. Her tutor looked behind him to the plant that turned slowly each day.

"Looks like it's time to end our lesson," he said, bringing his hands silently together in front of him. "Good work today, Highness."

Kyra nodded and gathered her books into a small bag. She did appreciate her lessons, but all of it was a calculated set-up for a future she would never survive long enough to see.

"Thank you," she replied.

"Enjoy your day, Highness," he said, as he cleaned his marks from the wall.

The door opened, and Kyra looked upon the familiar discomfort of Vujet's face. He said nothing as Kyra stood and left the room. He strapped a custom-made harness to her and tied it properly.

Silent still, he then lifted off the platform. Kyra clutched her bookbag. After all the time the guard captain had been improperly designated to fly her around, she'd never gotten accustomed to the movement. Even now, she felt nauseous whenever he turned abruptly. She noted, however, that he had sensed this and tried to fly as straight as possible.

The internal view of Daltay was genuinely beautiful. Kyra didn't see much of it, as all of her classes were close to her room. She was confident that if her room was bigger, her classes would be held there, but then Methis couldn't force her to be close to the guard who'd murdered her father. She was confident Methis very much enjoyed having the two together. It was another torment. Another use of his power over her.

Kyra hated Vujet. Not because he had murdered her father, but because it had been on Methis's discovery. She couldn't find a way to learn how the Iewen felt about him. Methis had made sure she knew that her father had been unpopular for all of the opposite reasons, so the Iewen must have loved him. Vujet wasn't just a bitter reminder of Methis' power (and of the absence of her father), but most of all, he reminded her that she was soon to meet the same fate.

As she neared her home, she thought that it was an especially keen cruelty to give him to her as her only friend. If this hadn't been the case, she thought she might quite appreciate him. Despite the cruelty of his presence and all it represented; she still would have much liked to invite him in. Everyone called her "Highness", but no one treated her as he did. He was unyielding, but somehow there was support for her that she didn't get from any other Iewen.

The duo landed on the platform in front of her room. Vujet started untying her, and a sudden horrific realisation dawned on her so abruptly that she felt herself panic.

"Stay calm," he said.

"I'm going to be killed," she said, almost in a whisper.

"No. You are the blood of Amaranthus," he replied as he worked the knot free and lifted the straps.

She moved away.

"Let us talk inside," he said.

"No," she said.

"If you know, I know, and soon he will too," he said.

"What do you know?" Kyra said, her voice shaking as she stepped back from him.

Vujet's face darkened as he lowered his head.

"How?" she said.

"I felt it," he said as he lifted his head again. "This needs to be spoken, planned."

"I can't if he knows…"

"He knows it's time. Only I know right now, so let's talk," he said, his hands lowered as he walked toward her.

"Are you threatening me?" Kyra asked, clasping her balled hands at her throat.

"Of course not," he said, stopping in his tracks. "I serve the kingdom first and foremost."

"Methis is the kingdom," Kyra said, narrowing her eyes.

"You are the kingdom, Highness," he promised.

"What do I do?" she asked.

"You can't run. There's nowhere he won't find you."

"Why was that your first suggestion?" she asked, looking away from him.

"Because it would be your first choice … but you won't make it out of Daltay."

"Instead of saying what I can't do, how about what I can?" she said, pulling her shoulders in tighter.

"He will discover the truth no matter what. We could find a way to tell him that you have romantic feelings for me, and that I return those feelings," Vujet said.

His words made her shiver. Kyra looked at him directly, and she knew her shock was plain in her face. She knew her own feelings, and that he sensed them, but not that he returned those feelings. She'd been too horrified and terrified by her realisation of both her maturity and affection for Methis's pet.

Kyra shook her head, not only to deny his suggestion, but also to deny feelings that would no doubt get her exiled and murdered, just like her beloved farther.

"The most likely and worst outcome is my murder and your further subjugation. If we tell him directly, he may have mercy," Vujet said.

Kyra looked at him, shocked. She was horrified in that moment that she hadn't worried about his life in all of this. In all of her planning about her dark future, she'd never imagined that Vujet cared for her. In a moment, she saw the most practical difference between the legacy of a warrior and a queen.

It wasn't comfortable, but the preservation of the royal line was important. Vujet was born to serve and even perhaps die defending that bloodline. She hated reality in that moment more than any other, because she so greatly wished she had the heart to risk herself for another. Then she had another horrible realisation: this was exactly what her father had done, and she was not capable of doing the same.

"We have to run," she said.

"You know we can't," he replied.

"A life of risk is better than certain death. Methis hasn't visited or summoned me for weeks. He won't call on me for a little bit longer. He thinks me weak, so he could easily think my maturity is stunted. We have time to plan," she said, opening her hands to rub them and keep them from shaking.

She looked up at the silent guard captain, who reluctantly nodded. The corners of her mouth curved almost imperceptibly.

"What do we do first?" she said.

Vujet gestured to the front door of her home. The young princess nodded and entered her home, like she realised she should have on his initial suggestion.

Reia

Dressed in simple clothing, carrying a large bag filled with lumpy fibre of in front of her, Reia looked like a farmer, like someone that no Iewen would look twice at. Which is how she'd gotten to her childhood home unnoticed. She opened the door with a rising feeling of delight. She missed her daughter sorely.

The house was brightly lit from the side of the tree and the numerous lights within. Her daughter loved the glow.

Her delight was shattered in the moment she opened the door, however. The house smelled like something that Reia knew well. She dropped her bundle and rushed to the body that lie on the floor. In one look she knew her aunt was long dead, for days at least.

She stood immediately in silence and made her way to Verina's room. It was empty, as she expected. She searched the rest of the house to ensure that she was alone. Neither her daughter or her aunt's killer were present.

She checked through her daughter's room to see if they'd taken anything else. She saw nothing missing. She looked the house over and saw no footprints.

When she'd seen the aftermath of other attacks, there were almost always footprints, but here, the blood around her aunt was undisturbed. It took skill to leave no footprints. She crouched beside the body and inspected the fatal wound. She'd been stabbed in the back, a single well-struck blow. Reia turned the body over to see usual mess that accompanies death, but most importantly, that there was a wound in the front of the body.

The attacker had been strong, precise, and clean. It was likely done by a professional such as herself, just as she'd left no marks when she'd killed the Yurelle princess's lover. She sat back against the wall on a section of floor not covered in blood. The stench of rot and thick blood hung in the air around her.

She let the grotesque scene and stench of her murdered family fuel her resolve. Most likely this was an intentional message from someone obsessed with power, someone who excelled at dramatics and child-stealing.

If Methis expected her to beg him, he'd never been more wrong about her. She loved her daughter deeply, but her absence didn't mean she was alive. He could have killed her elsewhere to motivate her. If she was alive, Reia refused to let Methis make her the tool of his malice and manipulation.

This moment would be Methis's downfall.

Unfortunately for the spy king, there was another option. A better option.

Guiyn

Guiyn waited in his brother Laur's study early in the morning. Laur trained every morning, which provided Guiyn the opportunity to sneak in effortlessly and go through his brother's papers. This morning, however, he had a motive other than snooping. On this morning, Guiyn stood behind the door and waited patiently.

When Laur finally entered his study, he closed the door behind him as he always did. And as he did so, he revealed Guiyn.

"Get out, Guiyn," he snarled.

"We're overdue for a discussion, brother," Guiyn said, his tone calm.

"I know why you're here. Get out," Laur snapped.

"Just tell me why you didn't stick to the plan and I'll leave," Guiyn said.

"There was no plan. You simply threatened me and left," Laur said.

"I assume you have a better plan, then?" Guiyn asked.

"I do, in fact. They have no child yet, so we have time. Let the kingdom see how much they hate having a foreign queen first," Laur said.

Guiyn was shocked. His brother had a plan, and it was rather cunning. Cunning was Guiyn's speciality. His brother was usually dull, stupid, and impatient. It almost seemed out of character for him to be so clever, and it was certainly unusual for him to wait to act.

Guiyn stood in silence for a time, eyeing his brother. He then sat on the close side of his brother's desk. Laur sighed as he walked around the desk. Guiyn watched him curiously.

"You're impressed," Laur said, smiling.

"Concerned," Guiyn said, his voice quiet.

Laur sat straight-backed in his chair, narrowed his eyes, and remained silent.

"Can you guess why, brother?" Guiyn asked.

Laur remained silent.

"You'll see how much I believe in the right of succession, brother. Leave my study," Laur said.

Guiyn remained seated. "I hope you have a backup plan, for if they love her, brother..." Guiyn said, finally standing.

"They can't love a foreigner," Laur snapped.

"Ptrey were born serving queens," Guiyn said as he left his brother's study.

Reia

It was late at night when the guard at Kyra's door changed. They gathered at the front of her house. After a soft king and now a spy king, it was unsurprising that a new generation of guards were so easily distracted. As they talked, Reia flew into a back window of the apartment.

She walked across the fungus floor in almost perfect silence. She listened for breathing but heard nothing; the princess must be a light sleeper. Interesting. She slowly opened a door and looked into a room with the shadow of a desk and chair. A study. She heard the sound of footsteps and turned abruptly.

In the darkness, she saw the outline of a tiny wingless form.

"Princess, I have come to your aid," Reia said, touching one knee to the ground with the other facing her princess. She leaned on her upright knee as she bowed.

"Who are you?" Kyra whispered.

"Reia, your spymaster, Highness," she said.

"Methis's spymaster," Kyra snapped.

"No, princess. I am yours," Reia said, her voice edged. She met the eye of her liege when she spoke. "Methis is no king to me, nor to our kingdom. He doesn't serve our kingdom, he weakens it."

Kyra sat on the floor both knees against the ground. "What can you do for me?" she whispered.

"I can help you dethrone the pretender," Reia said.

"Why?" Kyra asked.

"Because he is not my king," Reia said.

"Methis is cunning. Can you prove it?" Kyra asked.

Reia smiled. She'd met Kyra's father when she served her spymaster. He was trusting and soft. His daughter was nothing like him. It angered Reia that it took Methis to steal her child before she came to meet Kyra herself. She should have come sooner.

"I can, Highness," Reia said, her voice confident. "I will prove it time and again until my death. I have never failed my kingdom."

"Will you tell me what you've never failed with?" Kyra asked.

"I tell you everything I have done for this kingdom, and anything you need to know about Methis, the council, and your kingdom," Reia said.

Reia had lied, though. But she'd made a promise to herself: she'd only lie once. And only about one truth. She'd never tell her princess that it was she who discovered Farin's secret. His little hidden Kyra.

Kyra nodded. She took a deep breath and remained silent for a time. Reia stayed silent too, although she was concerned that the princess wouldn't accept her help. Because she needed it.

"How often can you visit me?" Kyra asked.

"You come back to your apartment for midday meal every day. I can come to you while you eat, if you permit me," Reia said.

"You can do so unseen every day?" Kyra asked.

"I can do so easily," Reia said.

Kyra was quiet for another minute. Reia felt what could have been a hint of interest in the air between them. Perhaps Kyra was even impressed at her work.

"Start from the beginning, if you would," Kyra said.

Reia nodded and took in the moment for a brief second. It felt good for her skills to be wanted. Methis had never wanted her advice; she'd had to push it on him. Kyra actually listened. What she chose to do with Reia's expertise remained to be seen.

Fiare

Fiare looked at her bare room in silence. She hadn't told anyone she was leaving. She'd wanted to pack everything first. She wanted to step onto the back of a hawk the moment after she'd told them. She understood completely why her father had waited so long to tell her.

She'd worn her simplest dress, but even still, she thought she looked like an overly adorned mess compared to the Yurelle. She'd only seen their clothing in pictures until the Grand Chancellor and her husband had walked into Velwrith. She was going to stand out, no matter what she wore.

She looked over at the chemically created glass tiara she'd grown up wearing. A princess's tiara was small and unadorned. Even as the first child of the king, her crown looked like a piece of jewellery rather than a symbol of her heritage. She picked it up.

A part of her wanted to break it. Like her whole life, it was fragile. It was everything she'd known. Knowing her place, taking her lessons, dressing properly, acting appropriately, all of her efforts felt like they'd been twisted against her. She'd never acted poor in her life. The reward for her unwavering servitude was just as that of the fanatic prince: exile.

She placed the tiara on the pillow where she kept it. It was the only thing left in her room. A room she would never, could never return to. Not while her suitor, the murderer of her brother and destroyer of her father's lineage, sat on the Iewen throne. She would watch her legacy bleed from Malarmha.

She made a promise to herself through all of this that she would be proud of it all. She'd not lose her composure and give insult to her whole life. She would joyfully leave everything she knew behind and begin a new life with strangers. Although she was confident, she'd cry at saying goodbye to her family, and she'd enter Malarmha with a smile on her face.

She left her room to see her cousin Tenro, with her father's crown on his purple head. There were few whom she adored more than him, so she was grateful that he wore it, despite the horrible reason why. He was impeccably dressed, as usual, his new bride standing beside him.

The couple were questioning a guard. The guard was holding Fiare's bags.

"Cousin!" Tenro said.

"Hello, sire," Fiare said, bowing her head.

"Don't do that, please," Tenro pleaded. "What is happening here, are you changing rooms?"

Fiare shook her head.

"Since it's always empty and a favoured place of Syriel, can we talk in the old library?" Fiare asked.

Tenro and Syriel both furrowed their brows, Syriel sensing the confusion in the air. Tenro nodded.

"Anywhere you want," he said, his tone echoing the confusion in the air.

Fiare then began walking to the library with Tenro and Syriel's footfalls echoing on the stones behind her. She thought about the words she could use to explain but all she could think to say was sorry. None of it was her choice, but she knew how much it would hurt them both. And she knew how much it would hurt to say.

She was Tenro's closest friend now that Zona was gone, and although she barely knew Syriel, she knew herself to be one of her only friends in the castle. They needed her. Fiare was confident they also knew how much they needed her.

The library smelt of history in the form of old pages and leather. She ran her hand over the smooth shelves and took in everything around her. She'd played here as a child and taken lessons when she was little. It seemed so strange now, that she'd seldom come here as an adult. Despite this, she would miss it sorely. At least Syriel would continue to enjoy such a treasured place.

"Are there libraries in Malarmha?" Fiare asked, looking directly at Syriel.

Syriel nodded as she looked at Tenro for guidance. When he offered no explanation, she faced Fiare again.

"There are a few, but none so grand or old as this, of course," Syriel said.

"Can anyone enter them?" Fiare asked.

"No. It's not open to anyone in the castle like this. Malarmha is a lot more open and larger, so there aren't guards on every corner.

Things of great value are closed behind guarded doors," Syriel said, her brow still furrowed.

"Why are you asking this, cousin?" Tenro asked.

Fiare felt the curiosity leave her face. She felt her features tighten, but she straightened her back, took a deep breath, and smiled at Tenro and Syriel.

"Because I am going to study there," she said, deceptively. "Father asked your mother if she would teach me her craft."

Syriel and Tenro's faces mirrored each other's confusion as they glanced at each other. They didn't need to, however, as their confusion was thick in the air.

"Malarmha isn't safe," Syriel said.

"I know," Fiare said quickly but gently, smiling appreciatively as she did.

"Olianna is a master of her craft, to be sure, but we have many incredible teachers here," Tenro said.

Fiare didn't want to tell them everything, but it seemed she'd have to. She took a moment to phrase her words carefully, so as not to make them worry. She wasn't exactly worried about how they felt, but more about how they would react. As king, Tenro could override what her father had decided, and she knew as well as Amer that this was their best choice.

"Father made an agreement with the Grand Chancellor because Methis made … an offer for me."

"What sort of offer?" Tenro asked as he furrowed his brow, his face darkening.

"He wanted me to be promised to him."

"You can't be serious?" Syriel said, her voice sharp as her face crinkled into a scowl.

Fiare was incredibly surprised by this reaction. She'd never known royalty to be so expressive and open. Malarmha must have been a very different place.

Tenro put his hand on Syriel's shoulder. "It is a clever move from him, unsurprisingly... and just as clever of a choice on your father's part," he said, smiling gently at her. Tenro was always as he should be; he was appropriate, gentle, patient, and clever. He was born and trained to be a king.

Fiare frowned sympathetically at Syriel. Fiare was mad too at first, but there was no point in being mad. It was wasted energy, and she needed to keep her head now most of all.

"It might not be my choice, but perhaps it's the best thing for me," she said.

"I think the Grand Chancellor might appreciate the company, too. What do you think, Syriel?" Tenro asked.

Syriel's face was still twisted. It was as obvious on her face as it was in the air. Fiare was quite confident that Tenro wanted her to voice her opinion so he could voice his, explain why they were both so calm. Tenro faced Syriel with a soft posture. He seemed to have been expecting this response from her.

"You can't both be serious, surely," Syriel said through gritted teeth.

It was obvious now that Yurelle passion was something Fiare was going to have to learn about and get accustomed to quickly. It was so utterly foreign she could hardly understand it.

"We don't always get the best choices. We can only choose the best options from what is provided," Tenro said.

"I could be mad. I was at first. Holding resentment and pain in your heart is like grabbing onto a poisoned frog; it would only hurt me, and I don't want to extend my displeasure. Most of all, I want Methis to have as little power over me as possible," Fiare said.

"I can't believe this, or how calm you both are. I clearly don't understand the She'ehlarah at all," Syriel said, turning to leave.

"Nor I the Yurelle. Can you teach me a few things?" Fiare asked as she stepped toward the door.

Syriel turned. Her posture relaxed.

"I don't understand what you're saying when the Yurelle, Iewen, and She'ehlarah are all defined by the hatred we have for each other," Syriel said in an intense tone.

Fiare looked at her curiously in that moment. It seemed Syriel was so furious, she had actually tired herself out nearly instantly.

"Hating another colony is different. It's almost like an ancient curse handed down from parent to child," Tenro said.

Syriel nodded. Syriel had to have known this. Faire thought Tenro was saying it to remind her how different it was from Yurelle passion.

"We so often are our history," Syriel said, her tone frustrated.

"What is it like in Malarmha?" Fiare asked.

It took a moment, but after Fiare had asked her about her home, the tension in her face relaxed.

"Incredible. I'm dreading the bloom here, as in Malarmha it's not just a season. It's hard to explain… but it's like a torrent of fresh air that sweeps the city like a spell. The bright colours of the city are somehow even brighter, and there is so much joy you think your heart can't take it, but it doesn't burst. It's filled in ways you never knew you were empty. We are passionate, we are consumed by what happens to us, in everything bad, but also everything good."

"I've heard you hug a lot," Fiare said.

Syriel nodded, walked back toward her, and put her arms around her.

"It probably feels strange at first, but you'll get used to it," Syriel said quietly.

"I've never liked it here," Fiare whispered back.

Syriel stepped back from their hug. Fiare felt Syriel's shock in the air. "It's complicated for me," Fiare said.

Fiare looked back to see Tenro standing patiently. "Thank you, Syriel," Tenro said.

"You will be happy there. It's often a hard place to live, and unsafe. But it's an incredible place," Syriel said.

The way Syriel spoke of her home sounded like she was homesick. Perhaps the two of them were even more similar than Fiare realised. Both expected to leave home without looking back.

"I should leave. I've packed everything, and this was the last thing I had to do," Fiare said.

"Already?" Tenro asked, shocked.

"Father told Methis the arrangements had already been made, but he couldn't bring himself to tell me until now," Fiare explained.

"How do your sisters feel?" Tenro said.

"I don't know. I guess I'll find that out in a moment. Father told them for me. Will you both walk me to the hawk port?" Fiare asked evasively, avoiding speaking on a subject that would upset her. She didn't want to fill her mind with sadness if she could help it. Syriel and Tenro both nodded.

"I love this archive," Fiare said. "I'm going to miss it a lot."

"My mother will show you a few places that you'll love. Ask her about the reading. I spent a lot of time there as a child instead of at my lessons," Syriel said.

"Thank you," Fiare said appreciatively. After a deep breath, she then gestured to the door. Syriel and Tenro nodded as they followed her from the archive. The short walk to the hawk port was quiet. Fiare could feel Syriel trying to calm herself.

Fiare's connection to Syriel was one of the reasons she was able to be so calm about going to Malarmha. As she realised it, they had taken the steps to the rooftop hawk port already, and Fiare turned around to say it.

"Fiare!" The voice of her mother called.

With a sigh, Fiare turned to face the hardest hurdle of leaving the city. Her mother, father, and two sisters were standing on the edge of the port. She could see tears in her mother's eyes and great fatigue in her posture. She'd lost a son, and now she had to lose a daughter. Fiare couldn't imagine how she was still standing. She wasn't dying, though, she reminded herself.

Little Maia was just about to celebrate her second season, and Alura her first. Alura was already walking, they'd grown so much, but they still looked so small. After the loss of their big brother, they'd need their big sister, especially with Maia about to come of age.

Fiare couldn't be there for them, and that was more heartbreaking than she could handle. She thought about the celebration of the bloom in Malarmha, as Syriel had described, and focused her thoughts on it.

She went straight to hug her mother as both of her sisters joined in the embrace, with her father's arms joining a moment later.

"Follow the Grand Chancellor's instructions carefully. Malarmha isn't safe," Mayala said.

"I know, Mother. I'll be careful and diligent," Fiare said, stepping out of their embrace. "I'll be just fine."

"Even still, listen to everything she says," Mayala repeated.

Fiare nodded, her eyes turning gently towards her mother. After everything she'd been through, she hadn't lost herself or her love for her daughters. Fiare was so lucky to have such a dedicated and loving mother.

"You'll do well there, Fiare. You always were the finest example of a She'ehlarah princess," Amer said.

His comment meant the world to her, and he knew why. She then looked down at her sisters who both just cried up at her. Fiare crouched down and hugged them again.

"Be good, little ones," she said gently.

"When will you come back?" Maia asked.

"I'll write to you. The moment I know, so will you," Fiare said, kissing her little sister on the head.

She stood and looked at her family one final time.

"I love you all so much, I feel I'm taking you with me," Fiare lied.

"Go on, then," Amer said, as stoic as ever.

She waved to Tenro and Syriel and then boarded the hawk beside her guards. She waved as the bird shook a little and then took off.

Like most She'ehlarah royalty, Fiare had never left the castle. She'd never even seen the painted garden that she'd heard so much about. She'd always been told that Castle Velwrith was safety and everything else was uncertainty.

The uncertainty of the tangle below her didn't frighten her, however, but rather excited her. It was so lush and wild, with vines twisting around its massive trees. At one point, she saw a creature she'd only heard of, its scaled slender body coiled around a tree too close for comfort. But still, she wasn't scared.

The verdant landscape was far more beautiful than Cthessa's vines and flowers, even more awe-inspiring than any painting she'd seen. Her stomach dropped as the hawk dipped sharply.

She'd had her own guard in the castle. Her two Dragonriders were specially picked for her life in Malarmha. She looked them over as they bowed their heads to her.

"We wanted to introduce ourselves sooner, but we didn't want to interrupt your goodbyes at the port. I am Oryza," the male said.

"Sativa," the female said.

"Thank you for leaving Velwrith for me," Fiare said.

"It's an honour," Oryza said.

"Truly," Sativa said.

Fiare smiled. She was glad Amer had asked them on her behalf, because she could never ask someone to leave their home for her.

She turned her attention back to her incredible surroundings, but the tangle was no longer below. She stared at the huge mushroom stalks that towered over the farmers below. Then her attention was drawn to a massive stone.

It was open at the top in sections, overgrown with moss and vines. She could see a tiny hint of the city within through those breaks in the great rock, and her excitement doubled. She never knew she could feel such excitement.

The hawks landed on a stony section of the forest floor. It was another place Fiare never imagined she'd be, not even in her most extreme dreams.

Sativa stepped off and turned to see if Fiare needed any help, but she climbed down the side without any problem.

"Welcome home, Princess Fiare," a familiar voice said.

Olianna herself had come to greet her. Fiare could hardly believe it. She hadn't even imagined she would take the time to do so; this was a favour, after all. For a moment, she couldn't find the words to express her surprise.

"Thank you," she said, bowing her head as she would to any queen. To her surprise, however, Olianna did the same.

"I've had a room prepared for you. I can only hope it's to your liking," Olianna said.

Fiare lifted her head as Olianna did too. Fiare couldn't think of a way to state her appreciation, so she just smiled and followed when Olianna turned.

"It was Syriel's old room. I'm certain she won't mind," Olianna said.

"Thank you," Fiare said.

Fiare then followed in silence, still in awe that the Grand Chancellor herself had braved the open city to collect her.

Chapter 2

The Celebration of Life

Remin

The sounds of incredible and curious music awoke him. It was a type of music he'd never heard before. He opened his heavy eyes and was greeted by a shocking sight. He was in a crude house, with leaves for a floor and mud for walls. The smell of earth and wetness was a more honest realisation of the crudeness of his house. That scent was stronger than the memory of building it.

When he smelt that foreign earthen smell, he instantly realised where he was. So much earth was only at the bottom of the tree. It was an overwhelming scent. The bitter moment of his exile consumed every corner of his mind, his daughter screaming and crying as she watched her father mutilated at what she thought was an execution.

He closed his eyes again, trying to take control of his thoughts. He couldn't change it, no matter how desperately he wanted to. And he couldn't find out what had happened to his daughter. He had to stop his thoughts from taunting and torturing him. Finally, he felt the thoughts recede, although the torment and agony of losing everything still remained.

He looked over to where his clothes hung. He only had one set of clothes, so making a place for them to hang had been rather simple. It was just sticks lashed together, dug into his earthen floor, but he'd seen the need for it and made it himself. That was his focus now: anytime he needed anything, he would make it. He took his clothes and dressed.

His home only had one room for now, but soon he hoped to see other houses and learn how to design them. He wanted to learn from the Therai how to make more complicated things. But for now, this hut that mostly blocked the cold night, where tiny bugs and fat drops of rain fell through the ceiling, was all his. He had a lot to appreciate, not to mention that he was alive to appreciate anything.

Ptery stayed in their cities because the world beyond them was deadly. So he was grateful that the bugs that fell through his roof were harmless. The fat water drops couldn't stop him from flying because he had no wings to wet and weight down. He could only hope a brutal murderous creature wouldn't fall through his makeshift roof. He'd heard stories of whole platoons being taken out by one hungry mantis. He then worried about his house flooding with water with him trapped inside. More thoughts to push out of his head.

Agitated he rushed his dressing. The clothing he had been given was crude, but he reminded himself over and over again that he was grateful for it all. Because he was alive to have it.

After a moment of calming himself, he then pushed aside the cloth door, that Gerathen had been kind enough to get for him. He'd weave his own cloth soon, that was another thing he was determined to learn for himself. Mentally, he put that on his list of things to look forward to. The list was short, but it was precious. And again and again, he was alive to write it.

On the other side of his makeshift door was a sound Remin had though he'd never hear again. He thought he'd imagined the music that flooded the muddy streets but outside his home he heard it clearly from outside the turmoil of his own head. He followed the feint sound of elation through the sprawl until he saw a small gathering of Ptery.

He stepped atop a small mound of drying mudbricks to see three musicians of a like he'd never know. They dressed brightly, of what looked like well-made fabric. played instruments of a like that Remin had never seen. They seemed quite well made everything about them conflicted with their surroundings.

They played string instruments that Remin couldn't identify, all with small square hollow bases covered in cloth. Connected to these were wooden struts with strings down the length of the instruments. There was no singer, like he preferred in the Daltay throne room, although every so often, one of them shouted a joyous sound or made an excited trill.

Through the crowd Remin saw Gerathen. Remin excitedly tried to draw his attention. Gerathen, however was too interested in the musicians. Remin couldn't blame him; they were incredible—and, no doubt, they were a rare sight.

"Remin."

Remin turned to see the face of the first Ptery he'd seen after exile. Tsune gestured for Remin to approach him. Remin closed the distance between them and greeted him with a nod, which Tsune returned.

"It's your first festival! I couldn't let you miss out," Tsune said.

"Miss out on what?" Remin asked.

"Seeing the city," Tsune answered.

When the older healer spoke, he turned and pushed gently through the yielding crowd. Remin followed, though with much less conviction. Ptery often appeared young until they died, even in their later seasons. Tsune, however, moved like a youth. He walked the city streets like he knew them well, despite the fact that Remin had exiled him soon before he himself was exiled. Tsune was a harsh comparison to Remin.

Remin had heard that not all of the exiled looked like mouldy masses of decay and rot, but even after such words, he still didn't know what to expect. Tsune guided him around the great tree for quite a long walk.

The buildings and even the road seemed to be better built the longer they walked. The muddy, mossy, leaf-covered ground became compacted earth. The buildings' rough mud brick walls were covered in a smooth material that Remin could only guess was some type of earth, while some houses were covered in different types of moss. Despite having built his own house, earth was still a foreign building material to Remin.

The She'ehlarah and Yurelle were builders, but the Iewen seldom built anything. Most of their houses were fungus disks that they farmed and then lived in. Despite the fungus disks having a hard outer shell, it seemed so utterly bizarre now. After having made his own bricks, Remin couldn't work out how the Iewen lived. The matter of the living hollow tree was another source of confusion altogether. The lush green leaves had always confused him. Perhaps the holy city was truly blessed by the perfect god, and he was now damned.

The scent of earth was always present as the duo walked, but the smell of rot and decay became less overwhelming. It was replaced with another organic smell Remin had barely smelt before. It was a similar fresh smell to the plants he'd kept in the king's room; but this was different, as the intensity of the smell redefined it entirely. It was just one more bizarre change between the great tree and the untamed rainforest below.

After quite a while, Remin thought he might be in a different city altogether. The ground was stone or at least very hard earth, and the buildings were painted! The smell of earth, plants, and life was incredible. It was the strongest perfume he'd ever smelled.

"It's so strange that the new sections of the settlement don't smell like this, like life, but like death instead," Remin remarked.

Tsune scoffed. "Life is consumption. The wild god's world is as much about death as the clean god's," he said.

All Ptery knew this, but Remin had never had reason to give it meaning in this context. It was a hard reality. Remin had always had trouble facing hard realities. His thoughts were ripped from this wonderful moment to Tsune's exile. He tried to control his thoughts, as he'd always been able to do so far. But then another thought invaded his calm: the memory of his screaming daughter and the indescribable pain in his back.

"Oh, they're getting started!" Tsune said.

Remin was beyond grateful for Tsune's words. He pushed down the feeling that he was about to vomit and forced his attention to an elevated forum a few centimetres above them.

The forum platform was made of what looked like wood and stone, adorned with masses of bright flowers and ribbons. The bloom in Daltay wasn't as bright and wondrous as this.

Seeing the Pterys' elation made sense to him in an instant. This was their afterlife, so they should all live it the best they can. It was the most honest celebration. With cheers and shouts surrounding him, he was enveloped by the overwhelming feeling of delight around him. He would keep this moment. This was his. Remin would always see his life here as an afterlife, and like the Ptery, he was determined to enjoy it.

"Welcome to Hald," Tsune said.

Remin could hardly believe what he was seeing. He was a poor judge of time, but it hadn't felt like they'd walked long enough to be standing in an entirely new city.

"Enjoy the Eclosure, Remin," Tsune said.

"Thank you," Remin turned to face his friend, but the healer was already leaving him.

Remin had thought they'd spend the day together, but Tsune was looking at a female yellow-haired Ptery who stared back at him. He couldn't blame him. It sickened Remin to think that he'd exiled Tsune, but he was grateful that he seemed happy here.

It was an entirely different city from where Remin lived. Here it was a celebration of colour and life. He expected the Eclosure, the hatching season, to be a gloomy affair. This was one of those moments he was immensely grateful to be wrong.

He had another vivid memory of the first time he saw his daughter, and felt the sheer delight and then torment of seeing her winglessness. It seemed cruel that every memory of his most precious connection was so tortured. He could only hope that the time he spent with her was enough to give her short life happiness.

That was all behind him. He had to stop thinking about his past. As everyone in exile had told him, the past was gone. He would take the present as it was intended: a gift. And he would enjoy the first Eclosure as a parent without a child. As horrible as that was, at least he had no secrets now. No one could take anything from him.

He breathed a deep sigh and looked over at a small cart beside him. It was filled with fruits that Remin couldn't identify. Jutting up from the cart were cut pieces of different fruit on wooden skewers. They looked so delicious that Remin's mouth watered at the sight of them.

"It's all free today," the vendor said, offering Remin some food on a stick.

Remin took it gratefully, his eyes wide. "Thank you!" he exclaimed loudly over the crowd.

He bit into the first piece and instantly tasted something he'd never known. It was very sweet, but a little tart. It was good, better food that he'd had in Daltay. Everything was going to be good from now on, he promised himself. He ventured forward into the festival grounds with growing joy in his broken heart.

Kyra

Reia reached Kyra's apartment at lunch time, as always, and entered with excitement. She nodded at Reia, who closed the window behind her as she entered.

"I have a few topics you might like for today," Reia whispered.

"I have a different idea," Kyra whispered back as the two walked across the small room to stand close together.

"Can you find a way to have this room better insulated against sound?" Kyra asked.

"I don't know if I could, but I could try to have this room made more comfortable," Reia said.

Kyra smiled.

"Another thing—do you have anything that would prevent conception?" Kyra asked, still whispering.

"I know of a safe oil, but I would advise my princess that if Methis caught you with it ..." Reia said, her words trailing off.

Kyra nodded. She knew it all.

"I know, just as meeting with you could be the end of us both," Kyra said.

"I can help you prevent your death by meeting you, and by getting you the oil. But again, princess, please, your life is the most valuable asset the kingdom has," Reia said.

Kyra nodded. She heard her spymaster's words loud and clear. But without Vujet, she would have died inside too many times over to be saved. She was most likely to die. She needed to keep whatever kept her alive for the longest time.

Syriel

Syriel stood in the king's chamber. She'd felt the presence of her husband behind her since their wedding. She'd been surprised how powerful his presence was to her. It was almost as if he were a tonic; she felt calmed just by knowing his closeness. She started tying up the back of her dress, but suddenly felt his hands on hers.

"I never thought I'd have a king tying my laces," she said.

"I never thought I'd be a king," he said. "Nor did I think I'd be married to a foreign beauty to tie the laces of."

Syriel laughed, making her husband's simple task a little harder. She coughed, feigning embarrassment at her loss of composure, then remained still as he finished assisting her.

"What is the Bloom like in Malarmha?" Tenro asked.

Syriel felt herself smile as she thought about the place where she'd spent almost all of her life. The Yurelle and even Iewen celebrated the same festival as the She'ehlarah did. Syriel had even heard her father speaking of the festivities in Khiar, the home of the Zrti. She had noted how many similarities there were among them all.

Syriel hadn't thought about it deeply before, but the next time the couple might be more excited about the Eclosure. That was, of course, because if all went well, they'd be greeting a prince or princess.

There were a great number of things she'd always miss about her home. She loved the vines and plants that grew over the stone buildings all the way from the stone ceiling above them. It wasn't like Velwrith, where such vines had a central mind. Malarmha's pieces of verdant artwork were each their own free entity.

"I can't yet compare it to your festivities, as I haven't seen them. In Malarmha there is so much colour. The city plants Bloom as we do. Bare footprints and handprints are stamped from luminous gel all over the city. We slingshot the gel as high as we can get it, with competitions revolving around it. Paper banners are strung from balconies that jut out or are cut from the stone buildings high above, proclaiming the gender of the hatched Yurelle. The city is so often divided; it's so broad, and so many of us live near strangers. But during the festivals, we're united," Syriel said.

Tenro circled around her as she spoke, which she only realised when she had finished. She looked to her left and smiled at him.

"What's it like here?" she asked.

"I can't relate to that separation. Everyone in the castle is family, though often quite distant. I wonder if that's what it's like beyond the castle walls in the outer city," Tenro mused.

"When it's safe again, do you think we could go and find out?" Syriel asked.

Tenro smiled and nodded. "I think we should. The heir, I mean, king's guard captain, Yune, would know the outer city incredibly well, as he lives there with his promised. You probably saw some of it flying over?"

"A little. I should have paid more attention. I was so nervous when I first came here, and when I got here the second time, I was..." Syriel stopped speaking, suddenly at a loss for words. She looked away from Tenro for a moment, trying to describe exactly her state of mind.

"Adrift," Tenro concluded.

"Do you think so?" she asked, looking at him again, evaluating his expression.

He nodded. "I was much the same." Syriel smiled for a moment. "I'm not now, though," he said.

Syriel felt deeply guilty that she had been able to move past losing her father, betrothed, and ex-boyfriend so quickly. It still hurt. If she thought about her feelings, it hurt too much to think about. She knew she'd carry that loss with her all of her days, and she only coped with it by pushing it down as deep as she could.

She smiled at her husband and patted down her now-fastened dress.

"For our first child, can we hang a banner from the castle balconies?" she asked.

"I think we should," Tenro said with a smile. "We've always spent our time in the castle gardens, but it's been deemed too dangerous, even now. I wish I could show you my favourite terrace, where I spent most of my happiest moments."

"Things will change," Syriel said.

"I'm sure of it. Let's go help set up for the festivities," Tenro said.

Kyra

Kyra was living on borrowed time, and every breath pulled her closer to the moment when Methis found out. She sat at the foot of her door in her tiny, windowless room. She had been waiting for her weekly schedule to be slipped under the door, like a hungry prisoner waiting for food.

Kyra held her week in her hand and looked over her schedule with horror. Her own time was shrinking with her freedom and, more brutally, her resolve. She'd been given a class for almost every waking moment. It was a tool designed to push her to Methis, but all it did it make her realise her finality.

It was bizarre to be given such an oppressive piece of information. The weight of this paper was too heavy to hold. She opened her hand and watched it float softly to the floor of her room. She stared at it, pulling her knees in tighter.

If Methis was ever close to her and Vujet, he would know in an instant that Kyra was an adult, and that she had desire for Vujet, the Ptery she pretended to hate deeply. Methis had thankfully bored of his toy and hadn't come to her, even during the Bloom. But he soon would. She only had up until the moment he came to her. She would die then. She'd be thrown from the tree, just like her father.

A hand rapped on her door. "Kyra, it's time for study," Vujet said from the other side.

When she heard his voice, her heart beat faster. He was her death, and she loathed him, yet she cherished the sound of his voice. In a moment, he would pick her up and carry her to her lessons. Fate had been so cruel to her, that he was the only male who'd ever held her.

The memory of him would forever be scarred with a moment of screaming in the throne room, as she lost her father. And even still, her skin shivered with excitement at the thought of his hands on her. Fate was too cruel. The wingless princess had fallen for her father's murderer and her warden.

"Kyra," Vujet said, knocking on the door again. Soon her door would open, and her exhausting, preplanned day would begin. "Kyra, please," Vujet said.

She sighed and then stood. She would not wait for him to open the door, as he always did. She unlocked the door and opened it. Vujet stood on the other side of the threshold with wide eyes.

"This day will be different," she said, holding her hand out to him.

With furrowed brow, he took her hand. Kyra pulled him into her small room and closed the door behind him.

"Methis will be my death, but that does not mean I should not live before I die," Kyra said.

"What?" Vujet stammered, pulling his hand from hers.

"I'll have one day," she said.

"If you're to say you're unwell, I must return to my duties and Methis would visit. My work is being poorly done by another in my absence. The kingdom too, suffers from our poor treatment," he said, his typically confident tone unsteady.

"They all suffer with a spy on the throne. I am the blood of

Amaranthus, and I will have one day before my legacy dies," she said as she unbuttoned her shirt.

"You would doom me too," Vujet said, stepping back from her.

"We're all doomed, let us be so together," she said, opening her shirt. "No one will have the opportunity to sleep with an Iewen princess ever again."

Vujet sighed as he too, began undoing his clothing.

Kyra felt his delight in the air between them, mixed with the torment of their combined oppression. She'd only ever known what it was to be a captive, so his feelings were her only outside existence, which only heightened her eagerness.

That must be what she loved about him: he too knew what it was like to be imprisoned. But also, to be an object of murder. Both of them had killed her father just by existing, just by being their legacies.

She justified her motives for bedding her captor as he stepped forward to kiss her. And then all need to reason melted away as she became clay in his experienced hands.

Mayala

She'd promised a day to her daughters, and so with a rare measure of clarity and extreme willpower, she'd woken early. Her girls had come to her room when she was already dressed. The girls were also dressed, talking at length about their hair and how it should be tied.

Alura stood poised, so proper that Mayala was reminded of Fiare. Maia held a luminous moss that grew brighter with warmth. Amer had given it to her for her first time going to the festival. It was good that she still had it with her, a full season later.

"Now that I'm an adult, Mother, can I wear my hair like a proper grown princess?" Maia asked.

Mayala looked at her daughter with a broken heart. If Methis wanted to make a child contract with her, she didn't know how she could protect her, other than by promising her to another suitor right away. She couldn't stand losing another child so soon; it threatened to break her. After a time, Mayala smiled and nodded.

"I want to wear my hair the same!" Alura said.

"No," Mayala said quickly.

Both of her daughters looked at her. "Just a moment ago, you were all curled up in my arms. Give me one more season before you're all grown up, Alura," Mayala said.

"But there's the new baby!" Alura protested.

"She means you, specifically," Maia said.

Alura looked at her mother with her eyes wide. She wasn't yet accustomed to thinking about others. One moment ago, her only thought was of her own survival. Ptery grew fast, but their maturity was tricky. Young adults often went from childish to adolescent to adult within the same moment. Parenting a young Ptery was an incredible challenge.

"I'm sorry, Mother," Alura said, lowering her head.

Mayala smiled. With one simple comment, Maia had helped shape her sister. Ptery siblings were an extraordinary aid to the younger ones—not just because they'd been young but one blink ago, but because they were still children in many ways.

"I count myself always lucky to have such wonderful daughters," Mayala said. She knelt down and opened her arms.

Alura hugged her mother, and Maia did soon after. They didn't know what it was to lose a child, but they knew how It felt to lose a brother and a sister. They were also in deep, ceaseless torment.

"We're going to have a great day, Mother. You'll see," Maia whispered.

Mayala nearly cried when her daughter consoled her. A mother was supposed to console her children, not the other way around. She had to find her strength for their sakes, but above all, she needed to find strength for her new child.

Her girls had grown so fast that she hadn't even realised it. It seemed only moments ago that little Alura was in her arms, but next season, the young girl would be celebrating her Bloom. It all seemed too hard ... too impossible.

When Mayala thought about her child yet to hatch her heart sank. How could she raise another child to die or leave her? She could barely leave her bed in the morning, yet she was to have another tiny life dependent on her diligence. She couldn't do it.

Creating life had taken a permanent toll on her. Mayala loved each of her children, even the ones she couldn't cuddle now or ever again. She didn't have a single regret for the strength she lost with Fiare and even Zona. Fiare was still alive, though it felt like she too had died, as Mayala might never see her again.

She lost so much more strength when she'd lost them because she'd cherished them so dearly. She didn't regret the joy they'd given her because of her pain. She was grateful for every precious moment she had with them. However, a part of her wanted the pain to stop at any cost.

Mayala thought about her youngest child. She had already paid the physical cost, and yet she couldn't bear for them to hatch. No matter how she felt about the child, they would hatch any day now. She had to find her strength. Perhaps they would give it back to her, just as Maia had in one whispered breath.

"Come now, girls, let's celebrate the festival," Mayala said.

"I can't wait to leave the castle!" Alura said, jumping back and then walking excitedly around the room.

"We can't leave the castle this season," Mayala said. Both young girls looked at their mother with wide eyes.

"You heard Father when he said we couldn't leave the castle after,"

Mayala stopped speaking when she realised the next words she needed to say.

"But we have to celebrate the Bloom, we always have," Maia said.

"It will be different now," Mayala said, her voice forceful. She surprised herself with the strength of her tone. She struggled to leave her bed in the morning, but she realised she still had the energy to keep her daughters safe. She could only hope that it would always be so.

"We have some merchants coming today. Since we can't go to the festival, we brought it to us," Maia said.

"It's not the same," Alura whispered.

"Nothing is the same," Mayala said, her voice quiet. "We have to do the best we can with everything."

"I'm going back to our room," Maia said.

"No, we're going to share in the festival together again," Mayala said.

"This isn't the festival, mother. The Bloom is outside the castle, in the sunshine," Maia said.

"The Bloom is a celebration of your growth, and a celebration for the little ones who are born. It's important to celebrate your adulthood this season, Maia. Just as it's important to celebrate your little sibling, who will first look at the world this season," Mayala said.

"The egg hasn't even hatched yet," Maia said.

"Can we see it again?" Alura asked.

Mayala smiled and nodded, but she could feel her strength leaving her. Maia wasn't like Fiare, Zona, or even Alura; she'd always been tiresome. Mayala didn't want to think about how much harder their lives would be if the new baby proved to be as exhausting as Maia.

"We'll sneak out later with Vira and Pame," Maia whispered.

Mayala ignored her children's whispers. She'd surprise them by making their guards stop them. Guiyn and Wyma can do as they pleased, but her children wouldn't be put in danger. She reached a hand out to her youngest daughter.

"Come, girls," she said, guiding them into the nursery room.

The egg sat in a curved stone bowl, a safe cradle, deep enough to ensure it wouldn't fall. Cthessa's vines provided a warm nest.

Alura took her hand from her mother's grip and approached the lone egg. She gently touched it, and Mayala felt her daughter's delight in the air.

The egg had hardened now, but soon Mayala would hear that cracking, tapping sound as her new child braved its dangerous new world. As she thought about the wonderful moment of her child's birth, Mayala knees buckled and she fell to the ground.

"Mother?" Alura said, as she ran the short distance to her mother.

Mayala couldn't respond. She hadn't been a mother to two of her children, and she had failed to guide one to adulthood. Only a moment ago, she was the mother of the prince heir, and now she had only one daughter for the king's legacy. Yet none of it mattered as the crown sat atop a foreign queen's head.

She couldn't keep her son alive, couldn't stop Fiare from being taken, nor could she make her daughters queen. She had once advocated for her son to marry Syriel. Now all she thought was that they had given a stranger the power over their kingdom. How had that even happened?

Amer said that Cthessa had guided him to Tenro, and that Tenro would marry the foreigner. Mayala's breathing become shallow as she struggled to find air.

"Mother?" Alura yelled.

"I'll get farther. Stay with her!" Maia said.

Mayala couldn't breathe. She felt a tightening in her chest. She still couldn't find breath, and the discomfort morphed into a sharp stabbing as the sensation intensified. It felt like hours and hours of pain twisting through her body like thorns. The weight on her chest grew heavier.

"Mayala?" Amer wrapped his arms around her. "I'm here, my love, breathe," he said. Mayala's breath started to slow, but the pain didn't stop. "I'm here, love, I have you," Amer said.

But still the pain didn't stop. Her head spun, she was breathing slightly slower, but she needed air. Her vision started to fade, and then she fell to the floor.

Kyra

The day had been Kyra's shortest yet, and it was not yet even time for their midday meal. Her bedsheets had never felt so smooth, nor the mattress so soft as it did at this moment. Her sense of touch was heightened, and though exhausted, she had never felt so complete.

She ran her fingers over Vujet's muscled chest and felt her skin tingle. Everything about him was like some ancient magic that soothed secret parts of her that she didn't even know ached. He was the greatest experience of her life, and she wanted more. She wanted her life flooded with stolen moments with him. She didn't know how many times she would be permitted to live in this dreamworld, so she would cherish every second.

She was as exhausted as he, and her only desire now was to pass out beside him. But she couldn't stand to miss out on any time with him. She had never known she could be so open, so honest in action. She'd never been intentionally naked in front of anyone, and for him she'd been utterly bare. She swirled her finger across his sleeping body, drawing imaginary circles on his skin.

She sat up abruptly at the realisation that when Methis killed her, it would likely be Vujet who did so. It was a horrible thought, but at least it would be someone who loved her who ended her life. In an instant, tears filled her eyes. Life was too cruel. Reality had stolen the happiest moment of her life.

"Kyra?" Vujet asked, his voice croaky.

"Sorry," she said, rubbing her eyes with her blanket.

"I'm sorry," he said, sitting up, thought labouring through his fatigue.

"No," she stammered, furrowing her brow, her antennae drooping. "I just didn't want the moment to end."

"All moments end," he said, his head lowered.

"I know," she said in a frustrated tone. "I know better than most."

"Of course," he said, looking at her directly. He smiled and touched his finger to her chin for a brief moment. "We can enjoy this one until it's gone."

His shoulders drooped so much that it was evident he was far more exhausted than she, but he too wanted to stay awake with her. She smiled.

"If I could design my own world, you would be at the centre of it," she said.

"I am already. I'll carry you wherever you need to go, for as long as I can," he said.

"That's not what I mean," she said, closing her eyes.

"I know. I feel the same," he said.

She felt his hand on her shoulder and jumped a little as she opened her eyes fully.

"Let's make a promise to only think about each moment we're in," he said.

Kyra's eyes widened.

"Yes," she said.

"And in this moment, I want to say how much I love your eyes," he said.

"I want to say how much I love your arms."

He laughed. "My arms?"

"I like the way they feel around me."

"I like the way you feel around me," he said.

Kyra blushed. "You, Mister Captain, are far too forward for your own good."

"Aren't I just?" he said, smiling.

She stared at him, still unable to believe they had successfully stolen this moment. She felt the wild god in her eyes as she looked into his.

"You really are," she said. "You're so bossy, and you overstep your station."

"Yes, I do, princess, and I regret nothing." He leaned forward, pulling her close to him as he kissed her.

They both leaned back from their short kiss, and Kyra pulled her naked shoulders back proudly.

"I also regret nothing, no matter what happens."

"No matter what happens," he agreed.

"Tell me about your life," she said.

His eyes widened for a moment, and then he smiled.

"I'm the oldest child in a small family."

"You have siblings?"

"Two. A sister and a brother. My mother died young. She was a scout, so my father raised us, just like you," he said.

Kyra smiled. "Do you remember your mother?"

"Yes, I remember her well," he said, as his antennae raised with his eyebrows. "She was like a force of nature, but she was patient. Scouts are something else."

"Did she see many great things in the tangle?" she asked.

"She did. Some she told us about, others she said she'd never talk about. We used to assault her with questions, and there was much she wouldn't say. But she did tell us about when she found a pool full of tadpoles. The mother frog guarding it didn't attack them. They didn't stay to test her tolerance, though. She said that the pool was so clear and clean; the little creatures had eaten all of the muck in the water. She said it was like a mirror."

Kyra sat in silence, her eyes wide.

"Other times, she spoke of circles of mushrooms, or other strange patterns that naturally occurred. Markings on trees made by other creatures. It's so incredible to think about how much life there is in the depth of the tangle."

"Did she know the creatures making those patterns? Were they like ours?"

"She didn't always know the creature, but she'd draw some of those patterns. Some did look like Ptery markings," he said, smiling.

"'So much of the world is ripples and echoes'. That's what my father used to say," Kyra said. Vujet smiled.

Kyra waited for him to tell her that her father had been a good king, but the lie never came. She felt sore about that, but then the soreness melted away when she realised that he didn't want to lie to her. She was grateful for his honesty as she tucked herself against him. She didn't know what a life without lies felt like.

Remin

Brightly coloured flowers were dotted on every makeshift house. Streamers were tied around every doorway and window. The excitement of the festival of life was celebrated in every realm. Even this far from the centre of Hald, music floated on the wind.

Tsune walked out of his house, straightening up his complicated and bright festival clothing. A young female emerged from his house, also straightening her clothing. Tsune looked confidently at Remin and waved. Remin waved back, but in shock. Remin had seen it before, but this was the most obvious example of how Tsune acted like he was many seasons younger than he was.

In a strange way, Remin thought exile might have been the best thing for Tsune. It seemed like life above had been more oppressive for him than for most Iewen. He defied Iewen culture in numerous ways. The more Remin learned, the more he felt that the life above was a place where no Ptery could flourish, even those who obeyed their harsh laws.

Tsune whispered something into the female's ear, and she giggled and waved as she walked off. Tsune watched her leave before approaching Remin.

"You're missing out on the festival, Remin! You're new to the city. Come make some friends," Tsune said.

Remin smiled. He wanted to see the joy of the season, but for Ptery who'd lost someone, the Bloom was all too often a reminder of a season the lost would never reach. He'd joined in a little, but thoughts of Kyra had gotten to him particularly hard on this day.

"You go ahead," Remin said.

"Not without you. We stand by each other here; we have to. And if you don't live life, you lose it," Tsune said.

Remin smiled. His friend was right.

"Why didn't you change your name?" Remin asked.

"The life of a commoner is similar from here to there. Nothing like the change you're enduring," Tsune said.

He looked at Remin for a moment. "Don't think about the past when the present is so much better," Tsune said.

Remin followed Tsune deeper into the city. "I like to stay on the edge of the new city. I'll show you my favourite place," Tsune said.

The pair stopped a short walk further at a small eatery. Tsune walked with his shoulders pulled back. Remin thought he must have looked quite different, with his comparatively slouched posture.

The eatery was surprisingly large for its small front. In each corner of the room, short tables were surrounded by connected benches against each wall. More toward the centre of the room there were taller tables with stools. The very centre was an open section, with a slightly raised middle section as a central stage.

A group of three musicians played on the central stage. They sounded and looked inebriated, but also seemed to be enjoying themselves as much as the small gathering within. Bright streamers hung from the high section of the central ceiling. Paint had been streaked across the walls and dotted with coloured sand.

"Tsune, back so soon," a female said, smiling broadly. She looked like the same female that Tsune had seen off just a moment ago. She was sitting with another female and a male. They were yellow-haired, not like the bright green of the Iewen, or the brown-haired Ptery Remin had still not identified. They were all winged.

Tsune sat beside her and looked at Remin intently. Remin seated himself beside Tsune.

"I'll get us a round of drinks," a male voice said.

"I'm Leisa. You're Remin, aren't you?" the other female said.

"Yes, Remin," he said.

"I'm Mesi. That's my brother, Yoci," the first female said.

"How long have you been here?" Remin asked.

"I've been here all my life. My mother was dropped here five seasons ago, but my father's been here all his life," Leisa said.

Remin nodded. It was his father who had exiled her mother.

"Me and Yoci are first-generation Hald," Mesi said.

Only Remin and Tsune knew what it was like above. In a moment, Remin realised why they looked to the future so much. It wasn't just about moving on from the painful past. Most of the people in the city would never have even seen the city above them. He couldn't imagine living beside those who had seen it if he hadn't.

The benefit of all originating from Khiar, the home of the Zrti, was that none of those who left it had ever seen it. Almost none of them even knew where it was. The Therai knew their origin was above them. They circled it knowing that their ancestors were on the other side of the hollow tree between them.

"Are you settling in okay?" Leisa asked.

Remin took a moment to reply. Before he did, Yoci returned with the drinks he'd ordered for them.

"This is made from flowers and fruit. It's sweet, but if you're not accustomed, it will intoxicate you quickly," Yoci said, taking a drink from his tray and placing it in front of Remin.

"Sip it," Tsune said.

Remin sipped the drink. It was fermented. The Iewen commonly drank a similar drink. He'd liked it and drank it a lot, especially toward the end of his reign. "I like it," he said, furrowing his brow slightly in feigned intrigue.

Remin didn't know what to say to the group. Most of what he wanted to talk about were things about his past, like the state of things above them, or the number of new houses that had been built near him. His substance was almost entirely from above. He didn't even know what to say to those from a different world.

"What was it like up there?" Leisa asked.

"Don't ask things like that," Yoci said.

"I don't mind. You can ask any questions you like; I'll tell you when I don't know or when it's too sad for me to answer," Remin said, glancing at Yoci.

"It was brutal, honestly, but my life was different than most. I lived in hiding up there," Remin said.

"Lshar said something like that once, about living in hiding," Leisa said.

Remin nodded. It took him a moment, but he smiled.

One moment ago, he'd been an actual king, and now he was lower than the poorest person in his kingdom. But he had to remember what he'd gained here. He didn't have to hide anymore. He was no longer living in fear. But most important of all, Kyra was dead, and he had to face that.

Remin realised he'd been silent for a moment and then looked at Leisa. "Are you an outlier?" he asked.

"No. Most of us aren't. My father was a tailor, my grandfather too, and my great-grandmother before. We don't call people who make their own way outliers here. We're the children of the lost," Leisa said, taking a sip of her drink.

Remin sipped his drink as he thought about that. Outliers were shunned in Daltay. Anyone different, like him, were never welcome.

"Building the queendom is our communal legacy. Every new exile I've met has been astounded how much we build. It seems to be something unique to Hald. Is it true there are housing shortages in them all?" Yoci asked.

Remin removed the sad thoughts from his mind and refocused on the conversation. "Yes. Housing is a problem in the kingdoms, particularly in the Senate. They can't build more in their rock. Parts of the upper shell that protects their main city have already broken from their digging. Daltay doesn't leave the tree. Both the She'eh and Yurelle push into the tangle, where they have dedicated scouts for that dangerous work," Remin said.

Tsune looked at Remin and then at Leisa.

"Our city is built on change. We welcome it. Anyplace you want to try and work, those within will offer to train you. They will often be harsh about it, and won't offer pay. They're especially rough to typical Iewen. It takes a while for those from above to adapt. You don't seem like a typical Iewen, though. You seem much more like one of us," Leisa said, leaning forward.

"Oh, I almost forgot, Mesi. You said you wanted to show me your new garden. The one you and Yoci built," Tsune said.

Remin lowered his head to hide his blushed cheeks. He could hardly believe Tsune would resort to such a cheap ploy.

"I did promise. Come on, Yoci, let's leave these two to chat," Mesi said.

Remin looked up to see the trio stand.

"It was lovely to meet you," Remin said, trying not to make it obvious how awkward he felt.

"That was not subtle," Leisa said, sliding over to him.

Remin smiled.

"The festival is about making strangers into friends, and I expect your world is full of strangers," Leisa said.

"That's too true," Remin said, sighing.

"I can help change that. I know we're not supposed to talk about the past, and I think that would go double for a past we were not present for. But Tsune thinks highly of you, and that has to mean something, given your history," Leisa said.

"I appreciate the honesty. I think he sees more in me than I do myself," Remin said.

As he finished speaking, Leisa slid across the chair and put her lips to his. It was an immense surprise, but an incredibly welcome one. She tasted like the fermented fruit drink. When she slid back, Remin just stared at her, his eyes soft though expectant.

"Can you forgive a fancy of someone who was never anyone?" Leisa asked.

"I don't understand," Remin said.

"I never dreamed I'd meet a king, nor get a chance to kiss one," Leisa said.

"I'm not a king," Remin said.

"You were once. We don't hold people to their past, but it never goes away," Leisa said.

Remin couldn't find the words to argue with her. Instead, he just nodded.

"Do you want to come back to my home? We can just sit and talk about your world and mine if you like, or we could celebrate the festival of new life and new adulthood in the traditional way," Leisa asked.

"I'd like that very much. Both, actually," Remin said, as he then downed the last of his almost full drink.

Leisa smiled before she drank the last of her drink. She stood and took his hand. He appreciated that she didn't waste any time. As she walked with him behind her, he noted that her confidence was much like Tsune's. All of the Therai he'd met had been confident. They had it right; he'd just have to learn how to emulate them.

The warmth of her hand in his made his skin tingle as he walked with her.

CHAPTER 3

A MATTER OF HEART

Methis

"You're a delight, as usual," Methis said. He stood from his bed and swung a robe around his shoulders.

"And you are the king we've been waiting for," Nayri said. She rolled over to face him. The blanket remained where it was, exposing her naked skin.

Methis turned to view her again. Curled locks of her vibrant green hair were strewn across the light grey sheets. Her naked form was an unusual delight to him because she'd been his lover before he was king.

"I am the king that follows Amaranthus. I am the killer of princes," Methis said, lifting his chin high.

"The whole kingdom waits in delight for you to kill the new queen and king," Nayri said.

Methis looked at her through narrowed eyes. "No doubt," he said, his tone sharp.

"I'm sorry, Highness, did I say something wrong?" Nayri asked, sitting up.

He shook his head, his wings twitching behind him. She stared at him for a time, sitting up on his bed. Her eyebrow furrowed as her antennae searched the air for an indication of his feelings.

"I should best get to work," Methis said.

Nayri nodded. She crawled to him to get off his bed. "I wanted to wait until it was more obvious, but I can't wait to tell you," she said, standing. There were only a few steps between them now.

"I carry your child," she said, stretching her wings out behind her.

Methis's mouth opened. He stood in silence for a time. "I'm to be a father at last," he finally said.

"You are," she said, pulling her wings closed. "You should think about a name."

He smiled at her suggestion, and not just because a name was important; giving him the responsibility was right. She knew better than to call it an heir to the throne.

"Are you hungry?" he asked, glancing at her naked belly.

"A little," she replied, reaching for her clothes.

"Stay and eat with me," he said.

She looked at him with wide eyes. He had never asked her to eat with him before, but clearly it was time.

"As his Highness wishes," she said, bowing.

Lon

The unarmoured second-in-command of the king's guard sat silently in the painted garden. The sound of music always lifted her up, and this night was no different. The scent of the flowers around her paired perfectly with the music and flavour of nectar in her mouth.

The painted garden was a jubilation of colour, passion, and vitality. The garden was filled with flowers, the painted dancers that tended their garden enveloped in verdure. It was a dream for the sleepless, a home for the lost.

Almost all Ptery left the garden unburdened. Surrounded by life and light on all sides, it was no surprise. It was one of the only places Lon felt at rest. Always on guard everywhere else, this was a precious place for her and many other Dragonriders.

Lon watched her favourite dancer. He was naked of all but underwear. He didn't look naked to her; he looked liberated. Covered in luminescent paint, he danced on his toes with a skill equivalent to that of any soldier. When he saw her, the bounce in his toes became even more practised as he danced toward her.

"Lon," he said, his voice thick and sweet, like honey.

"Eryngi," Lon said, resting her chin on her hand.

"You look ever like a light in the darkness, the arm between us and destruction," he said.

"And you, effervescent as ever," Lon said.

Eryngi looked at her with delight as she smiled.

"How much time do you have, my forever stoic curiosity?" he asked. When Eryngi had danced close enough, he kneeled and held out his hand to her.

Lon took his hand without reply. She stood quickly and pushed into his arms that circled around her. As she did, however she felt a strangeness. She smelled pollen on his skin. It was the turning of the season.

Lon's skin prickled with excitement, but then, like any Dragonrider of a strong legacy, she felt the familiar sensation of heightened awareness. The most magnificent celebrations were when all Ptery were most vulnerable. And after the murder of their prince, the She'ehlarah had never been so vulnerable.

Life was the greatest reason any Ptery had to celebrate, and the pollen in the air spoke of dormant life soon to emerge. It was spring, the season of Eclosure, when young Ptery cracked from their eggs and cried for their mother's breast. It was not only the meeting of these little ones that was reason for celebration. Since all Ptery hatched at the same time, it was the anniversary of each of their emergence from their eggs. The anniversary of their introduction to their world and family. She thought she would have more time before such a wondrous and dangerous occasion.

"What is it?" Eryngi asked.

"I smell the Bloom," Lon said.

"Yes. I know what that means for you. We should get to work quickly," he said, smiling.

Lon smiled back and then pressed her lips against his. She was certainly going to enjoy herself before she'd have no time to herself at all, especially because Dragonriders didn't always make it home.

Amer

The stone walls around Amer were covered with Cthessa's vines, like most of the castle. In the physicians' pools, the tendrils were dotted with blue flowers. The scent of perfumed water calmed his emotions, but the deep, heavy worry in his heart remained. The air was thick with moisture from the many herb-infused water pools built into the stone ground.

Wooden walls divided each pool from the next. This was not for the privacy of the naked occupant within, but to keep those in the room calm. The She'ehlarah had learned from the perfect god that self-connection through isolation was sometimes imperative for healing.

Amer sat beside Mayala, who was submerged in a scented pool. Her already weightless, pale face looked gaunt, her tiny body frail. Shamihi, the head physician, walked into the room quietly. Amer looked over his shoulder to see her standing behind him.

"Apologies, Sire, I had come to check on Queen Mayala, but it is not required. Just overly cautious," Shamihi said.

"Will she recover?" Amer asked.

"Yes, she is expected to recover fully. It was an isolated incident," she said.

"What precisely was it?" he said.

"A tightness in her chest. Not a heart attack, but similar," Shamihi said.

"Thank you," Amer said.

"I'll give you privacy, but if you need me at any time, Sire, I'll be behind my desk," she said.

"Thank you," he said.

Shamihi walked away. Amer looked over his shoulder again to make sure, and then he went to take Mayala's hand. As he touched the water, her eyes slowly opened.

"Are the children all right?" she asked, her voice quiet.

"They are. Are you all right?" he asked.

"I am in the best care in the kingdom. The children might not understand. They need comfort," she said.

"I can check on them," he said.

"Please, I will recover," she said.

Amer wanted to believe her words, but her voice was so weak. She looked at him through barely open eyes. Her physical weakness was reflected in his own mental fatigue and scarring. Amer hadn't been able to find the strength to be there for them when Mayala was in danger.

Amer crinkled his brow and then nodded reluctantly. He only wanted to stay with her. But she was right. He pulled his fingers from the thickened, scented water and wiped them on a towel on the wall behind him.

"I'll be here, I'll be safe," she said.

Amer nodded again and then quickly left the room. He couldn't linger or he wouldn't go. He left the room and stood in the hallway for a moment. The two king's guards he'd travelled with started walking when he did.

It was a short walk to his children's room, but he used the time to try and think about what he should say. He realised while on his way that a part of him was worried that their actions had worsened Malaya's sickness. Then he remembered that they were still so young, and that they required guidance. He thought of Fiare at their age and sighed. She was always such a dutiful listener, such a patient creature. All of his children were so different. Amer reached his daughters' room soon after and knocked on their door.

Maia opened it immediately. It was so hard to believe that Maia was fully grown. She'd reached adulthood and they hadn't even celebrated it. She frowned upon seeing him.

"Is Mother all right?" she asked.

"Yes," Amer said.

He walked into the room and sat on the floor. Both of his daughters sat with him. They were the only remaining of his four children in what had once been his kingdom.

"Mother will recover, but we're going to need your help now," Amer said.

"We can't get anything we want, why do we have to do more?" Alura said with a pout.

Amer looked at her with a frown. She was only one season old, but she was old enough to know better than to act so poorly.

"Because your mother needs you. You saw what happened to her, and you feel what she's gone through," Amer said. His tone was strict; such bluntness was usually reserved for his subjects. It silenced both of the girls at once.

Both of the princesses hung their heads. Amer had to remind himself that they too were suffering, and they had not learned how to deal with such emotions. Focusing on shallow thoughts was likely one of the only choices they believed they had.

In his own torment, he couldn't think of any subject on which they could easily focus. Even he was concerned about losing the new child so much that just like Mayala, he didn't want to connect with them. But he needed the help of his daughters.

"You are princesses, and just as I was required to be king, you too are to play your roles with grace. You live in a castle with limited space, and yet your room is spacious. You don't labour in the orchard farms, and yet you are never hungry. We all have our place in life, and yours is to help your mother care for your sister," he said, his tone soft.

"But we also have servants," Maia said, with her head still lowered and humiliation in her tone.

"They cannot draw out the legacy in your sister, as they are not princesses," Amer said, moving closer to his daughters.

"I know things are hard, but we will never rule. There is no point to living a harder life when we'll never need to use our skills," Maia said.

"You *will* need our legacy. Syriel is a queen with powers not seen since before our ancestors left Xndao. I've told you before that queens used to rule, and that their kings sat by their side. It changed once, and it could change again. We need to be ready for whatever happens because the thing that matters most is the legacy of our kingdom. It can only live through us," he said. His tone had softened even more now, and the frustration in his voice was gone.

He loved his daughters so dearly. He realised that he didn't want to remember how much he loved them, for the loss of Zona and Fiare was still too raw. As expected, when his frustration cleared, the memory of such conversations with Zona overwhelmed him, near taking the air from his lungs. He breathed slowly in an attempt to hide the ache of missing Zona from his girls.

He lowered his head for a moment, and when he lifted it he saw both of his daughters staring at him. Both of their faces were crinkled, with no sign of their previous foul mood. His suffering was thick in the air, and both leaned forward to hug their father.

Amer looked over to Zona's leaf bed and then to Fiare's. He missed Fiare as if she too were no longer alive.

"We will try to look after her," Alura said.

"What's her name?" Maia asked, leaning her head on her father's shoulder.

"We haven't decided," Amer said.

"I want to name her!" Alura said, her little voice still quiet. "If she's going to be ours, we should get to."

"They're not your child. That's not how it works," Amer said, his voice quiet.

"Father, we can't do all the work and get no reward," Alura said.

Amer gently moved out of the embrace with his daughters. "Fiare got no reward, but she always did what was expected of her," he said.

"We're not her, Father," Maia said, defeat in her tone.

"You are both my daughters, and so you are very much like your big sister," Amer said, smiling.

"You don't see it, Father but we can't be like her," Maia said.

"She was always perfect, always telling us we'd made mistakes," Alura said.

"*Teaching* you. You both have yet to grow, and you will be as elegant as her," Amer said.

"If you think that, then you don't know how different we all are," Maia said.

"Maia, enough. You are as much your mother as your sister is, and that is how your sister got her grace," Amer said, his tone again sharp.

Maia furrowed her brow and lowered her head. She pulled her legs closer to her. Amer wanted to say something to make her feel better, but this was their life. They had to accept the things that were, and they had to move forward.

Amer looked around his children's room again. There were many rooms like it in the castle; all who lived within the great stone walls lived well. Amer had moved into his own room when he'd wed Mayala, but his daughters would never move from this room.

They chose to spend most of their nights in sleep in the nursery. He sympathised with their limited life, but his life too had always been restricted. He had freedoms they would never have as king, but he too was a servant to the crown. They were all marked by the same fate, the same legacy.

"Any Ptery who spends their life dwelling on what they can't do and what they don't have, lives badly, regardless of what they do or do not endure. The only way to live well is to focus on what you have, and use it to create your own great life," Amer said.

"That's easy to say for you, now, Father," Maia said.

"With my experience, yes. It's how the weight of the crown never broke me. Ruling an entire kingdom is an incredible freedom, but also an immense burden," he said.

"But you get to choose everything," Maia said.

"Just as you will, for your sister," he said. The new baby's sex was not known, but Amer decided to make it most relevant to his daughters by saying sister.

"Oh," Alura said. Amer smiled, his features softening.

"What do we do?" Maia asked.

"Remember what Fiare, your mother, and even I taught you. Then teach that to your little sister and help your mother when she needs you. She has always helped you whenever you needed her," Amer said.

Maia nodded, though her shoulders slumped. Amer put his hand on his daughter's shoulder.

"You are both legacies of the crown, and you're far more incredible than you yet realise," he said.

Trauma was hard on everyone, but more so on a developing Ptery mind. There was the possibility that Maia and Alura would never properly mature. It should have been unlikely in two with such a strong legacy. They needed more guidance now than ever, and Mayala and Amer could hardly guide their own feet.

Lshar

Lshar stood amidst a crowd. They flicked their long green hair behind their shoulders. The music and shouts of street musicians delighted Lshar from many different places. A group of females wearing strips of cloth on their chests and tiny skirts pushed past Lshar. One stopped to kiss them on the cheek and wink before she disappeared into the thickest part of the crowd. Lshar smiled as they disappeared.

The buildings in the old city were a design not seen in any other. Their multi-storied brown stone walls shadowed what little light touched the undergrowth floor. Their green crested roofs were unique in all the world Lshar knew. The high windows were typically closed, but almost every shutter was open for the festival. Almost every window was filled with faces enjoying the festival from within.

Lshar smiled broadly. This was a moment when they could all truly show who they were. Since being here, Lshar had never hidden themselves, but it was more liberating now, even for them.

Lshar saw a few faces that looked out of place, but none more than Remin. He looked happier than the last time Lshar had seen him. Like he'd replenished something, but Lshar didn't know what. And Rein still didn't look happy enough surrounded by so much beauty and light. Lshar waved him over.

Remin slowly moved through the crowd to join them.

"You do not look like you've had enough free food and drinks," Lshar said, their androgynous tone kind.

"Don't I?" Remin said, furrowing his brow.

Lshar tapped him on the shoulder.

"Come now," Lshar said, turning from the crowd.

Lshar found a place that was a less crowded amidst the beautiful and tall buildings. They knocked on the open door of a nearby house. A young male walked into view from inside their home.

"Captain!" he said.

"Do you have any fruit for my friend here?" Lshar asked, turning to point at Remin, who looked out of place.

Lshar turned back to see the young male smile and nod.

"Anything for a friend of Lshar," he said, disappearing from view.

Lshar turned back to Remin.

"With a little food and drink, you'll see what the excitement is all about," Lshar said.

Remin smiled, but his eyes stayed sad. Lshar wanted to help him, but the transition from king to no one was something they couldn't even comprehend. Seeing more of the festival was key, they were sure. The chatter of a young couple caught Remin's attention as they talked about their excitement about the festival.

"Did you hear that there's another new exile?" a female voice said.

Lshar raised their eyebrows as Remin's attention focused on them.

"What's his count now, twenty?" the male asked.

"More. Not all survived the fall. Tsune said this one might not wake up. He hit his head against the tree," the female said.

"He might survive it. I've heard they can," the male said.

"Tsune said he wasn't from a great house, so at least he's not more important, anyway," the female said.

They continued to talk, but the moment their topic changed, Remin turned to Lshar again.

"You've been watching for your daughter," Lshar said.

"I was trying not to, but yes. I thought I wasn't supposed to talk about my old life," he said.

"That rule is to prevent hostility and sadness, but sometimes reflection is the only way we learn," Lshar said.

"The freshest and juiciest fruit," the male behind Lshar declared.

Lshar took the offered fruit on a stick and handed the other to Remin.

"Thank you," Lshar said, their tone sincere.

"Enjoy the festival." The male bowed their head and disappeared again.

"Can you just ask anyone for food?" Remin asked, confused.

"His partner is an old friend. It's a long story. But you're not interested in that, you want to hear my story," Lshar said, taking a bite of their fruit on a stick.

Remin nodded. "Was it so obvious?"

"Everyone wants to know the story of someone like me. I'm sure you heard that I hid wingless, right?" Lshar said.

"Yes, I heard that," Remin said.

Lshar could see that Remin wanted to say more. Lshar thought it might be something in admiration. There was a darker shade on Remin's face. Perhaps it was regret, as Remin had exiled Tsune for the same reason.

"I was destined to be exiled, anyway. I was of a great house, but I never had desire for anyone. I thought I might try to save some others before I was exiled," Lshar said, their tone flat.

They'd told the story so many times that they were numb to it. They'd heard too many times that things had been assumed about their sexuality, so Lshar preferred to talk about it openly.

Remin frowned deeply. "If I were king at the time you were found out, things might have been very different for us both," he said.

"You're right," Lshar agreed. "But then we would both still be prisoners to morals that conflicted with the rules of our society."

Remin rested his full attention on Lshar. Lshar knew that might perk him up. They watched as Remin ate the first piece of fruit from the stick. He smiled then, and so too did Lshar. Lshar then saw three treetop visitors walk into view behind Remin. They would certainly cheer him up; if nothing more, they'd be a great distraction.

"Look, it's the Mesren," Lshar said, nodding their head behind Remin.

Remin turned and Lshar enjoyed the wide-eyed stare that all new exiles got when they saw them. They were completely covered in dark green fur, except their faces. They traded with Hald often but only visited the old city, so it wasn't common for Lshar to see them. They were pretty special, as there was nothing like them in any of the Zrti descendant colonies.

"What are they?" Remin whispered.

"They're Ptery like us, but much older," Lshar said.

Remin's mouth was wide open. Lshar would have appreciated a conversation with them, but Remin looked unprepared. Discovering exile isn't death was often too much for newcomers, let alone seeing another type of Ptery.

Lshar wanted to make Remin feel welcome, not encourage him to shut himself in his newly built house. Lshar remembered learning all of this. A world view shattered in the first moments of being here. Learning about the other types of Ptery would have to wait.

"I want to show you my favourite tradition," Lshar said, steering Remin away from the Mesren.

The duo walked a short distance through a city, celebrating lives that they once thought they'd lost. No civilisation celebrated like the exiles. Lshar looked back at Remin, whose wide eyes were looking around him. Lshar pointed out a group of Therai in a particularly vibrant costume. Although clearly overwhelmed, Remin smiled.

Lshar took Remin to the main stage in the centre of the sprawl, upon which stood the incomparably beautiful painted throne. Carved, painted wooden struts supported embedded pieces of coloured translucent crystal. Coloured crystal wings extended from either side of it.

Atop the throne was the jewel of Hald. She was clad in too many vibrant colours to name. Her yellow hair was knotted with ribbons and beads, her skirt inspired by many different flowers. It was deigned to look like it blossomed around her, making her form look far greater than the tiny figure Lshar knew was beneath.

The winged queen was the symbol of transformation and of life after what the exiles thought was death. She was a promise of the creation of a better world. No other colony was actively building their city like they were. Her bright colours promised a wonderful future that no onlooker could deny. Lshar glanced at Remin to see that he too, was transfixed by the visage of their metamorphic queen. She leaned forward on her throne, her hands on her knees as she listened to the words of one of her kneeling subjects.

"Thank you, Your Grace," the yellow-haired winged Therai said.

She waved her hand as her subject rose. "Enjoy the celebration," she said. Her voice was musical and warm.

"During the festival, she encourages her people to speak to her, even more than usual," Lshar said.

"An approachable monarch?" Remin said.

"Seems fitting from an exile culture, doesn't it?" Lshar said.

"Yes, I just ..." Remin's words trailed off. Remin's eyes were still as wide as before, but Lshar felt his excitement in the air rather than apprehension.

"Do you want to meet her?" Lshar asked. Remin quickly shook his head. Lshar nodded as they approached the throne. Lshar knelt before the Therai queen. "Thank you, Phelendra, for another wonderful celebration."

"Lshar! You deserve more celebration than most, my dear," Phelendra said.

Lshar stood and walked back to Remin. They turned to see the queen looking curiously at Remin.

"I expect you might one day receive a private invitation from her," Lshar said.

Phelendra's attention returned to her stage as Remin looked at Lshar. "I don't know about that," he said.

"You'll have to trust me on that, then," Lshar said with a smile. "She even meets with the Ascent on the other side of the tree."

"What's the Ascent?" Remin said.

"Rebels, really. They want to rebel against exile and ascend up the tree. It's an ideal that's as absurd as their name," Lshar said.

Remin nodded. His demeanour had changed drastically from when Lshar saw him in the crowd.

"Have they made any progress?" Remin said.

"I don't think anything meaningful. They rely on us for their survival," Lshar said.

Remin frowned. Lshar thought he might like to meet them. It was a surprise that he didn't ask how to get to them. Remin needed time, Lshar decided. He'd find out if he wanted to stay here or ty to get back up, eventually. He'd find his place, wherever that was.

"You should mingle. There are many Ptery here I think you'd like to meet. This is a big city," Lshar said.

"Thank you, Captain," Remin said, bowing his head.

Lshar watched Remin walk into the crowd. Remin was going to be a great asset to the Therai, and everyone knew it but him.

Fiare

Fiare woke up in her new room, still exhausted. Malarmha didn't have servants to awaken her, so she stayed in bed for a time. She couldn't even imagine her life here. She rolled over and looked around the room from her bed. Early morning light subtly painted the walls a warm colour. The bed was surrounded by shelves where many plants had been placed.

The scent of those leafy plants, their soil, and vibrant flowers helped rouse Fiare to waking. Natural light and plants were a fine way to wake up and something Fiare would delight in becoming accustomed to. Natural light wasn't seen within the castle, which was why her favourite place in Velwrith had always been the garden balcony.

Syriel had collected a number of different plants, but even more intriguing was her collection of oddities. All around her room were little treasures of different origins, like the hoard of a sentimental shut-in. She had never seen Syriel as a shut-in, nor as someone who held onto things from the past. It seemed utterly bizarre for someone who'd been promised to another colony at birth. She had to have grown up knowing that she was going to leave her whole life behind at maturity. Perhaps that's why she had such a big collection.

As delighted as Fiare was by Syriel's trinkets, she was also confronted by them. The little objects made her feel like she, too, was a curiosity that didn't belong. Syriel must have never felt like that, being born here, but Fiare wasn't from here.

She sat up and walked to the little desk against the wall. The light from the window bathed it in warm shades. Just as with the bed, the desk had shelves on each wall around it that also held plants. She seated herself at the desk. There were a few sheets of paper and a quill beside them.

The first thing she would do was to write home. Her father and mother would receive Olianna's letter, but she wanted to write them of her safety in her own hand. She would write to Syriel first. Fiare wanted to tell her that she was staying in her room. She wanted to ask about Syriel's collection. She most wanted to ask about Syriel's life. She wanted to speak with Syriel, but she couldn't walk down the hall anymore. She wanted to speak to all of her family. She sighed and sat up straighter.

"No point looking at what you can't have," Fiare told herself.

Dear Syriel, I've been given your room. Fiare said as she wrote.

A knock at the door interrupted her. Fiare stood immediately and stared at it with a furrowed brow. Who would want to speak to her so early? She then realised she wasn't dressed. She scurried around her room, trying to find something to wear for the day. All of her bags had been packed so neatly, but her clothes were so heavy and complicated.

She opened Syriel's cupboard and took out a simple shirt and pair of pants.

"Princess Fiare?"

"One moment," she said, dressing quickly.

She looked herself over and decided she would get used to the discomfort of the bizarrely simple clothing.

"Who is it?"

"I am Diplomat Semath. I work for the Grand Chancellor, but also for your father in Velwrith. The Grand Chancellor thought I might make a suitable guide to Malarmha."

With her wings pulled behind her back, Fiare opened the door slightly.

A red-haired, handsome male stood at her door and bowed when it was opened. He was dressed in well-made, simple clothing and had a number of pouches and cases hanging from his belt. Beside him stood a beetle rider, like the one who followed Syriel. The beetle rider was carrying a box, and he too bowed. The diplomat stood up quickly and handed her a letter.

"It's from the Grand Chancellor. It confirms who I am," he said.

Fiare nodded and gently closed the door to read it. She looked it over carefully. It said all he'd explained, and so she opened the door again, this time wide.

"The Grand Chancellor suggested we go for a walk together, but I asked if I could talk to you first about our history a little," Semath said.

Fiare smiled. "I'd like that, thank you," she said.

"Wonderful. Might I come in?" he asked.

Fiare nodded and stepped away from the doorway. Semath took the box from his guard and then walked into the little apartment. He placed the box on the table.

"I brought some refreshments," he said, gesturing to the table in Fiare's room.

Fiare seated herself at the table, and then he sat too.

"I'm sorry if this was an early appointment. I had intended to tell you a little about our fair city before you went out into it," he said.

"I appreciate that. Pardon my bluntness, but I had heard there were dangers in the city," she said.

"Yes, there are, princess," Semath said, taking a small crystal bottle and two glasses from the box. "There are areas of the city you should avoid. I would advise until you learn the city better to stick to the main streets. The Grand Chancellor does not expect you to come to harm here, but she would rather you be cautious," he said, pouring a liquid from the bottle into the two glasses.

"The main streets are safe?"

"Certainly. They're well-lit and well-guarded. The city has many snaking alleyways that can't be patrolled. You have been assigned a guard, but it's best to stick to the main streets for now," Semath said, placing Fiare's glass before her. "This is just a simple juice. We have nothing fermented here," he said, lifting his glass.

Fiare copied him and sipped from the glass. It was a strange flavour. It wasn't as sweet as the She'ehlarah nectar. Delighted by the new flavour, she smiled. Semath smiled back.

"I brought a map of the city," he said, opening a case on his hip. "I can point out some places you might like to see, such as our market and shopping district."

Fiare held her glass to her nose, smelling the strange drink. She was trying to identify the flavours as Semath pointed out some important locations. Life was going to be incredibly different here, but it seemed she was soon to enjoy a vast number of new flavours.

Kyra

A loud knock at Kyra's door interrupted her study. She closed her book and sat up in her chair. He hadn't visited her in the middle of the day before, as it was when he was working in the throne room.

"Enter," she said, her voice demure.

When the door opened, she didn't see her secret lover enter. Instead, she saw the imposing visage of Methis. The shadow of the twisted crown made darkened spikes on her ceiling.

Her heart thundered in her chest as he closed the door behind him. She was an adult now, and this was the moment when he was going to try and take something she couldn't give him. She stood and pulled her shoulders back, but she could feel her knees shaking so violently that she knew he saw it.

"You don't feel desire for me, I understand that. I expect you find me intimidating, and I can't blame you for that," Methis said.

He sat at her tutor's chair at the side of her desk. She did not seat herself, however. She searched but couldn't find the words to reply to him. All she could think was that he was sitting where Vujet sat when she studied late at night. Her skin prickled.

"No matter how anyone feels, the blood of Amaranthus must not be broken. It's the only unwavering thread that holds this great kingdom together," Methis said, looking over the table at the book she was reading.

"What would you have me do?" Kyra asked in a shaking voice.

"We take the less dignified but effective route of countless other kings and their ideal and unable chosen. It's a simple medical procedure. A physician will see you tomorrow to confirm you've reached your maturity, and if so, they'll begin the procedure soon after," Methis said.

Kyra was horrified, but it was less frightening than she had initially thought. Every time she saw Methis, she was mortified at the prospect of his finding out about Vujet. Somewhat calmed, she sat in the chair.

"It's been described to me as an unpleasant process, and it can be lengthy. But I don't do this out of cruelty, but necessity. The bloodline cannot be broken," Methis said.

"You already said that," Kyra said. "The kingdom has other options."

Methis smiled. "If you think you can go out and find love, you're fooling yourself. No one in the kingdom could care for you; you're wingless. You are nothing but a means to an end."

Kyra narrowed her eyes. She wanted to dispute him but she knew he was mostly right. Except that Vujet loved her. She was seen as property; she saw how even her teachers looked at her. She was seen as a problem, not a solution.

There were two positives. Methis didn't even think to suspect Vujet of what Methis would see as transgressions against the crown. And Kyra had time. She could bear the discomfort and indignity of a lengthy medical procedure. Every moment she didn't have his child was more time she was secretly free to be with Vujet.

It was possible that Methis thought his line so strong that he would kill her when she bore him a son. So, she'd have to listen, and learn how to ensure he would never have a child.

"For the kingdom," she said.

Methis smiled. It sickened her to see it.

"Good, then," he said, standing. "You will be excused from classes tomorrow. I will have Vujet informed that you won't need to be transported."

Methis left her room, but the discomfort he'd brought with him remained.

She lifted her legs onto her chair and curled into a ball. What an unfeeling creature. What a disgusting excuse for an Iewen. He wasn't worthy of his green hair, let alone her father's crown. She couldn't let a son of his survive.

She gasped. She could do better; she could try and ensure it was Vujet's child who grew within her. No one would know. The child would always take after her, even the child of a legacy as strong as Methis's, because nothing was stronger than Amaranthus's legacy. Vujet had a far better legacy than Methis. There was loyalty and love in his veins.

She would never have freedom nor happiness, but her father's kingdom could have a bold king who served the kingdom. It was all as simple as continuing to take the oil Reia had procured for her and then stopping after she'd had the procedure.

Mayala

Mayala watched her two children from her table in the soft early light of Cthessa's luminous flowers. Amer wasn't yet awake, so she alone held a warm bundle as her children played. She felt an unfamiliar feeling of a warm heart and tapped her feet, bouncing the precious bundle.

Maia giggled as she Imitated her bigger sister's voice in play. She adored Fiare most of all. Mayala couldn't imagine how she had raised such an elegant little princess, but she knew she had two more little princesses, and her heart felt full.

"No, princesses don't talk like that," Maia said, giggling.

"I will rule my subjects with a stone fist," Alura said.

"No, princesses can't rule," Maia laughed, her whole face warmed by a broad smile.

"I will build another castle just for me," Alura said.

"You can't do that, Zona," Alura said.

Mayala's face went pale as she looked down to see that the baby in her arms was Maia. Shaking, she stood. She placed the baby in her crib and walked around the two children to see the beloved face of her only son. The warmth in her heart was replaced by a horrific ripping sensation. She felt the intense torment of losing her son again as she stared at him.

She gasped awake as her leaf bed opened immediately. She stepped out and leaned against the wall, gasping for breath. Over and over, she'd dreamed of him. His memory tortured her from the corners of her memory, like shadows calling to her, whispering of her failings.

Cthessa's light warmed the room slightly, just enough to see the floor. Malaya didn't want to recreate anything from the memory, so she didn't touch the wall. She picked up a soft, durable moss from beside her bed and closed her hand around it, warming it. After a moment, it started to glow. She pointed the moss around the room to see it was empty. She walked into her small lounge to see no sign of any of her children.

She stared at the egg with rising anger. The egg wasn't full of promise and pure love now. It felt twisted, knowing she could lose it, her sacrifice of health wasted. She sat at the table and breathed deeply. She flopped onto the table, the moss rolling from her open hand. She tapped her other hand on the table as she tensed it and intensified the tapping. She wanted to punch something, but she was of two great houses who both wouldn't lose their temper, so she rapped her hand on the cool wood.

She didn't know she'd heard it at first, but there was an offbeat echo to her tapping. She stopped, picking up the moss and sitting up abruptly. She tensed her wings and uncurled her antennae into the air, feeling around her. She saw and felt nothing, but still heard the tapping. She then realised that she knew that sound and looked over at her egg.

She stood, her knees shaking so much that she stumbled a little. Her heart was flooded with fear as she crinkled her brow and made her way across the small room. She wasn't ready to give her last years to another child. She'd lived six seasons, and with her health already failing her, she might not live to see her child into adulthood. She couldn't even be sure she'd see them grow up. She certainly might not see them get married like her nephew. She heard the tapping as tears welled in her eyes.

She didn't have the strength or time to raise the tiny creature, even if her breaking heart could handle it. She placed her shaking hand on the soft protective shell and felt the warmth from within. The egg sat on a bed of vines in a raised bowl; she could feel the warmth of the vines this close. Memories of first seeing Fiare, then Zona, Maia, and finally tiny Alura swirled in her mind.

She felt the excitement of the hatching just as she felt now, and shivers crawled the length of her body as she felt happy for a moment. She loved her children so dearly. Few things mattered as much to her as them. Her heart started thumping as she felt the tapping at her hand. When the tears in her eyes finally fell, it wasn't in horror but relief. She didn't know she could feel so much happiness for her last child, so she cried unhindered.

She placed the moss on the vines, its light shining brightly from the warmth as she placed her other hand on the shell. She'd carried the egg within her for only a short time, but it was such a precious feeling. As she listened to the tapping and felt it under her hands, she realised she wouldn't give any of it away. The true joy of first seeing her children and then helping them grow filled her heart.

She knew now that she wouldn't trade the torment of losing her children for anything because it came with the wonder of their existence. She could raise another child. She had enough strength left for one more, no matter much they'd be altered by knowing they had two siblings they'd never meet. Or the shattering ache her family felt for their loss. She would bring this baby into a world of privilege and extraordinary love. Most of all, this tiny baby was wanted.

Her eyes were too blurred to see the egg crack, but she felt it.

"I want to meet you now," she whispered. "I didn't know I could stand it, but all I want is to see you."

"You'll be Raishy if you're a girl. Named after my grandmother. If you're..." she choked on her words. "If you're a boy ..." She lost her words completely for a moment as her thoughts went again to Zona.

"You'll be mine, no matter what. And you'll be so loved, I promise. I promise."

The cracking under her fingers intensified. The light of the moss faded as the vines cooled. It encouraged the tiny creature to emerge into the world faster, and as always it did. The cracking beneath Mayala's shaking hands intensified. She felt the first touch of her child's hand into the world as their sharp little nails poked through.

Malaya's tears were so thick now, she was scared she wouldn't be able to see well enough to hold her child. She'd never cried this much in her life, but she didn't know if she could love another child. She was overwhelmed with love and pain.

She was also released from the crippling restraint of her despair and terror that she wouldn't be able to raise her own child. She had enough heart for two lost children, and another baby. Nothing surprised her more. Not even the murder of her son shocked her more than knowing she had the selflessness to raise another child through her torment.

She quietly gasped as the egg fully cracked and she wrapped her arms around her tiny child. The tiny infant cried softly at the harsh cold against their skin for the first time. She couldn't imagine how scared the little creature must be. She pulled them close and rocked them gently, as with her warmth and support their crying hushed.

She fell to her knees with the baby in her trembling arms. She realised that she'd never wanted anything more than their tiny existence. She held her child close to her healing heart as she cried against their head. She wiped her eye with her arm just enough to see a little boy in her arms. She cried then. Not the nearly silent cry from a moment ago, but loud and uncontrolled. It didn't matter that he was a boy; it only mattered that he was alive. She held hope and healing in her arms as she sobbed.

"May?" Amer said, running to her.

"It's a boy," she whispered, cradling her tiny son.

"I missed it," Amer said, his voice pained.

"I'm sorry," Mayala whispered.

"I won't miss a moment of his life," Amer said. His arms wrapped around her as they cradled their last son together.

"I want to call him Raishy," Mayala said.

"Your grandmother's name. It's perfect, May. Perfect," Amer said, kissing her head.

"He's perfect," she whispered.

CHAPTER 4

THE LAST HATCHLINGS

Hye

Hye held his one-season-old daughter's hands as she stood for the first time. His legacy was secrecy, and he'd lived his life concealing his emotions to the point where he seldom felt anything. He watched her tiny legs walk, with the assistance of her growing wings. She was so tiny, and yet he witnessed her walking. The flapping of her wings echoed the beating of his heart as it thumped within him.

Because of his legacy and skill, Hye hadn't even imagined that he could feel anything so deeply, and yet he was in awe of the tiny creature. He had stolen her, but in this moment, it didn't feel like she was anything but his own legacy. Above all else, he was saved from the grim truths of life by the realisation that she was truly his daughter, no matter who her creators had been.

She wasn't of his direct legacy, but she was the child of a master spy. Legacy was a birthright—what a child had the capacity to learn *and* what they were taught. Each was equally important, so for all intents and purposes she was his daughter, and there was a whole world of things he would teach her.

She lifted up from the floor, and then lost her footing and flew softly on the ground. Her first fall, and she'd caught herself. It was utterly baffling that such a small creature held so much potential. Hye sat in silence as he was overwhelmed with awe.

"If she doesn't catch herself, you should never reach to pick her up. It's important for her to try to stand on her own," Caise said.

Hye looked at her abruptly, his eyes briefly wide. For the first time in his life, he hadn't realised someone had entered the room he was in. Caise tilted her head to the side, and Hye returned his full attention to his daughter.

He had to be careful not to let his emotions prevent him from completing his work. That was one of the biggest reasons spies could suppress their emotions. Less noise to sort through provided more accurate results, but it was also for their safety. No one had ever snuck up on him before now. He had known of this danger before, but now he understood why so many spies died when they had children to teach their legacy to.

A part of him didn't want that legacy for his daughter. He didn't want her to be in danger when she felt the joy of her own child's first steps. But the legacy of a spy, especially that of a great house, was more important than any single life, no matter how personally precious. He smiled. It was bittersweet, but the delight of a child was worth a short life to him.

"She looks hungry," Caise said, handing him a bowl.

Hye looked at the bowl, confused, and then looked back at Caise.

Caise smiled and sat down next to him. She handed him a spoon.

"Do you have a name yet?" Caise asked.

Hye shook his head. Caise smiled as she leaned forward, gently taking the little one by the waist and pulling her back to her father. She put her gently onto his lap as he scrambled to adjust enough to make room for her on his knee.

"Are you hungry?" she asked her.

The child nodded.

"One spoon at a time, don't rush," Caise said.

Hye looked at Caise when he realised he'd have to feed her. He hadn't been around children, before and he didn't know the stages of their growth. He had always thought that one-season-old children could feed themselves.

Hye carefully took a spoon full of the unknown food from the bowl and spoonfed his daughter. She opened her mouth and chewed the almost liquid substance. She then opened her mouth for another spoonful. Hye utterly beamed. She was so wonderfully adorable. She didn't even know him, and yet she trusted him so much.

"She needs a name. I'll have to name her soon," Caise said.

"Names are important," Hye said.

"Yes, but better to have a bad one than none," Caise said. Hye looked at Caise again as she sighed.

"I'll leave you two to it," Caise said, smiling as she stood.

Hye didn't respond. Caise was right that she needed a name. It was overdue. But it was an impossible task for him; he was still unable to believe how much he loved a creature he'd only just met.

Fiare

Clad in Yurelle fashion, the foreign princess stood in the marketplace, holding a piece of silk cloth.

"This is the prettiest silk I've ever seen," she said, her voice so quiet it was almost a whisper.

"The She'ehlarah have far better silk," a female voice said. The voice was soft and airy, like the smooth silk in Fiare's fingertips.

Fiare turned to see a bright red-haired, beautiful female standing beside her. She too held a length of silk in her hands. Her clothing wasn't the typical, practical Yurelle style. It was more feminine, slightly less colourful, but somehow far more beautiful.

"We may make beautiful things, but they're nearly impossible to live in," Fiare said.

The stranger tilted her head slightly, her antenna bouncing gently in the air.

"I should tell you that I know who you are. I'm a senator, and when I heard you were coming here, I studied your face. I didn't intend to do so; I was just fascinated by how different your world is from mine," she said.

Fiare looked at her in silence for a time, pulling her bright wings behind her back.

"I see that you feel the same way about my culture as I do about yours," she said, honestly.

The stranger smiled. "How are you adjusting?" she asked.

"It was … intimidating at first, scary. There was so much that I thought I knew, but still surprised me," Fiare said.

"And now?" the stranger asked, releasing the silk in her hands.

Fiare thought on her words carefully. There were so many things she should have said, but there was only one thing she wanted to say. Whether she should say it or not was her dilemma. She took a breath. "It's enrapturing," Fiare said.

The stranger smiled. "I'm Avena."

Before Fiare could respond, her thoughts were interrupted. "Mistress Fiare." Fiare dropped the fine silk and on the table below it as she turned to see a male dressed in messenger's clothing.

"Princess," Avena corrected.

"Apologies," the messenger said, holding out a letter with the Grand Chancellor's seal.

Fiare noted he didn't correct his mistake. Many Yurelle didn't want to call a foreigner "princess", as she wasn't *their* princess. It had bothered her at first, but now she respected their ideals. They treasured the leadership of many ruling lineages, and they'd worked hard to achieve it. it resonated with her that they refused to give up on what they believed in. Fiare broke the seal and read the short statement.

Princess Fiare Dairsen,
  I'd like to meet with you to see how you're settling in and if you need anything.
  Grand Chancellor Olianna.

"I don't want to pry, but is everything all right?" Avena asked.

Fiare looked up at Avena and nodded. She then turned her attention to the messenger.

"Please tell the Grand Chancellor I will be happy to meet with her," Fiare said.

The messenger nodded and sped off through the busy market.

"Everything is just fine," Fiare said.

Avena smiled. Fiare looked at her in silence for another moment. She again wanted to say something, but she wasn't sure if she should. She thought it over carefully before she decided to listen to the long-silenced voice deep inside her.

"I haven't been here long enough to get to know the city. As someone of good taste, do you think you could introduce me?" Fiare asked.

"Nothing would delight me more, princess," Avena said.

"You should just call me Fiare," she said.

Avena smiled as she gestured for Fiare to follow her.

Syriel

Syriel sat in in one of the comfortable chairs in the She'ehlarah library. It was her favourite chair, as it was far too big for her and soft enough to almost swallow her whole. A think book about stone working lay heavily in her lap. It was an important book. As she sat taking in the scent of old paper and wooden book covers, all she could think about was the numerous happy mothers and fathers trotting around the castle. The same castle that she couldn't leave. She'd never been so confined, and she'd never felt such a failure as a queen without a child. She shook her head and read from the book.

The She'ehlarah, masters of the earth … what if she couldn't have a child? Her mother had problems having a child. No, she would return to her studies. At least she'd make a good ruler, even if she might be the last of her line. The only blue-haired creature in the whole world, and never to have a child.

"Stop," she whispered.

She returned her attention to the book on her lap, but the carefully written words wouldn't fight the torrent of thoughts in her mind. She closed the book.

She breathed in deeply and tried to listen for the echoing drip of water from Fasier. She could hear the sound in her memory, but not in her ears. She reached out again, pushing gently through the veil of darkness created by her closed eyes.

Nothing was beyond. The comfort of the familiarity she carried with her was out of reach. Her legacy was unattainable, just like the continuation of her line.

She closed her eyes and reached out again. This time, she sought her father and his promise that they would dream together. Her eyes flashed open as the memory of his unseeing eyes took control of her imagination.

She thought about the time they'd spent together, playing hide and seek around their Malarmhan apartment, his voice reading her too many stories to remember. She closed her eyes again and reached out to him. She breathed in the wet scent of the cave. But again, all she smelt was books, and all she felt was the comfort of the too-big chair.

"Syriel?" Tenro said.

Syriel opened her eyes and looked at her husband. He wasn't tall, but his stature was powerful. His shoulders held so confidently that in the moment of seeing him, her torment eased. In such moments, she remembered why she'd decided to leave her entire world behind.

"I've been looking everywhere for you," Tenro said, closing the distance between them.

"Why?" Syriel said, closing the book on her lap.

"Mayala's child is a boy," Tenro said.

Syriel smiled, but she felt her deception in the air. The furrow of Tenro's brow showed that he felt it, too. She tried to control her feelings, but the scent in the air didn't go away.

"We have so much time, Syriel," Tenro said, his antennae bouncing in the air.

"My mother struggled to have children," Syriel said.

"Couples can take a season or two to have a child, and we have nothing but time. And if we can't, we have options. Don't worry about a future we can't see. Enjoy the present," Tenro said.

Syriel smiled. Now if only he understood why it was such a torment to be disconnected from Fasier. Perhaps he had some magic words to console her about that.

"Come share some joy," Tenro said. He took her hand and pulled her out of the too-big chair.

"All right," Syriel said, hugging her husband for a moment.

"We only get this moment once, and once-in-a-lifetime moments need to be savoured. We should only worry about problems when we meet them," Tenro said.

"What is 'should' when the mind does what it wills?" Syriel said.

"We need to practice, then. When I was little, we had a meditation session every morning. We would focus our thoughts and take control of our complicated young minds. It was difficult, but me, Zona, and Fiare got a lot out of it. Fiare was the best of all of us," Tenro said.

"I wish she was here to talk to," Syriel said.

"When we're safe again, we could have her come visit us," Tenro said.

"*If* we're ever safe again," Syriel corrected.

"We will be," Tenro said.

"We are from such different worlds," Syriel said, her face darkening.

"Our worlds are of our own making, particularly ours, as we are king and queen. Whatever we want, we can make it. We just have to know what we want," Tenro said.

"How do you turn my every negative into something positive?" Syriel said.

"Because everything you say is positive. You just don't see it yet," Tenro said.

Syriel smiled.

"Let's not think about it now. We have a little person to meet," Tenro said.

"Right," Syriel said.

"Oh, I hope he's cute. Sometimes babies look so weird," Tenro said, laughing.

"Tenro!" Syriel said.

"I'm sure he'll be a great person, but sometimes babies are incredibly unfortunate-looking. It's just true," Tenro said.

Versai

Versai was one of four Dragonriders who stood at the barred doors to the castle with stiffened shoulders. Two She'ehlarah in servant clothing stood patiently with them.

Siah and Wyma with their children and Amer's two daughters approached.

Things seldom bothered Versai. Seeing Maia and Alura beside their aunt Siah, however, made her narrow her eyes. She thought it as possible that the children had asked to come with their aunts as that their aunts had convinced them to join. Whatever the case, their mother was ill and likely still too weak to stop them. Their aunts should know better than to endanger the children of their chosen's brother.

"It's the last day of the festival. Please have heart," Siah pleaded.

"I'm sorry, I truly am. I know how important the Bloom is. I just know that your safety is more important," Versai said. She looked specifically at Alura and Maia, who stood beside their aunt.

"We won't go far, and I will watch the children. They have never missed the festival, and their people will be scared when they don't see the girls," Siah said.

"I have orders to not let direct royal family into the city," Versai said.

"The doors have never been barred!" Siah said.

"They have been barred before, but it was a long time ago. They will be barred again whenever those within the castle need protecting again," Versai said.

"The Dairsen daughters wish to leave, and so they shall," Siah said.

She furrowed her brow. There had not been such danger since Amaranthus was killing queens and their children. She put her hand on her chitin blade and saw the faces of the gathered nobles change in an instant.

"By order of the king, these doors will not open," Versai said.

"We'll speak to Tenro," Wyma whispered.

Versai said nothing as the group walked away from the castle doors. When they were gone, Versai sighed. "Thank you for the tip," she said, looking at the two servants. Her attention then fell on the one who only wore a servant's clothing.

"Walk with me," she said, as she then looked at the other. "Please return to your work."

Both of them nodded, and the servant left. The pair walked in silence until they reached Versai's post. She walked through and turned to wait as the impostor closed the door.

"Thank you yet again, Hye," Versai said.

"I'm, sorry that this is our use during this time, general," Hye said. Versai nodded.

"Tell me about Guiyn and Laur's plan," she said.

"I still don't have exact numbers on Laur's army. The group training outside the city are a minimal threat," Hye said.

"Is there any indication of when they will attack?" Versai asked.

"None as yet," Hye said. "We're still not sure why they didn't stop the wedding as they originally planned."

"Wyma and Siah were overtly defiant. Is there friction between them and their coupled?" Versai said.

"I think it's the opposite. I expect they're feeling power that's not theirs, but if that changes, you'll be the first to know. General, I want to tell the king. Tenro is not like his uncle. This is a new reign, and we don't need to protect our king this time," Hye said.

"I cannot function with disbelief from our king. Our highest charge is to protect the crown," Versai said.

"I know our charge. Just like Tarind and Amer's relationship is vastly different from Laur and Tenro's. Tenro knows his father. My professional advice is that Tenro needs to know," Hye said.

"I regret saying this, but *I* have never made an error in judgement regarding the safety of the king," Versai said and pulled her shoulders back as she raised her chin.

Hye did not react, but she knew he'd grasped her meaning.

Hye sighed. "With respect, I think this is one, General," Hye said.

Versai furrowed her brow. She had not expected him to challenge her. He had to be confident to stand his ground. It was possible there was merit to what he said, but he'd said such things before. She let a silence grow between them as she weighed the possibilities. After a time, she realised that she couldn't make a decision yet. She moved on.

"Are we still prepared for an attack?" Versai said.

"Yes, General. Yune and Lon are ready to lead the king and queen to the Painted Garden until things calm down," Hye said.

"When did they last practice their alternate routes?" Versai said.

"I'm not sure of that, but when I last spoke to Yune, he said Lon is still going to the garden often. I am certain that they are ready at any moment," Hye said.

Versai nodded.

"I've said it before, but I have to restate this. Amer's choice to crown Tenro means that he sees his brothers clearly now. And he will be the secondary if not primary target of the attack ..." Hye began.

"I remember this. If the threat looks more dangerous, we will tell Amer," Versai said.

Hye raised his eyebrows. Versai made note of what was an extreme reaction from the usually stone-faced spymaster. "Thank you," Hye said.

Versai nodded. "That's all we needed to discuss," she said.

Hye nodded, then turned and left the room, closing the door behind him. Versai's thoughts returned to Hye's words.

Remin

The throne room of Daltay was bright and warm. Light poured in from the holes in the great tree. Remin felt the breath of the world upon his face. Tears streaked down his cheeks as his naked feet touched the soft fungus that was the floor of his world. He wiggled his feet and felt his body writhing. His hands touched the soft, warm ground as he looked up.

In one moment, the love for his home turned to agony. Methis stood above him, utterly unaware of his presence. It had been a blink when it happened, but now it was slow, as if a painter had drawn every moment second by second. The gallery of his torture was extensive. He was frozen in the moment when his second wing had hit the ground.

He'd felt it, and he heard it fall, but all he cared about then and now was her. The tiny girl in Methis's grasp sought to reach him. She pulled and writhed against his grip, but she couldn't get away, not then and not now. Tears flooded her little red eyes as she screamed and thrashed against her captor. But his one hand held her in an iron grip.

Immeasurable pain splintered through his body from his back, but still he stared at her, desperate to reach her. In an instant, her immature face changed to the face of someone he barely knew. Curious eyes watched him like a student learning from their teacher. Bright green hair was tied neatly behind her head.

Methis looked at Remin in that moment. "They're all mine," he scowled.

His attention then turned to the throne. Remin couldn't understand. He stared unblinking at what was the face of his daughter again. As he was still trying to save her, it happened again. The pinnacle of the worst moment of his tattered life. Kyra fainted.

When she fainted, he too felt the darkness in his mind protect him from the torture as he joined her in unconsciousness. It was the only way they'd ever be joined now.

His eyes opened to see a simple house. The walls had been painted in welcoming bright colours. The lower half was green, with a yellow band in the middle and blue above.

Like a field of flowers, Leisa had said. He focused on this imagined world of a whole field of yellow flowers as he tainted another happy moment with his nightmare.

He was truly confused as to whether she had been there or not. He had to remind himself she'd never even been to the city. He untangled the mess of his memories. It made him think about that moment again and again. She hadn't been there. It was his mind ruining the only good moment he'd found. Perfect god save him, he wasn't even in command of his own mind.

He looked at the body of his lover and reminded himself over and over that he wasn't up there. He was in a different world, free of it all. He ran a finger over the curve of the female sleeping next to him. She moaned and turned over, lifting up just enough to move her wing out from under her. Her yellow hair rolled over her shoulder.

"Good morning," she said. Her sweet voice was more welcome than the nectar they'd shared the night before. She sat up when she saw him. Her brow was furrowed, her mouth slightly open.

"Are you alright?" she asked, touching her soft hand to his cheek.

"Yes. Yes. I'm fine," he lied.

She narrowed her eyes at him, tilting her head slightly.

"I dreamed of Daltay," he said.

"A not-so-sweet dream?" she asked.

"Never sweet. It's always the worst moment," Remin said. Leisa curled up against him with her whole body.

"It has to ruin the only good mornings I've had here," Remin said.

91

"Then let's rebuilt it," she said, gently kissing him.

Remin smiled. He lowered his head to hide the shame of his weakness. He tried as hard as he could to stop it, but he felt both of his eyes well up with tears. Leisa kissed them away. "I don't know all the horrible things you've been through. But I can promise to give you some wonderful memories," she said.

"You are the source of all my good memories in recent times," Remin whispered.

He felt a fool for saying it. She was sure to leave him. Instead, he glanced up to see her smile. She threaded her fingers through his hair and gently rested his head on the front of her shoulder. Curled around each other, he felt the nightmare, the violence, and the agony melt away. At least for now.

He wrapped his hand around her back and touched his fingers to her wings. He missed them sorely. But if the cost of them was her, he'd make that exchange ten times over.

"I'm sorry I'm asking so many questions," she said, her voice quiet.

"You didn't cause my nightmare; I always have them. I like talking about the few good things of Daltay," he said.

"Can I spend another day with you?" she asked.

Remin could hardly believe it. It had to be pity. But even still, he nodded against her shoulder. She kissed his head and hugged him a little tighter for a moment. This could all end at any time; this surely had to be born of pity or the desire to conquer a king.

This was nothing like he'd known before. His brief affair with his servant had ended with her leaving him in shame and promised secrecy. She'd taken one look at their daughter and ran.

"We can stay here if you like, or I have this wonderful eatery where they make little cakes both sweet and savoury," she said.

"I love cakes," Remin said.

He squeezed his eyes shut. What a childish thing to say!

"Me too," she said. "I'd love to share them with you."

Remin snapped his eyes open and couldn't help but laugh.

"What's so funny?" Leisa asked.

Remin tried to find the words to define his state, but he simply couldn't. From one moment to the next his feelings shifted. He went from being sure this couldn't last to thinking maybe he could spend more days with her.

She sat up and caught his gaze.

"What?" she demanded, a smile stretched across her face, her eyes wide.

"Nothing," Remin replied.

"Laughing at nothing, hmm?" Leisa said.

"It's a little too much to believe, really," Remin said.

Leisa smiled, her eyes no longer wide. "Yes," she said, leaning back down to kiss him.

"You know … if you work with Tsune, you could come visit me all the time," Leisa said, looking away from him for a moment and then shifting her gaze back.

She wasn't subtle and he was certain she hadn't meant to be, that much was plain. She didn't strike him as any type of subtle, and he found that refreshing. He lay for a while in silence before he too smiled.

"I think I'd like that," Remin said.

"I think you'd make a good healer," Leisa said, biting her lip.

Remin laughed. She had to know he meant both parts of her suggestion. He took a deep breath and enjoyed the sight of her sitting beside him, leaning over him. Her naked body was so confidently shown it was a particularly precious moment. She had no shame of her intentions or method of pursuing them, and he found that incredibly desirable. A moment after his desire heightened, he knew she felt it in the air as she leaned back and flicked her hair out. She then looked at him the same way as she had the night before.

"I think I might know what you're seeking this morning," Remin said as he pulled her against his body.

"You'll have to show me to prove it," she said, biting her lip.

Tenro

Tenro approached Amer and Mayala's chamber door. One of the guards who flanked the door tapped gently.

"King Tenro and Queen Syriel to see you, Sire," the guard said.

Syriel took Tenro's hand and squeezed it lightly. Tenro looked over at his wife to see her wearing the same smile now as she did when Tenro had heard of his aunt's health problems. Her brow was furrowed and her antennae were curled inwards, but the smile on her face was genuine. He went to complement her, but the door opened and his attention snapped to the doorway.

"Tenro, Syriel, thank you for agreeing to visit," Amer said, his voice warm. He stepped from his room and embraced his nephew, then Syriel.

"It's good to see you, Uncle, but we're really here to see one of our newest subjects," Tenro said with a smile.

Amer stiffened his shoulders. "The crown has changed you, nephew," he said, breaking his straight face halfway through his sentence. Amer tapped Tenro roughly on the shoulder. "I don't think anything could change you," he said, stepping back into his chambers.

Tenro nodded as he entered Amer's chamber. Instead of the scent of paper and books, flowers and herbs were thick in the air. The air was slightly damp, signifying their pool was likely full. Amer and Mayala had largely kept their pool empty, as they were almost never home when Amer was king.

"Tenro," Mayala said, stepping into the entryway to hug him.

"Hello, Mayala," Tenro replied.

"Dear Syriel," Mayala said, hugging her.

"Good to see you both," Syriel said.

"I'll get Raishy," Mayala said.

"Don't wake him for us," Tenro said.

"Nonsense, you should meet your cousin," Mayala said warmly.

Tenro laughed as Mayala went off to get Raishy. It was so good to see her standing. Losing Zona had shaken him, and he was his cousin, not his parent. He had been beside Mayala through it, but he still didn't know how she was handling it, let alone the pain she felt. Of all of living Dairsens' mothers, she was the most committed. She had even been like a mother to Tenro when his own mother had been distant.

"I'm sorry I haven't come by much," Tenro said.

"No, it's expected that you'll need to prioritise your work. We know better than most how heavy that crown is on your head," Amer said.

"Family is important," Tenro said.

"We're not going anywhere. Your kingdom needs you to learn quickly," Amer said.

Tenro nodded. He knew Amer was right, but he realised he'd expected scolding. He had to remind himself that he wasn't Amer's student anymore. Their relationship was different; Amer couldn't guide him like he had. Tenro was king now. These were all things he knew, but seeing it in practice still surprised him.

The cry of a baby brought all attention to the tiny bundle in Mayala's arms. "Oh, there, there," she said, quietly.

Tenro stepped forward and reached his hand out to the fussing infant. The baby ignored him as he wiggled in his mother's arms. Mayala bounced him up and down until he went silent.

"Nice trick," Tenro said.

"You learn a few, after having four little ones. Take him," Mayala said, handing the bundle to Tenro.

Surprised, Tenro received the little child. "He's heavy," he said.

Mayala laughed as Raishy fussed in his arms. Mayala guided Tenro's arms to hold him securely and helped him rock the baby. A huge smile grew on Tenro's face. He was excited to meet his cousin, but he was surprised at how natural it felt to hold him. He looked at his new wife and shared a smile with her. She returned the smile, and from the look in her eye, she had the same thought.

"The shared look of a new couple," Amer said.

Tenro looked at his uncle abruptly. "Are we that obvious?" he asked.

"We all are. All kings and queens know the significance of children," Amer replied.

Syriel moved closer and put her hand on Tenro's arm. "I can only hope we can juggle the kingdom and the importance of the next generation," she said.

"You won't have any trouble with that. The two of you will love your kingdom and children just as much," Mayala said.

Syriel smiled at Mayala.

"Speaking of children, we asked you here not just for the delight of your company or for you to meet Raishy. My daughters went with their aunts in an attempt to leave the castle at the end of the festival," Mayala said.

Still gently bouncing his baby cousin, Tenro gave Mayala his full attention.

"I made it law that no one of the royal family will leave the castle until it's safe. This law has not changed when you became king, but they still tried to leave the castle," Amer said.

"Versai herself stopped them at the castle gate," Mayala said.

"Are you sure?" Tenro asked.

Mayala nodded.

"Certain," Amer said.

"You're insinuating that my position has to be made clear, too?" Tenro asked.

"Yes," Amer said.

"Would it be as simple as a proclamation, or should I speak to my mother and aunt personally?" Tenro asked.

"That's a question I don't have an answer for. Usually the father and mother of the king are entirely compliant with his rule because they chose him to be king," Amer said.

"You warned me that my rule would be difficult. And I know Syriel knew her journey was more challenging than mine," Tenro said.

Syriel nodded.

"We're walking new ground already, but we will handle this and keep to tradition," Syriel said.

"Typically, the new king would restate current laws in the first season of his rule. He'd add new laws too as he desired. I don't know if that will be enough to make it clear how important these laws are to a defiant family," Amer said.

"Let's try tradition before we're made to be unconventional," Tenro said.

"That sounds like a good start," Mayala said.

"I know you chose me, but I'm sorry for the trouble this puts the both of you in. Especially now," Tenro said.

"We *both* chose you," Amer said.

"I appreciate you saying that," Tenro said, looking at Amer and then Mayala.

"We can help you write a statement too. But later, we'll have lunch brought for us. I thought you might like to try and feed Raishy," Mayala said.

Tenro's face went from tense to relaxed in a moment. The way he and Syriel went forward was critically important, but that would be a short-lived problem. The parenting skills they'd learn now would help them with their own children, and they were the greatest future of their kingdom.

"I'd love that," Tenro said.

"Come sit down here. I'll bring it all out," Mayala said.

"Can I help?" Syriel asked.

"Please," Mayala said.

As the two females left the room, Tenro saw Amer go to say something. Tenro tilted his head.

"Don't make light of your mother and aunt's defiance, as I did of my brothers. I think a statement is a good first step. Your mother and aunt should be given the positions of respect and authority that they desire," Amer said.

Tenro moved Raishy in his arms, then nodded. He'd have to think about what it was that they even wanted.

"The food is out," Mayala said across the small dining room.

"Thank you, I won't make light of this," Tenro said, walking into the dining room.

Kyra

Kyra walked slowly out of the hospital. She saw Vujet waiting. He stood tall, as always watching diligently from the landing outside the building.

"You can walk faster than that, but just take it easy," the doctor said behind her.

"Thank you," Kyra said, her voice drained.

When he heard her voice, Vujet turned. His face went pale when he saw her. He closed the distance between them and picked her up gently. He didn't bring a harness anymore, which was a great relief.

"Do I look so poorly?" she whispered.

Vujet said nothing as he took off for her apartment. Every beat of his wings sent a jolt of pain through her body. She tried to sit still, but she wiggled in his arms a little. Vujet tightened his grip and sped up. It made the jostling worse, but Kyra knew it was because he cared.

It felt like hours, but they arrived at her home after Kyra thought she couldn't fly any further three times over. Vujet pushed past her guard and opened the door immediately. He put her on the floor of one room apartment and left quickly again.

She lay on her back in the middle of her floor, exhausted and sore. When Methis had told her that a medical procedure would be simple, she hadn't expected to feel so awful. She rolled onto her side and held her stomach loosely.

"The princess looks ill and I'd like to give her privacy, if you would be so kind as to give her that. Please don't tell Methis, again. I will stay here to ensure her personal security," Vujet said from outside. "As you will," the guard said as they left.

It was a moment longer before Vujet re-entered. "I'll dismiss the next guard shift, too," he said, sitting down next to her.

"You don't look well," Vujet said quietly.

"At least this time when you dismiss the guards, I don't worry about getting caught," Kyra said.

Vujet nodded. He flattened himself out on her floor and moved closer to her.

"You're worried something went wrong?" Kyra said.

"Yes. Everyone I asked said it can feel awful, but you look like you feel truly terrible," he said.

"I know this is a bad time, but while you were in the hospital, I talked to Reia as you asked. She found a female having the same procedure and had her ask the physician if she could take the oil if something went wrong with the pregnancy. The physician said it would be the best option, and it would surely end the growing life.

She said there would be no damage done, but are you sure you want to try this?" Vujet said.

"I'm certain," Kyra said, her voice even weaker.

"The physician was talking to a typical person, not the future of the kingdom. Reia has been incredible, but if she's working against you, this would be the perfect time to end Amaranthus's line. And what if she was wrong?" Vujet asked.

Kyra felt her eyes closing.

"Methis will come to see me, remember," she said, her voice barely a whisper now. Despite the awful feeling and the horrible pain, she felt herself falling into a much-appreciated sleep.

Reia

Reia was early, yet when she opened the door to her office, Kimure was already seated. He sat at her own desk, leaning back in her chair. It didn't bother her, but she still feigned irritation.

"You're early," Reia said.

"So are you, just less so. Which means I get the good seat," Kimure said.

"Fitting, that seems to be the way the kingdom is ruled," Reia said.

Kimure sat up. "You speak so openly against our rightful king," Kimure said.

Reia smiled. "I'm genuinely surprised you could say that with a straight face," she said.

"It was difficult," Kimure said, leaning back into her chair again.

Reia seated herself facing her own desk.

"Did you bring him up simply to jest, or is he the topic of this secret meeting?" Kimure said.

"He is," Reia said.

Kimure's face darkened a little. He was terrible at hiding his emotions. She felt the despondence in the air between them. His antennae twitched, likely in an attempt to feel any evidence of her mood.

Cute, she thought. She was delighted that so many key players in the political game thought her an amateur. She'd have surpassed Methis but for her purple hair. Like any skilled player, she'd use this to her advantage.

"We could talk about Daltay or walk around the point, but with such a busy and well-respected tactician such as yourself, it's better to get to the point, is it not?" Reia said.

"It is, of course. Woo me, girl," Kimure said.

Reia smiled, then furrowed her brow and lowered her head slightly.

"I have lost everything. If Methis dies, so does my chance to get it back. But we have a chance to stop Methis and restore the blood of Amaranthus to the throne. Restore the only royal bloodline that's ever ruled the Iewen. There is no certainty with Methis on the throne. Not even a certainty of our historic royal stability," Reia said.

"It's time for a change. There is a Yurelle in Velwrith," Kimure said.

"The only thing Iewen have ever agreed upon is who's head the crown belongs on," Reia said.

"The right head for the crown could finally be the end of the She'ehlarah. Methis is calling for war," Kimure said.

"A betrayal of the blood of the first king is more likely to be our end than theirs," Reia said.

"And your suggestion is to put a child on the throne just because she has Amaranthus's markings?"

"Kyra is young. She has no family, no guidance. She's proven to listen to a captain of the guard and me," Reia said.

"We simply don't want the same thing. You want to protect your people," Kimure said.

"The Iewen are my people. Listen to my words. Kyra's council is her spymaster and a soldier. Methis will do what brings him more power, but Kyra," Reia said, stepping forward, "Kyra is desperate to prove she is Iewen, and she'd destroy the She'ehlarah to do it."

"That's a gamble," Kimure said.

"No. I gave her poison to prevent a child from Methis," Reia said.

"You poisoned the last of Amaranthus's line?" Kimure said, standing.

"I told her it was poison. The point is, I watched her take the last dose," Reia said.

"Why would she do that?" Kimure said.

Reia sighed. "I already told you. She trusts me. We can convince her to attack the She'ehlarah as they fight among themselves from within," Reia said.

"Why do you think they're fighting internally?" Kimure said.

Reia pinched the bridge of her nose. "They have a blue-haired Yurelle ruling beside a king out of sequence," Reia said.

"And you assume ..." Kimure started.

"You know what a spymaster does, don't you?" Reia said.

Kimure slammed his fist on the table. "I know what you do, Reia. I want to know if you're guessing or ..." Kimure said.

"I *do not* guess," Reia said.

"You could be wrongly informed," Kimure said.

"I'm not," Reia said, looking at Kimure, unblinking. "I have nothing left but this kingdom. I am not taking chances, and I am not acting on anything but certainty."

"You're too late; I've been removed from the king's council. By letter ... not that Methis attends anymore," Kimure said.

"That's why I've come to you. The eyes of the public aren't on a former council member," Reia said.

"But Iewen treat their spymaster like royalty," Kimure said.

"That's why one could be crowned king. But he is not a king, and before even the most uninformed person realises this, we have to act. We have to restore the rightful legacy, and in so doing, have the most mouldable monarch we've ever had," Reia said.

"All right. Let's say I agree with you. What's to stop someone else form moulding her?" Kimure said.

"That's the most elegant part," Reia said, standing. "Methis had contorted our spy network to spy on his own people. I'm restoring it, but currently I see everything in Daltay. I know everyone who speaks to her. She's sheltered now, and I'm entirely confident I can keep it that way," Reia said.

Kimure smiled. Reia didn't know him well, but in all the time she'd been watching him, she'd never seen him smile with his eyes, until now.

"For Daltay," Kimure said.

"For Daltay. To be the only colony left when the dust settles," Reia said.

Kimure left the study, closing the door behind him.

Reia sat, breathing a sigh of relief. Kimure hated spies. She'd watched as part of Methis's network as he'd argued with even Methis himself. She thought she'd have to twist his hatred for spies into a hatred for Methis. He seemed to believe that she'd been angry at him, and that had helped greatly.

In truth, she *was* desperate. He wasn't her only contact, but he was an important one. He was an old soldier with too many friends to count. He had more pull than anyone else on the council had given him credit for. He'd help Kyra's rise just as he'd help her obliterate the She'ehlarah, at last.

Reia's purple hair would soon be a remnant of a non-existent people.

Yune

Yune opened his front door with gusto and kicked off his boots as he ran to his bedroom. Irda sat on their bed and put her finger to her lips when she saw him. Now without boots, he slowed and sat beside her.

"You got my note," Irda whispered.

"I did. I was lucky enough to be given leave to see our child hatch," Yune said, his voice matching her quietness.

Irda smiled broadly. "It's not progressed much, but look, we'll see our first child soon," she whispered.

Yune moved closer to his chosen as she leaned her head on his shoulder. "I never thought about how I would feel in this moment. I never expected to feel such concern," he said.

"In what way?" Irda said.

"I've trained numerous soldiers, but a child is something entirely different. I'll have to learn a whole new set of skills," Yune said.

"Well, you know, I've helped mothers in the Painted Garden. If you do it wrong, it could be the hardest thing you'll ever do. But if you're patient and gentle, and you try to impart the skills of your legacy, it is still a great challenge, but it will be one you rise to meet together," she said.

Yune smiled. So many of those of the Painted Garden never left it. She **was** her legacy as much as he was his. She believed in a better world through sharing and growing together. It was what he loved about her most, what he himself knew he'd never be. He also found it somewhat reductive. Her view of the world was so colourful, and that simply hadn't been his experience at all.

Irda gasped as another crack formed. There were numerous breaks in the eggshell now, and both parents sat forward on their bed.

"Any moment," Irda whispered.

The couple sat in silence for another few minutes as a little finger poked through the fragile egg. Irda, cloth in hand, jumped up and went to catch the child as if it might leap out. Yune moved from the bed and sat kneeling beside her. After another few minutes, a little face pushed through the egg as a healthy, but tiny baby crawled out. Irda took the infant up in a moment.

"A girl!" she said.

"Eri," Yune said, repeating the name they'd agreed on earlier.

"She's so tiny," Irda said, covering her in the cloth she'd held for her.

Yune gently patted some of the residue from the egg from his daughter's head.

"Careful," Irda said.

"Of course," Yune said with a smile.

He stared at his daughter in awe. He saw the pure joy in Irda's eyes as her emotion magnified his.

"We have a daughter, and she hatched late," he said quietly.

CHAPTER 5

WHAT IS TO COME

Tenro

A young Ptery sat in a domed underground garden of the Great Plant, Cthessa in the She'ehlarah castle of Velwrith. The seed chamber. Two braids that started at his temple coiled around the glass crown upon his head.

The scent of earth was thick in the cool central room of the undercity. Deep green vines crawled over the light grey stone walls that all connected to the huge bulb in the only earthen section of the room behind him. The bulb sat atop a mass of roots that over generations had grown so much that the bulb had lifted off the dirt where it had been planted. Teardrop-shaped leaves encircled the bulb, connecting at the very top. Some of her teardrop leaves were open, cradling her like a waking rosebud. The bulb was Cthessa, the beating heart of all She'ehlarahs' life. Tenro watched the bulb from the corner of his eye and imagined the bud opening.

With eyes forever closed, Aspect Leatti lifted her head. It was uncommon for their heads to move.

"Your brother would come to me often," Leatti said.

"You mean my cousin Zona," Tenro corrected.

"One and the same," Leatti said.

"The Iewen murdered him," Tenro said.

"Amaranthus's line is broken, and blood is shed again," Leatti said.

"That's what I just said. I know what happened. I want to know what *will* happen and what I should do," Tenro said.

"There is an old story about a time when the gods walked with us," Leatti said.

Tenro crossed his arms and furrowed his brow. She was distracted today.

"I remember that story, but it's old. Why do you speak of this now?" Tenro asked.

"I'd like to see that," she said.

"It's a story from the past. You mean you *have* seen it. Your tense is always wrong," Tenro said, his tone flat.

"We see things differently," Leatti said.

"I didn't come here to talk about perspective or history," Tenro said.

"Stay with the little one. Keep the egg," she said.

"In the great library of memories and legacies from our past, that is what Cthessa advises?" Tenro asked.

"It is," Leatti said, her tone final. "Leave her when she comes to me."

"Leatti, I can't bring her here," Tenro said.

"It was written on paper," Leatti said.

"You're talking about my marriage contract. She signed an agreement that we are equal in all things but your governance," Tenro said.

"I am not governed by any king or queen," Leatti said.

"Perspective again," Tenro noted.

"Time reveals," Leatti said.

Tenro sighed deeply.

"The Iewen are a serious threat," Tenro said.

"They will focus their hatred internally," Leatti said.

"You told me once before that the true enemy of the Iewen are themselves, but I never thought I'd see them kill their own king. You talked about them like they didn't have the strength to fight us, but they were able to kill my cousin. Are you underestimating them?" Tenro said, unfolding his arms.

"Zona didn't have the confidence or conviction of a Dairsen," Leatti said.

Tenro was disturbed by what she could mean. She'd been cryptic and confusing before, but this conversation seemed different.

"The way you say that …" Tenro furrowed his brow.

"You were born to be king; it was always you," Leatti said.

For the first time, it was Tenro who ended the conversation with the Aspect. He couldn't believe what her words could mean. Cthessa had so much information that she had been known to predict the future. Until this moment, Tenro had never expected that Cthessa could design her own future. Loyalty to the Great Plant was literally in his blood, but in this moment, he questioned everything.

Had she played a part in his cousin's murder? He wanted to ask her, but for the first time he was frightened about her answer, and even more worried about how it could affect his future. He had wanted to ask her about Sirathen, an Aspect who had died too soon, but now he thought he might already have the answer, but not her reasons. He was confident he'd have to learn her reasons himself.

Fiare

Clad in bright and practical Yurelle fashion, Fiare sat at her desk, studying numerous books of governmental protocol. It was so foreign but so clever that it felt familiar. So many things she'd talked to her father about were here. They'd been here all along. It was incredible, dizzying. She'd been told her whole life that the Yurelle were reckless and defiant, but all she saw here was intellect, careful, thorough, and forward thinking. More so, she found home in the words she read. A world where she could fit.

There was a knock at the door. She desperately wanted to keep reading, but she opened the door. Olianna greeted her with wide eyes.

"You're looking different," Olianna said, gesturing at Fiare's clothing.

"Hello, Grand Chancellor. It's nice to be comfortable when I'm reading," Fiare said, blushing.

"Don't be embarrassed. Anyone in the city would think it a compliment. And call me Olianna," Olianna said.

Fiare nodded. "No one back home would fail to recognise me," Fiare said.

"Are you concerned about that?" Olianna said.

"Only that I find myself not caring about it at all," Fiare said.

Just when Fiare thought she was being too informal, Olianna's face brightened. "Oh, I'm sorry, please come in," Fiare said, moving out of the doorway.

Olianna walked into the room that had previously been her daughter's. Fiare closed the door behind her.

"I don't have the heart to change much," Fiare said.

"Syriel has a new home; you should change whatever you like," Olianna said.

"Well … I also like her style," Fiare said.

Olianna looked over her desk. "Heavy reading," Olianna said.

"Surprisingly easy reading," Fiare said.

"Really?" Olianna said, focusing her attention on Fiare.

"It's smart and practical," Fiare said.

"That's why the pioneers first left Velwrith," Olianna said.

"Kindred," Fiare whispered.

From the smile tugging at the corners of Olianna's mouth, Fiare knew she must have heard her.

"Would you like to attend a Senate meeting?" Olianna said.

Fiare's eyes went wide. "I would be allowed?" she said.

"It hasn't been done before, but nor has a Yurelle marrying a She'ehlarah," Olianna said.

"It feels utterly bizarre to be the one walking new ground," Fiare said.

"Before you came here, I researched you and your family carefully. Every account was that you were definingly dutiful. You were as She'ehlarah as a person could be. But it also seems that you're an outstanding daughter of your people, and walked a path that wasn't right for you without a single misstep," Olianna said.

Fiare didn't know how to reply. In one chilling moment someone had seen right through her, when her family hadn't. It hurt. Not only because before Olianna's daughter had married her cousin, their people's relationship was strained. Yet all this time, she was somewhere she felt more at home than with her own people.

"I'm sorry, was that too forward?" Olianna said.

"No. You're completely right, I just wish ..." Fiare's words trailed off.

"From one pioneer to another, you belong with us as long as you want to stay." Olianna said.

"Thank you, Olianna," Fiare said, feeling utterly strange using her name instead of her title.

"I'll see what I can do about the Senate meeting. If there is anything you need, please don't hesitate to ask me," Olianna said.

Fiare smiled. "Thank you, truly," she said. Fiare could sense her own pain in the air, and she knew Olianna felt it too. She didn't know if Olianna understood why it hung between them, but it was clearly there. Fiare had spent her whole life concealing her true feelings. To be so transparent in this moment was a shock even to herself. Perhaps the Yurelle were rubbing off on her.

"Well, you have a lot to do," Olianna said, gesturing at Fiare's desk. Fiare nodded. Olianna let herself out.

Fiare sat at her desk again. She was too shaken to resume the reading that had been a revelation just a moment before. She wanted to go home. She felt like she was betraying her people by being so comfortable in a foreign place. But most of all, she wanted her family to see her as Olianna did. She reminded herself of what she always had: dreams were for rest, not for waking.

Yune

The heir's guards' commander stood beside the royal training yard in the upper part of the castle. The upper level of the castle was the main entrance to Velwrith from other nations. Travelling by hawk was fast and safe. It had taken many generations for the She'ehlarah to utilise the great creatures. It is written that before the hawk port, visitors were scarce and mail carriers disappeared often. The great birds changed life in ways too numerous to imagine life without them.

The huge doors at the front of the castle were open for She'ehlarah farmers and those who lived outside the castle, like Yune. The top part of the castle had the least of Cthessa's vines, being the highest point away from the bulbous plant far below in the undercity.

Yune was slightly distracted from only just hearing about a number of secret passages through the castle. They were secrets for him, his king, and his queen. Being part of the king's guard was the highest honour for any Dragonrider, and of far greater significance than heir guard. He never dreamed he'd get promoted, especially after Zona had died in his care. It was an incredible responsibility, and he had vowed not to fail. His whole unit needed to be stronger for him to keep his word.

Commander Yune watched Saf train on the field as his weakest soldier's weapon was again knocked from his hand. Saf fell to the hardy moss that lined the training field. Every She'ehlarah soldier had fallen in these training grounds, and they all knew it wasn't as soft as it looked. It needed to be firm enough to not restrict movement at all.

"Damn it!" Saf yelled.

"Again," Yune said dryly.

With a heavy sigh and laboured movements, Saf retrieved his wooden weapon and regained his composure, then his stance. He and his opponent turned to Yune, who nodded. Then they fought again.

Saf launched himself into the air and then forward toward his opponent. His opponent stepped away easily and brought her wooden weapon down on Saf's exposed arm. In one attack, Saf again stood without a weapon. Saf wrinkled his nose, ready to retrieve his weapon upon command.

"Enough for today. Thank you," Yune said.

"Anything for the heir guard. And for you, Commander Yune. Well fought, Saf," she said, her tone genuine.

The young soldier placed her sword hand as a balled fist on her armoured chest, retrieved her weapon, and left the training grounds.

"You did well. You're getting better," Yune said.

"I'm not, Commander," Saf said mournfully.

"You are. Far better," Yune said.

The look on Saf's face was unnerving to Yune. For the first time, Saf didn't believe his commander. Until that moment, Yune thought he'd taken the loss of their charge the worst. Bren and Lon had been doing poorly, and he knew Saf was doing even worse, but he seemed uncharacteristically wounded. At first Yune had continued his training without pause, but now he thought Saf needed something else.

"Come with me," Yune said.

Saf picked up his sword and walked the distance to return it to the shelf beside the training grounds. When Saf reached Yune, the commander turned and led his soldier away from the upper castle. He walked intentionally slow as he searched for the words he knew Saf needed to hear.

"You were the only soldier I chose," he said.

In the corner of his eye, he could see Saf's eyes widen. He felt his shock in the air. Saf was the rawest of his soldiers when it came to his emotions. Yune thought for another moment on his words. He needed to convey this correctly, or it could wound Saf instead of heal him.

"Lon is one of the most exceptional fighters of all within our ranks. Bren is extremely talented also. Well respected, high achieving, and loyal. Soldiers of a strong legacy have their emotions deadened to think clearer and to fight through whatever pain and torment we face," Yune said.

Saf nodded, and in the corner of his eye Yune saw him look away. The pair hadn't yet reached the stairs to the lower level. The stairs were fast approaching, though. Yune didn't want to have their conversation on the stairs, so he stopped walking. When he did, Saf did also.

"You have a rare set of skills for a Dragonrider. You're a brave and strong fighter, but also part of an elite group who are far beyond strong. I didn't choose you for what you lack, but for what we lack. Despite your fighting skill, you feel. You're genuine, warm, and you point us all to where we need to face. You are the beating heart of the king's guard." Yune said.

Saf's eyes went wide. He seemed as lost in spirit as he was for words.

"We need you," Yune said simply.

"I don't understand," Saf said.

"How can I help?" Yune asked.

"Help me?" Saf said, pointing to himself. Yune nodded.

"So, you can help us," Yune explained.

Saf smiled. "One day off," he said.

Yune nodded. It was a trivial request, but if it was what Saf needed, he would have it.

"Enjoy the festivities. Spend some time with your promised."

Saf looked at his commander with great appreciation, and the single look held a lot of information. Dragonriders were not emotional. Saf's legacy was weak, however, and most would think that a bad thing in such an important unit, but Yune had chosen him for it.

Yune was honest; Saf was the group's heart. But anyone could see his strength was failing him. Just as in a Ptery's body, the heart needed to be protected so it could keep beating strong.

After a moment of silence, Yune turned to the stairs again and continued walking. He heard Saf's footsteps behind him shortly after.

Syriel

Syriel watched Tenro pacing in his private study. "They put my sisters in danger," Tenro said, a hint of irritation in his voice.

Syriel observed what seemed an almost uncharacteristic display of emotion. She was more shocked that concerned for him. A part of her found it appealing; his care for his family had never been more apparent. She sat down and gestured for him to do the same.

"What can be done about it?" she asked, taking on what was usually his role and steering the conversation in a conclusive direction.

Tenro stopped pacing and looked at her. He smiled briefly and seated himself. Syriel watched as he went from a moment of concern to the clever king she'd married. She was grateful for the change, as she couldn't even imagine how she would handle this if he couldn't. Well, she knew how; she wouldn't. But something needed to be done about it.

"Tell me how to help," Syriel said.

"To 'help'?" Tenro asked, his eyebrows raised. "What do you think we should do?"

"We?" Syriel asked.

"This is your family as well as mine. You are just as much a part of this as me, and to be honest, I need your opinion," he said.

"I don't think we should reward them," Syriel said.

"Nor do I," Tenro said.

Syriel smiled. "Before we decide what to do, why isn't General Versai on the king's council?" she asked.

"She was. My father convinced Amer that as head of the Dragonriders, he was a better choice," he said.

"Why did he remove her instead of creating an additional position for your father?" Syriel asked.

Tenro furrowed his brow.

"I never understood that either," he said. "I think there's more to it than that, but I only heard my father talk about it. I never asked Amer."

"Perhaps it's what he spoke about at lunch. He wanted to make his brothers feel important," Syriel said.

"Not both his brothers. He never made a position on the council for my uncle," Tenro said.

"I think we should speak to Versai before we decide," Syriel said.

"Perhaps. We should have an idea of what we want to do now, just in case," Tenro said.

"I love the way you think," Syriel said.

Tenro walked toward her and let her lean against his chest, as she so often did.

"I think we should tighten the guards on the front gate and at the hawk port and say nothing about it," Tenro said.

"Everyone will notice higher security, which sounds like a strong message without embarrassing anyone," Syriel said.

"I expect they'll feel angry at least, though," Tenro said.

"It's likely that's unavoidable," Syriel said.

"I'd like to talk to my oldest cousins personally to understand what they were thinking. Maia especially knows her mother needs her right now, and it's not the time to act up," Tenro said.

"I think it might be a bad time to remind her that she's not the king's daughter right now," Syriel said.

"I know. I lost a brother too. I'm older, but Maia, Vira, and Pame are not children any longer. My sister Meri and cousin Alura still are, though. This is a dangerous time when we've already had one prince die. How long do you think we should wait?" Tenro asked.

"That I don't know. Perhaps you're right to tell them now. I don't have any siblings, so ..." Syriel said.

"You didn't. I told you before, you do now. It will take time to get to know Meri, but she's your sister now too," Tenro said.

Syriel stepped back and nodded. "You're right. I should get to know her," she said.

"Certainly," Tenro said. "We'll go see Versai, tighten security, and have our older cousins meet with us."

"Did you expect to have to manage your own family?" Syriel asked.

"No. Amer said it would be hard, and I knew my family would resist from the first moment. When I was named king, my father was furious. It took Lon to tell him to step back for him to get out of my way when I left the throne room," Tenro said.

"You talk about Amer as your father, but what about your actual father? Can I ask about your relationship?" Syriel said.

"Amer was my father, and my real father was absent. It's not complicated or painful," Tenro said.

"I don't get along with my mother right now. She's mad that I didn't want to come here," Syriel said.

"I can understand that. I've lived my whole life for this kingdom, and I honestly don't know if I could give it up," Tenro said.

"I think if you thought it was for the good of your kingdom, you'd do anything. I envy your faith and conviction," Syriel said.

"You have it too; it just takes you a little longer," Tenro said.

"You think so?" Syriel asked, her antenna feeling the air for more of a hint of his opinion.

"I think you're the bravest person I know, and you have no idea how much I respect you for that. I'll always remember that first night we met, when all you talked about was the best choice for everyone," Tenro said.

"I love you," Syriel said.

Tenro smiled. "And I you," he said, closing the distance between them to kiss.

Remin

It was early when Remin approached the same hospital where he'd woken up. It was far from his lover's house, but further into the city than his home. Thinking about her, he knocked on the wall of the curtained doorway into the building. The curtain parted as the familiar form of Tsune stepped through.

"Remin. What can I do for you?" Tsune said.

"I'd like to help," Remin said.

Tsune nodded. "It's hard work, but we need more people than ever."

"I need to work hard right now," Remin said.

"I expect so. I thought you'd get into construction with Gerathin, honestly," Tsune said in a whisper as he stepped back into the doorway. "Had my heart set on you making a door for us."

"A part of my roof fell in soon after I built it. I think it's not my calling," Remin said, matching Tsune's quiet voice.

"Everything takes time down here. Learning a new legacy is almost as painful as the fall. Come on in," Tsune said.

Remin stepped through the curtain. The familiar smell of the tangle creeping into the newly built hospital was familiar and comforting to him now. It smelt like his own home.

"I was just about to check on someone in this room," Tsune said, pointing to a curtained doorway.

He pulled the doorway open and spoke directly to the sleeping, wingless Iewen within.

"Good morning. I'd like to check your bandages again," Tsune said.

The Iewen woke slowly and turned. His face turned pale and his eyes went wide as he stared at Remin.

"Good morning," Remin whispered.

Tsune looked back at Remin and then to the patient. "He's not a king anymore, and he has a new name. Remin is here to help you," Tsune said.

The patient didn't blink, however. Tsune gestured for Remin to leave the room, and he did as he was requested.

He stood out of sight as he heard the sound of sticky bandages being removed. The poor Iewen complained slightly. From that, Remin thought that he wasn't a soldier, but that he wasn't inexperienced with pain. Remin couldn't guess what his legacy was. He stood silently as the Iewen was seen to.

Tsune left the room and pulled the curtain closed again. "If everyone reacts to you like this, it's not going to be the right place for you," he whispered. Remin nodded.

"Your daughter is alive," the male whispered from behind the curtain.

Remin moved past Tsune and opened the curtain. He stated at the Iewen in disbelief.

"The first thing Methis did was make a new law that any Iewen of a great house could claim a wingless. And then Methis claimed her," the Iewen said.

Remin's jaw dropped.

"She's been seen leaving her apartment to study every day. That's all I know, but I know she's alive and well," he said.

"Thank you. I'm sorry for the discomfort I caused you," Remin said.

The Iewen shook his head. "I thought I was dreaming until I saw you," the Iewen said.

"I thought the same, but I think you'll find it's better to be here than up there," Remin said.

"If you're saying that, then I'd believe it. You're not king here, but you'd still prefer to be here," the Iewen said. A curtain opened behind him.

"Careful, you shouldn't be walking yet," Tsune said, rushing to another patient. "And you need sleep. Not rest, sleep. You haven't slept even nearly enough," Tsune pointed back at the Iewen Remin was talking to.

Remin turned to see another Iewen looking at him with wide eyes.

Remin rushed to help Tsune steady him. Remin and Tsune got him back to his bed. When he was safely in bed, the wounded Iewen laughed. "Never thought a king would carry me to my sickbed after exile," he said.

"I'm not a king here," Remin said.

"He's just a healer," Tsune said.

"Can he come to see me?" a voice asked.

"I can," Remin said quietly. "Do you need any help?"

Remin drew back the curtain of the calling Iewen to see another surprised face. "No, I just wanted to see you," the Iewen said.

Remin looked at Tsune. "How many are there?" Remin asked.

"All six rooms here are full," Tsune said. "We had to build another male hospital, which is why we didn't yet get a door. And at this time of day, I try to change the bandages of every occupant."

"Show me how," Remin said.

Tsune nodded. "We'll start with our adventurer in there who just had to get up. Be warned, though, his adventure would have made his back look worse. I hope you have a strong stomach," Tsune said.

"I developed one," Remin said.

Tsune looked at him for a moment. Remin was confident that his meaning was understood. Tsune nodded and gestured at the room they'd just left.

Tsune took the bandages off the Iewen's back and heard no cry of pain. "Were you a soldier?" Remin asked.

"Yes," the Iewen replied.

Tsune dabbed his back with a cloth that had been hanging in the room. It did look bad, but far less bad than when the gruesome violence had occurred.

Tsune pointed to a pile of clean bandages on a table beside the bed. Remin handed them to Tsune. Tsune applied a viscous liquid to the Iewen's back and then wrapped the bandaged around his middle.

"It's an herb mix. It keeps the wound clean, stops the bandages from sticking a little, and promotes healing. It's quite a marvel; the wounded heal much faster here than they do up there because of it," Tsune said.

Remin attentively watched Tsune work. It seemed simple enough.

"We only need to make sure everyone's bandages are replaced in the morning, given water all day, food at mealtimes, and that their pots are emptied when they need it. The physician stitches wounds and sees them every few days. We just take care of the constant work," Tsune said.

Remin nodded, but he was already thinking it was the wrong work for him. Tsune looked over his shoulder when Remin hadn't replied.

"It gets easier. When I first worked here, I felt the pain in my wound, but I wanted to help enough that it went away," Tsune said.

That seemed far worse than what Remin felt. His back still hurt from time to time, particularly when he instinctively tried to flick his wings. The sound was ever repeating in his mind, but a part of Remin thought he deserved it for what he'd done to Tsune and others like him.

"All done, next patient," Tsune said, standing and hanging up the wet cloth he'd used to clean the Iewen's back. "We'll clean these later with another herb mix."

Tsune left the room with Remin following him. "Your time to try it now," Tsune said.

Remin nodded and started to remove the bandages from the next wounded exile, who stared at him unblinking, making no cry of pain. When he was done, Tsune handed him the hanging wet cloth.

Remin gently wiped down the exile's back, and then Tsune dabbed it with the mix from his belt. Remin then slowly wrapped the bandages around his middle. All of it was harder than it looked, but with a little adjustment from Tsune along the way, another of the wounded had fresh bandages.

It was surreal to work beside Tsune. Remin smiled at him with a furrowed brow.

"It really does get easier, all of it. That goes to all of you," Tsune said.

Tenro

Tenro looked at his wife seated beside him in the king's council room. It felt powerful to be enveloped by the gentle purple wall panels that covered the otherwise bare stone. Most rooms in the castle were just bare stone, so those that were painted were intentionally made more significant.

Syriel looked over multiple different reports. Tenro felt her nervousness in the air. Her worry about their choice somehow made him more confident. He couldn't imagine how his uncle had ruled the kingdom without his chosen beside him in power. He couldn't imagine how the kingdom had been so successful with the king having to ask for the opinion of his chosen in private. He could see how sharing power could go wrong, but perhaps Syriel's people still had the right idea.

Nothing about Amer's choice was ever going to be easy. Tenro had been thrust into a precarious position, in large part due to his marriage to an equal and foreign queen. Even without her, he was a king out of line in direct contest with his own father. Syriel's presence complicated it further, but Tenro cherished her beside him. He always excelled when faced with any challenge he'd been given. Challenge inspired him.

A knock at the door interrupted his thoughts.

"She's here," Syriel said, unnecessarily.

Tenro took her now-unoccupied hand and received a faint smile as a reward. "Enter the General," he said.

The door opened, and the seasoned General Versai stepped into the room and closed the door behind her.

"Thank you for meeting with us right away. Were you able to clear your afternoon?" Tenro asked.

"Yes, sire," Versai said, bowing her head.

"Please be seated. We have much to discuss," Tenro said.

Versai did as she was asked as Syriel sat up in her chair. Tenro looked at her and gestured to Versai with his free hand. Tenro didn't have to be feel her delight in the air to know she was excited to deliver their decision herself.

"We would like to ask that you re-join the king's council," Syriel said, her voice flat and decisive.

Tenro could hardly believe it, but he caught a distinct feeling of shock for a brief moment. He wouldn't have thought it had originated from Versai from the unchanged expression on her face, but he knew it could only be from her.

"I accept the position gladly, Majesties," Versai said.

"'Majesties' … that's the royal address used by the Zrti," Syriel said, her tone turning light, her voice quiet.

"We used it here once, too, just as the Feularah did," Tenro said.

"Until kings took the crown after our queens were attacked by Amaranthus and his followers," Versai said.

"History is always important, but we did have an agenda in returning you into the council at this moment," Tenro said.

"Yes, of course. We'd like to raise security, but we wanted to hear your thoughts on the matter before we brought it up at council today," Syriel said as her tone returned to decisive and filled with the conviction befitting a queen.

"I think that would be a wise yet unwelcome decision," Versai said.

"We thought the same," Tenro said.

"The lives of those within this castle are more important than their comfort," Syriel added.

"Agreed," Versai said.

"That was a lot easier than I expected," Syriel said, with a slight giggle.

"Indeed," Tenro agreed.

Syriel looked at Tenro with a furrowed brow. Tenro guessed she wanted permission for something, as she had been asking. He leaned closer to her to whisper. "If you want to ask something, you have as much power as me," Tenro reminded.

Syriel nodded. "I want to ask a question that may be uncomfortable," Syriel said, focusing her full attention on Versai.

"Please ask," Versai said.

Tenro thought Versai might already know what Syriel was going to ask, but as an exemplar of a Dragonrider, she waited to hear the question rather than assume it.

"Why was the council changed in the first place?" Syriel asked.

Tenro didn't appreciate how gently Syriel had asked. She needed to believe she had the right to rule. Versai nodded, showing Tenro was right that she already knew what Syriel was going to ask.

"I advised King Amer to remove his brothers from power, and at the time he disagreed," Versai said.

"I feel like that's an understatement," Tenro said.

"It certainly is," Versai said with a slight smile.

"The council gathers soon. Could you brief us on the current security in the kingdom?" Tenro asked.

Versai smiled, a sight Tenro couldn't remember seeing before.

"Gladly, Majesties," Versai said.

Kyra

Kyra's door opened to the sight of Methis standing in the doorway. She didn't know how many hours it had been, but she felt well enough to sit up. Nothing made her more alert than the sight of the person she hated most in the world.

"You look well," Methis said, walking across the room as if it were his own.

Kyra turned in her bed and went to stand up, but felt her knees buckle as she fell back to the safety of her bed. Methis crossed the room quickly and took her arm.

"Careful, you're holding our future," he said.

Kyra nodded; she didn't think she could voice a lie that would deceive him.

"Sorry, Highness, I feel weak," she said.

"I was told you might, so I waited to see you," he said as he pressed his hand on her belly.

She wanted to scream. She wanted to hit him, but somehow, she didn't.

"Forgive me, I feel awful. I must sleep," she said, sliding back into her bed.

"Yes, rest. I'll come back to see you in a few days," Methis said.

Kyra pulled her blanket over her poorly clothed body and turned away from him. He stayed in the room, however. She felt the bed move as he lay down next to her. She closed her eyes and tried to think only about the child her and Vujet would have. She hoped he'd have his sweet eyes, but her chin. *He,* she thought to herself. What a dream.

A tap on the door roused her from her distraction.

"Highness, there is an emissary looking for you," Vujet said from beyond the door.

Methis got up quickly and left the room.

"They sent a letter," Vujet said.

"Look after her, please," Methis said, his voice muffled from behind the door.

After a moment, the door opened again. This time, it was Vujet in the doorway.

"I asked Reia to deliver him a new consort," Vujet said.

"Thank you!" Kyra said. Her voice was loud, which she only

realised when she heard it. Vujet seemed to notice too and frowned.

"The landing *is* empty," he said.

"I know, I didn't mean to be loud. I just ..." Kyra said.

Vujet crossed the room to touch her, but she recoiled from him.

"I need to bathe," Kyra said.

"You did great," Vujet said.

Kyra nodded, but she didn't feel like she'd done anything. She was grateful she hadn't vomited on Methis. "Join me in a few minutes," she said, getting up carefully.

Vujet gave her space, but held out his arm in case she needed his support. With her hand on the wall, she made her way to her bathroom and closed the door.

Hye

Dressed as a servant, Hye made his way into the council room last. He was taken aback at the sight of Versai already sitting at the table. She nodded at him as he entered, and Hye returned the gesture. Regardless of why she was here, it was important that she was.

"Thank you all for being here. I have an important matter to speak on today," Tenro said.

"Security," Syriel said.

Hye found his seat quickly.

"We'd like to discuss increasing the guard presence in the castle," Tenro said.

Surely Versai hadn't told them about the coming attack. He glanced at her, but she remained incredibly hard to read, even for Hye, as usual.

"Pardon, Highness, but do we believe security is not already sufficient?" Hye asked.

"Some of the castle residents have seemed to have forgotten why no royal may leave the castle. We hope to remind them of the danger or making mistakes," Tenro said.

Hye nodded.

"I realise safety is important, but it's been difficult, even for those who live outside the castle and work here," Natai, the advocate said.

"I have certainly seen the discomfort on the faces of more and more castle residents," Shara the High Priest said.

"The protection of those within the castle has never been more important," Versai said.

"No one can reasonably disagree with that. But there's another serious problem when castle residents are forced to be reminded of the danger in the form of more soldiers. It's already more oppressive than ever in history, other than when Amaranthus was rampaging in our new city. I think we need to give people a little freedom for the sake of their sanity," Natai said.

"That would harm the economy. It's been incredibly difficult to trade when the castle isn't accepting many hawks. Not to mention the loss the outskirts of the castle took from anyone of a royal line not participating in the festival," Craime the economist said.

Tenro leaned back in his chair. He looked at Syriel as he seemed to think for a time. Hye already knew the problems the kingdom faced from the murder of their prince. It ran deeper than even those in this room had already voiced.

A divide was growing. There were many who didn't want Tenro to be their king, and above all, the people didn't want a queen, let alone a foreign one. Security was important, with the potential incoming domestic attack. But it was still a force outside their legacy against the full might of the Dragonriders.

Above all, their kingdom was on shakier legs than anyone in the room seemed to realise. The whole kingdom needed a little freedom now more than ever, especially if the Iewen were to attack again.

Those within the castle wouldn't see sky for an unknown length of time, perhaps even long enough to end the Iewen entirely.

"A few days of letting those within the castle walk outside of it would do a great deal of good," Hye said.

All heads in the room turned to face him. "It's surely too dangerous to let everyone have a few days," Alina the Archivist said, looking at Versai.

"It's far too dangerous," Versai said.

"Two days won't be enough for an attack to be made, and the Iewen won't expect it if it's announced to be directly following the announcement," Hye said.

"Zona's assassin waited almost quarter-season. You know that, Hye," Tenro said.

"Yes. She waited on the order from Methis after he'd overthrown his king. Methis was that confident he'd succeed. He has no reason to believe we'd let the royal family out of the castle," Hye said.

"What if they get a taste of it and can't go back?" Natai said.

"As the advocate of the people, do you think that would happen?" Hye said.

"I don't know. We have the old books about this time in history, and it was only ever described as having been awful. We didn't always keep such good records, and we lost a lot of books over time," Natai said.

"Nothing compares to this, exactly. Any choice we make could be our last, so it's best not to make any choice we might regret," Versai said, looking at Hye.

Hye grasped her meaning, but it was because of the attack that he wanted to give those in the castle a little more freedom. "Ultimately, it is the decision of our King and Queen, so I would advise that whatever you choose, you don't do so lightly," he said.

"Every decision we make has been based on the learned opinions of those around us, and only after careful deliberation," Syriel said.

"Let us call for a vote from the experts. All for increasing security in the castle?" Tenro said.

A single hand went up, and didn't waver when she saw she was the only one in favour. Hye expected that Versai already knew she'd be the only one who wanted additional security, but cast her vote regardless.

"All those for maintaining the same level of security," Tenro said.

Shara and Alina's hands went up.

"So that leaves three votes to give the residents in the castle two days of freedom," Tenro said.

The three who hadn't voted nodded. Syriel leaned over to Tenro and whispered in his ear. Tenro nodded and then looked at Natai.

"I was going to speak with Syriel about this in private, but it seems we agree. I expected to leave this room with more guards posted in the castle, at least. Instead, we'll all leave with the residents of the castle seeing two days of time beyond the walls. That is, except for myself and Syriel, who will be kept under guard during that time. Please make the announcement, Natai," Tenro said.

Natai nodded. "I surprised myself with my vote in the end. I'll make the announcement right away," she said.

"It's going to be an incredible celebration. I'll keep guards close to anyone who leaves the castle, with your permission, Majesties," Versai said. "Certainly," Syriel said. Tenro nodded, too.

"Thank you all for attending this impromptu meeting and for all of your incredibly important opinions. We'll meet at our regular time this week," Tenro said, standing.

He nodded to Hye as he then left the room with Syriel beside him.

The room emptied quickly, soon leaving only Hye and Versai. Hye closed the door and looked at Versai in silence.

"They came to me after Tenro's aunts acted out. They asked why

I was removed from my position, but I told them nothing of what you asked me not to speak of. I still think it's a poor choice," Versai said.

"They're going to need us. When the coming events fail, there will likely be instability like we've never known," Hye said.

"I'll be ready. It's my life's work to be ready," Versai said, standing.

Hye also stood. "It's good to have you back . You're needed in the council room," he said as he left the room.

Laur

He sat in an open tent that otherwise obscured him from vision. He watched his soldiers at practice with a cup of orchid nectar in his hand. Reth, the commander of his private army, stepped into view. He was tall and stood with the imposing posture of a trained Dragonrider.

"There you are," Laur said.

"Apologies. I only just learned you were here," Reth said, striking his armoured chest with a fist.

"Never mind that. How soon will they be ready?" Laur said, returning the gesture.

"They are ready," Reth said.

"Good," Laur said with a smile.

"It doesn't serve me to ask, but I feel I must do so. You are certain of our success and the protection of the Dairsen lineage?" Reth's words were cautious, but his tone was confident.

Laur turned his attention from his soldiers to his commander.

"I protect my own legacy just as that of my family and my kingdom. If nothing is done, the boy king would ruin too many things to fix," he said.

"Can I speak more openly?" Reth asked. Laur nodded.

"Are you certain you want to oppose your own son?"

"You want to ask me why I don't believe in the way I raised my boy. You should ask me. That's a simple answer: I didn't raise him. His mother did. She is not of the king's line, and he was not raised to be a king like me. This is our only chance to preserve the integrity of the kingdom and restore stability," Laur said, his tone flat.

Reth stood for a moment as Laur looked past him to the training soldiers. Laur didn't watch his commander's face because he knew his cause was just. Reth knew it too. He had to.

"I'll see it done. The clean god will have her fill," Reth said.

"Send someone to tell my brother that I will attack in ten days. And make sure you end his line when you attack before," Laur said.

Reth nodded and placed a closed fist against his armoured chest.

Laur mimicked the gesture.

"You know just as well as I that a good king is the stability of this kingdom," Laur said as he turned and left.

CHAPTER 6

THE FALL

Kyra

A sharp knock on the door interrupted their precious moment. Kyra snapped out of her daydream in an instant. She jumped up from her bed, completely naked, and dressed immediately. Vujet reached for his flexible armour in the same moment.

Both of them didn't say what they felt. Kyra felt Vujet's fear in the air. It was such an unfamiliar feeling coming from him that she couldn't control her own concern. She knew that he was only worried for her, but that somehow made it much more terrifying. Within a few seconds, his fear was gone.

"One moment," Kyra said.

"Open up, by order of King Methis," a voice at the door said.

Kyra dressed quickly in the clothes she'd worn that morning, a simple brown shirt and green pants. Vujet needed a moment with his armour, however.

The longer they took, the more guilty they looked, but it was already suspicious. Kyra pulled his bone-infused armoured silk shirt over his arms and tightened the buckles between his wings. She helped him with the final fastener when she heard the door unlock.

There was only one explanation for why they'd not opened the door, and for the unmade bed in the single-room apartment.

A female guard stood in the doorway.

"Good afternoon," Kyra said immediately.

"Your morning teacher said you were not in class," the guard said.

"I didn't have class this morning," Kyra said.

"Methis wants to see you," the guard said.

"All right," Vujet said.

"I was asked to carry her," the guard said.

"Of course," Vujet said, his tone completely calm.

The guard held out her hand as Kyra calmly walked toward her. The guard stepped back from the door, allowing Kyra to exit her small room. The guard picked her up from behind and then flew off. She didn't wait for Vujet, but Kyra knew he'd follow right behind them. Kyra looked over the guard's shoulder, but she couldn't see him.

It was a short flight, but it still felt horrifyingly long. Kyra was confident that while her life was soon to end, Vujet could survive. By involving him, she might have killed him. Methis enjoyed cruelty, so her punishment might be to watch him die.

The guard carefully let Kyra stand on the landing platform to the throne room. She'd been here so few times that it made her stomach drop. She walked in, pushing by the guard without looking behind her.

Methis sat atop the gnarled throne like he'd been born to sit in it. Soldiers flanked him like he was a true son of Amaranthus. He was such a flamboyant pretender that it sickened her. Kyra walked through the throne room with humility and respect, but her knees were shaking. She stopped walking at the foot of the throne platform.

"You took the liberty to create your own lesson, I see," Methis said.

"Forgive me, Highness, I thought I had no lesson in the morning.

I asked Vujet to teach me about his life as a soldier and a captain."

"I'll bet you did. Vujet also has your schedule," Methis said, his tone dry.

"I do, Highness," Vujet said.

When Kyra heard his voice, she felt relieved. She was worried he'd flown off and left her to her own fate. She wouldn't have blamed him, since it was she who'd dragged him into this. She then felt even more horrified. He'd willingly flown to what was likely his own death for her sake. She then wished he'd flown off.

She glanced behind her to see him kneeling before the throne.

"Princess Kyra had some significant questions that I thought were more important for the heir of Amaranthus," Vujet said.

"More important than what her king desires?" Methis said.

"Her king was not privy to these questions," Vujet said.

"What were these important questions?" Methis asked, scowling at Vujet.

"Of policy, highness. She asked about the ranks of the soldiers and their responsibility to the crown. Her questions were more specific, indicating that what she should know, she didn't. Her education has been excellent, but without this early information, I've seen things she has been missing before that I could easily explain. This was simply more important," Vujet said.

"Why was I not simply informed, so it could be added to her lessons?" Methis said.

"The questions went on longer than expected, Highness. I thought to give one simple answer, but before I realised it I had held my own lesson, as you said," Vujet said.

"I gave you the simplest task in the kingdom," Methis said.

"I skipped the lesson," Kyra said. "I asked questions I knew Vujet would want to answer because I didn't want to go to class. I exploited his loyalty to the kingdom."

Methis was silent for a moment, looking from Kyra to Vujet. He knew. He had to know. He had to see through them. Kyra could feel her heart thumping, possibly beating its last beats.

"The fact that he can be so simply exploited by a child is another problem," Methis said.

"I'm not a child, Highness," Kyra said.

"You're becoming an adult, that's true," he said, waving off her words.

"I'm an adult. I have known desire," she said.

"Kyra," Vujet whispered.

"Then we should arrange a wedding ceremony," Methis said, smiling.

"Not for his Highness," Kyra said.

Methis stood and focused his full attention on Vujet. "You were conducting an entirely different lesson," he accused.

"I do not think it is I, Highness. I did as I said, and taught her about soldiery," Vujet said.

"We should give these lovers a proper send-off," Methis said.

"I am the last blood of Amaranthus, but I can't control how I feel. No one can control whom they do or do not desire," Kyra said.

"Well, you are no longer useful to the kingdom. Exile them both!" Methis shouted.

The guards in the throne room did not move, however. Kyra looked around with eyes wide, her antennae feeling the air. Methis too looked at his guards, his brow furrowed.

"Exile them!" Methis repeated, his deep voice thundering through the throne room.

All was silent in the throne room as Methis looked around him, trying to discover why his orders were being ignored. Kyra too looked at the guards and then to Vujet, who stood silently. She didn't understand.

As Kyra looked around, she saw the figure of Reia standing in the doorway to the throne room. Her spymaster's familiar silhouetted pose gave her confidence. Reia had helped in this, she must have. Kyra was sure of it. She looked back at Methis and watched the events unfold as if she were part of the audience to a play.

"They won't," Vujet said, as he looked at Kyra.

His eyes showed so much confidence, that in one look Kyra completely understood. It was like an idea that had been forming in her mind this whole time was suddenly made real, like a dream she'd barely dared to hope for had come to fruition. Was she dreaming? No.

Vujet had once yelled at her when she'd tried to end her life. He'd been honest with her. She realised he desired her so deeply because of his legacy, by which he'd been born to serve her. Soldiers were deeply loyal to the crown. She now knew what she'd wanted to believe all along. The crown wasn't Methis. It never was.

It was her.

Her entire life she'd crumpled herself as small a space as she could, but the king's legacy couldn't be denied. If cultivated, it would always bloom. She turned her attention to Methis.

"You changed the law, pretending to preserve Amaranthus's legacy. You did it for yourself, not for this kingdom. You don't have what it is to be a king," Kyra said quietly.

Her posture changed from hunched to straight-backed as she spoke. She walked the few steps toward Methis with a new, powerful stance. She then looked around her to see that the guards still stood unmoving, and then glanced back at Reia, who stood smiling on the edge of the throne room. With the image of Reia and Vujet firmly in her mind, she locked eyes with Methis—her captor, her betrayer, and the murderer of her father.

"Amaranthus could have killed the She'ehlarah king when he was cornered. He chose to keep his followers safe. You are so self-serving that would exile me and end our deepest legacy simply because I don't desire you. You would destroy the only stability we have ever known. You are not one of us. You are not a king. You're a parasite," Kyra said, her voice still quiet, but growing slightly louder.

She closed the distance between her and Methis and whispered, "You know better than most how we deal with such problems." She paused a moment. "Methis is not a king - and that despite my being wingless and female, I am. I am the sole heir of the only legacy the Iewen have ever followed. He tried to use our law, our conviction, and our perfection against us. He is a betrayer to the crown. Exile him," Kyra said, finally speaking normally.

With her back to Methis, Kyra turned to her head to Reia before she confidently proclaimed, "just as he did my father."

Vujet walked past her and held his knife to the spymaster. She felt her skin shiver as she turned her head and watched her beloved behind her. She'd never wanted to be with her partner more than at this moment. Their shared love for their kingdom heightened her desire to a point she didn't know it could reach.

Methis had placed Vujet right in her arms and doomed himself in what was supposed to be her torment. It had been intended to break her, but Vujet had helped create her instead.

"No!" Methis yelled, "I earned this crown."

Kyra turned her body to face him as she watched him squirm. The kingdom's instability had begun in her childhood, but it would end in her adulthood. She watched the grim scene as Vujet bloodied his hands, tearing Methis's wings from his back.

The first time she'd seen this horrific display she'd fainted, but it was different this time. Now the circle had been closed, and the kingdom would be safe. She'd never felt powerful, let alone with anther Iewen's life in her hands. It was intoxicating. Overwhelming.

Fiare

The steady gait of a Yurelle beetle was smoother than Fiare had even imagined. The scenery surrounding her was breathtaking. Giant mushrooms, tall as any Iewen apartment, spilt an almost endless shadow over the comparatively small beetle. The smell of fresh earth and new growth was intoxicating and all-consuming, to the point that she couldn't feel Avena's excitement in the air anymore. A glance to her right showed her that her only companion was smiling broadly. Avena was delighted to have her company when travelling home. Fiare couldn't help but smile. It was truly like a dream.

Her skin tingled as another gust of cold air ran across her naked shoulders, but she didn't reach for her coat, even as she shivered. The sensation of everything around her was too precious. Every moment of it was incomparable. She'd never even imagined anything like the far fields, as the Yurelle called them. They were like something out of an orchid nectar dream.

"You look cold," Avena said.

Fiare shook her head. "Oh, I mean, yes," Fiare said.

Avena reached for her coat, but Fiare shook her head. She leaned closer to her friend.

"I like it, is that strange?" Fiare said, almost in a whisper.

"Everything about you is strange to me. That's why I enjoy your company," Avena said.

"Tell me again that I won't make your family uncomfortable," Fiare said.

Avena laughed. "They're as curious as me. I promise if you say something strange, they'll only want to know why. But stop worrying, we're almost there. You can't turn back now," she said.

"Nothing makes the nerves fade like being told a choice is irreversible," Fiare said, pulling her wings in tight against her back.

"Doesn't matter how nervous you are; you and they will have a wonderful time," Avena said.

Fiare looked at Avena and smiled. She trusted Avena. It seemed strange to think it of a stranger she'd spent the festival with, but she really did trust her.

"Look, that's it, there," Avena said, pointing right in front.

Fiare placed both hands on the saddle in front of her and leaned forward, trying to see a house. She hadn't seen many on the whole journey here.

Avena laughed. "There," she said, again.

Fiare shook her head.

"I don't see your house," Fiare said.

"But you do," Avena said, pulling the reins on the giant beetle.

The creature came to a stop as Avena took her bag and a bundle of silk from its back. Fiare took her own small bag, but she still couldn't see any house.

Avent walked toward one of the giant mushrooms and tapped on a door that had been coloured white. Fiare didn't even know it was there. She could hardly believe it. Surely Avena couldn't have actually grown up inside a mushroom?

The door opened to the warm face of a female who looked much like Avena. Her red hair curled and coiled all about her head, and her clothing was simple, but was in all manner of bright colours. Fiare felt overdressed, in even her toned-down, more practical dress.

"Avena!" the female said, hugging her.

"Mother, this is Princess Fiare. Fiare, this is my mother, Solanece," Avena said.

"We've heard so much about you. Please come in," she said, stepping back into the house.

Fiare followed Avena into the giant mushroom flooded with disbelief and confusion. Inside it looked very similar to the Malarmha apartments—small, but well-used and bright. A little window let in a small amount of light. Parts of the walls were covered in a strange plant that seemed to give the majority of the light to the room.

The furniture seemed strange; it didn't seem to be wood like back in Velwrith, but even still, it was all brightly coloured or covered in numerous bright things. There was more life in one Yurelle room that she'd seen in all her rooms in the castle. It was almost overwhelming.

"Edulis, come tie up Avena's beetle, please," Solanece said to a male sitting at a desk, reading.

"Hey, sis," Edulis said as he looked up from his book. He put his book down and crossed the room to hug his sister.

Avena had talked about them both a little, but they seemed warmer and more Yurelle than she'd described. Edulis was clad in colour as much as his mother, but his hair was short, and his clothing was slightly tighter.

"This is Princess Fiare. Fiare, this is my brother, Edulis," Avena said.

"A pleasure, Your Highness," Edulis said, bowing extravagantly.

"Please don't. I'm not a princess here," Fiare said, blushing.

"Well, not a princess. Might I extend a more inviting gesture, known to us common folk as a hug?" Edulis said, standing straight-backed.

"By Nethlethi, I am so sorry, Fiare. Had I known my big brother would be so embarrassing, I would have suggested we go to a restaurant instead," Avena said.

Fiare laughed and in an attempt to end the awkwardness of the moment, stepped forward and hugged him. She felt his body tense in surprise and stepped back a moment later.

"Apparently you do like the gestures of the common people," Eduli said.

Fiare looked to Avena beside her, who sighed.

"So … about that food," Avena said, looking at her mother.

Solanece stood smiling at the side of the small room. "I've got a number of delicious things for sampling, if that suffices," she said, looking from Avena to Fiare.

"That sounds amazing. Thank you for having me, it's so kind of you. But I do have a question that I can only hope is not too strange," Fiare said.

"Ask anything," Solanece said.

"Can I get a tour of your home? If it's not inappropriate, of course," Fiare said.

"Have you ever been in a mushroom home before?" Edulis asked.

"I've never even seen something so tall. I didn't know you could make a home in here," Fiare said. "I mean…." she started, realising she may have just said something insulting.

"Oooh, then you simply must get a full tour, please come with me," Solanece said, taking Fiare's hand.

"Mushroom homes are tall; we don't cut into the edge of the mushroom unless we make a little window. But you have to be careful, or it will fall down. You can spend numerous generations in one home if you don't expand too much," Solanece said, leading Fiare to a set of stairs.

"The kitchen is the heart of any home, but we keep ours underground to keep our food longer," Solanece said, letting Fiare's hand go as she descended the stairs.

Fiare followed, folding her wings back in the narrow stairs. The little room below looked like a dining room. It was another small room that was well-used, brightly lit and covered in colour. The table was already set with a space for Fiare. An open archway led to the kitchen. Numerous pots sat on the counter.

"Mother, you didn't have to go to so much trouble," Avena said, stopping next to Fiare as she looked into the kitchen.

"You don't come home much now. You're here even less than you father when he was alive. Plus, you have an important guest who hasn't tasted our family cooking yet," Solanece said, making her way into the kitchen.

"I'm sorry, Mother, I'll come home more," Avena said quietly as she joined her mother in the kitchen.

"They're a lot alike, despite Avena taking father's legacy," Edulis said.

"Avena said her mother was a mushroom farmer. Is that what you do, too?" Faire asked.

Edulis nodded, a broad smile on his face. "It's a proud legacy, the backbone of the Yurelle," he said.

"Like orchid farming in Velwrith. It's the basis of our economy and the foundation of our world," Fiare said.

"Do you like it?" Fiare asked.

"I love it. How about being a princess?" Edulis asked.

Fiare's face went tight. "In all honesty, not so much," Fiare said.

"What about your role in the Senate?" Edulis said.

"I love it," Fiare said.

Edulis nodded. "Yurelle are a different people, aren't they?" he said.

"You really are all something special," Fiare said, looking at Avena and her mother in the kitchen.

Edulis smiled at Fiare. "I hope you stay in Malarmha. If you like the senate, hopefully you can stay," he said.

"I hope for that, too," Fiare said.

Her honesty shocked her, but it felt incredible to speak the truth. It was incredibly liberating. She wanted more honesty in her life.

"Edulis, help me with the pots," Solanece said.

"Can I help?" Fiare asked.

"No, dear," Solanece said, leaving the kitchen with a pot. "Guests don't help, but they do pick first." She opened the lid of the pot she was carrying, releasing a delicious smell that Fiare couldn't identify.

Tenro

Light of the luminescent plants on his wall crept through Tenro's sleeping leaf. Syriel always woke early. The scratching of a writing instrument was ever-present. His family were known to be dutiful, hardworking, and devoted, but she still woke before him. Her colony was known for their unending passion. He'd simply never seen it in practice. It seemed such a strange comparison, since there were so many of them to govern one city.

His leaf bed opened, revealing his wife who was indeed hard at work at her desk. The leaf moved almost silently, and she didn't see the movement in the corner of her eye, so Tenro stared at her. She worked with a furrowed brow, her wings flicking every so often.

He slid out of his bed, walked to their table, and served himself some orchid nectar. She still hadn't acclimated to alcohol and never drank it while she worked, so he didn't pour her a glass. He walked to his own desk and seated himself to look over his work for the day He was interrupted by a knock on his door. Syriel looked up and saw him for the first time this morning.

"Good morning, husband," she said, the crinkle in her brow softening.

"Good morning. You keep working. I'll get the door," he said, standing.

He took a moment to look Syriel over. She looked a little pale. She must have been working too hard. She'd been looking a little pale for a while. He'd have to find a way to let her regain her strength. But first the door.

"Who is it?" he asked.

"I have a message for the King and Queen," Yune said from the other side of the door.

Tenro opened the door quickly. "Must be important to be in your hand," he said.

"Quite," Yune said. He handed over the letter and remained standing at the door.

Tenro opened it quickly as Syriel walked up beside him. Tenro's wings opened as his eyes went wide when he first saw who had signed the letter.

King Tenro and Queen Syriel

The usurper Methis has been exiled. I now rightly sit on my father Farin's throne. I would like to express my extraordinary apologies for the conduct of my people when I was too young to stop them. I can't undo what was done, but I want to make efforts to amend anything I can in the wake of his tyranny.

Please send an emissary and we can discuss terms for our first true peace. I've asked my pilot and hawk to wait on your reply if you can accommodate them.

Queen Kyra.

Rightful Queen of the Iewen and last daughter of Amaranthus.

"Was Amer informed of this?" Tenro asked.

"A letter is being delivered to him at this moment, and to Fiare, Sire," Yune said.

"She can come home!" Syriel said, her face brightening.

"Fiare *was* trained to meet with foreign rulers," Tenro said, as he furrowed his brow.

Syriel leaned her head against his arm. He looked at her with a brief smile.

"Commander, can you see that the hawk pilot is given a room near the port, please? I'll need time to decide on this before I have an answer," Tenro said.

"Of course, Sire, I'll inform the guard right away. How long should I tell them to wait?" Yune said.

"The next morning, at least. Make sure they're extremely well taken care of," Tenro said.

Yune bowed his head and then left. It seemed inappropriate to ask the captain of his personal guard to be a messenger. He had, however, chosen to take the letter to his king himself.

"A queen on both kingdom's thrones," Syriel whispered.

Tenro hadn't thought about that. He looked at his wife with a raised brow. "A return to our history," he said.

"So, what will we do?" Syriel said as Tenro closed the door.

"We'll have an emergency meeting tomorrow to seek the guidance of the King's Council," Tenro said.

"Do you have any thoughts about our options?" Syriel asked.

"I think asking Fiare to meet with him would be a good choice, but I honestly don't trust this new queen. As we understand it, she was locked up for most of her life. That has to damage one's understanding of the world," Tenro said.

"She writes well enough, or at least her adviser does," Syriel said.

"I don't want to send Fiare, though I do want her to return. We'll have to inform her at once," Tenro said, returning to his desk.

Remin

Remin lay in his bed sore and exhausted, yet he woke with an unfamiliar feeling of usefulness. He hadn't slept. His mind was a blur. She was alive. That single sentence circled his mind like a typhoon. Over and over, it ravaged his mind. She was in danger. She had to be, and only he could save her.

Methis was a cold and cruel entity who thrived on hatred and bile. Remin had worked with him too long not to know him. Kyra was in danger.

A knock on the wall beyond his cloth door forced him to raise his head. He had to lift his head high, as his bed was on the floor. His cloth door remained closed.

"Remin?" Leisa's voice called.

Even for her, he couldn't get up. She wouldn't understand. None of them would.

"Tsune took his lunch break to visit me. He said you might need me," she said.

"Lunch" … was it so late already?

He heard the sound of cloth pulling back as light pierced his single-room house. He rolled over to avoid the light. Leisa's shadow entered his home as he pulled his thin blanket over his head.

"Tsune told me what the wounded Iewen said," Leisa said, her footsteps approaching his bed.

She sat down beside his bed and placed her arm on her pillow. Remin turned and hugged her, glancing her tensed face. Her expression and the scent of her fear in the air meant he looked as bad as he felt.

"The best thing about being on the floor of the world is that there isn't anywhere lower to go. There's only up," Leisa said. She was right. He had to go up. "Get dressed, come stay with me," she said.

Remin couldn't find the strength to move. He wanted to, but it felt like there was a hole in his middle from which every part of him was slowly seeping out.

"Okay," Leisa whispered. "We'll stay here." She kicked off her shoes, then pushed against him and crawled into his bed.

She hugged him tightly as he did the same. "Get some sleep. I'll get food for us later. Just sleep now," Leisa said.

The warmth of her presence and person rested his twisted and tortured mind. It was enough for the fatigue of the day and night to finally bring him to rest. The last thought in his mind was that he had to go up. He had to go to her.

Syriel

The small council room felt crowded this afternoon. The seated council were surrounded by family members and other prospective volunteers. The usual scent of paper and ink was drowned out by royal perfumes. The typically soft and inviting floral perfumes were oppressive when mingling in the too-small space. The normally airy room felt too warm, which was all Syriel could think about.

She focused her circling thoughts on the topic at hand, but still felt her thoughts weighed down by her discomfort. It was a strange feeling. She couldn't remember a time where she felt nauseated by such lovely smells and the comfort of warmth. She felt unreasonably uneasy. She put her hand on her belly under the table. It felt harder than yesterday. She'd felt it a week ago, and it had stayed hard. She only knew that to mean one thing.

Syriel looked around the room to try and ground herself. The council was seated at their table with the extended royal family seated around the edge of the room. Despite her feelings, the room was spacious enough to hold everyone in comfort. Her practice seemed to work as her head cleared slightly.

Methis's downfall was talked about in every corner of the castle, so all present knew their king and queen were going to ask complicated questions this day. It needed more minds than the typical questions the council gathered for, but it wasn't just to ensure the greatest success for a dangerous and difficult request. It was also to ensure all those who were to be spoken of were present.

Tenro nodded to Amer, and then to his uncle Guiyn. Syriel knew it pained him that his father wasn't present. She secretly slid her hand into his underneath the table.

"I'm certain that you're all aware of why you were asked here today. But I think it only right to ensure it is said. We seek an envoy to send to the Iewen queen," Tenro said.

"Fiare has been my diplomat and representative. By your leave, Sire, I sent her a letter detailing the situation and asking her to return home," Amer said.

"We should all be together," Wyma said.

"We expect her to arrive any day now. We need to be careful, as we have to consider that this might well be a trap, as the Iewen have never extended their hand to us before. It could be the start of a new era, but I'd rather not risk anyone from this family," Tenro said.

"What if the new Iewen queen takes your refusal to send a family member as an insult?" Hye asked.

"My queen and I have thought of something to prevent that. We propose a new council seat be opened. We think it well overdue, with our growing yet delicate relationship with the Yurelle. It would be a diplomatic position. We think it's imperative now that we are finally beginning to restore the ancient rift with neighbours," Tenro said.

The tone in the room immediately shifted from slumped shoulders and crossed arms to opened eyes, raised eyebrows, and the occasional smile. Syriel noted that some faces in the room such as those of Tenro's uncles had frowns along with their wide eyes.

"One job for two incredibly different colonies seems impossible. It should be two seats," Natai said.

Syriel looked at Natai in surprise. She'd replied almost without pause after Tenro's suggestion. Her tone was clear, and her words were confident. Despite the visible and distinct feeling that had changed in the room, Syriel was greatly soothed by Natai's honest positive reaction.

"I am honoured to be present, that I can agree," Craime said.

"I think the position should be made, but it should have an agenda of ensuring we get what we need from our neighbours, not the development of dependence. Apologies to my queen, but I am concerned we could get carried away with another colony's agenda.

First, two seats at the council for them. Then where next?" Alina said.

"Alina is right. With no intended insult to my queen, if we dedicate two or even one more seat of this council's time to benefiting our neighbours, our decline will be quick," Laur said.

"With respect in return, we're already working with Daltay. The council position would give us more power to use that position to benefit us," Syriel said.

"Who would be the 'us' here?" Guiyn asked.

"The She'ehlarah, my colony," Syriel said, looking unblinking at Guiyn.

Tenro raised his hand to his council. "Let us remember, this is about protecting She'ehlarah interests first and foremost. If the position or positions do us a disservice, the seats will be removed. Syriel left her home to begin to bring an end to the long bitterness we shared with her former colony. If there was ever a time to turn an enemy into an ally, if nothing else but for against the Iewen, it's now. I would not hope to say it's probable, but we need to try and create the possibility to lower the cold hostility between us and the Iewen for fear of the friendship we build with the Yurelle," Tenro said.

"Even my Yurelle are not friends with us. But we must build on a future, not our present," Syriel said.

"Well, if the Yurelle princess herself says we're not friends, why are we even trying this?" Guiyn said.

Syriel furrowed her brow. That was a bitter sentiment, even for one of his dark reputation.

"The likelihood of another moment such as this in our future shrinks to impossibility if we don't use what we have now. If we don't use the wedding between enemies to forge a better future, then what was it for?" Hye said.

"We're creating two council seats to justify their marriage?" Guiyn said.

"No. We're using my sacrifice of identity to build a new one between our two colonies," Syriel said.

"Not sacrificing much," Alina said, her voice almost a whisper.

Syriel shifted her eyes to Tenro's. He was watching his uncle Amer, who had been quiet during the conversation.

"I call a vote. Two council seats for diplomacy," Tenro said, standing. He raised his hand as he stood, commanding the room with his presence.

After a moment, hands in the room went up: Hye, Natai, Versai, Shara, and Craime. Syriel raised her own hand and had easily won the council vote. None of the royal family voted, as they were not permitted, other than Amer, whom Tenro had given a position of honour. Just as Tenro opened his mouth, Amer's hand went up.

"Thank you. We will discuss who will fill these seats at a later date. For now, the meeting will conclude. Thank you all for your voices and attendance," Tenro said.

Syriel stood. She and Tenro hadn't expected his father to attend, and seeing him had rattled Syriel a little. She had thought it would rattle Tenro, but as he left the room, with his hand in hers, Tenro looked directly at Laur.

"Thank you all again," Tenro said as he left the room.

Syriel pushed on her stomach again and felt its hardness. It had to be that she was with child. She wanted to tell Tenro, but she wasn't yet sure. She'd go to the physician in the morning and if she was right, then she'd tell him. She didn't want him to get excited unless she was sure.

More than anything, she didn't want to get excited just in case she wasn't carrying the heir to the She'ehlarah in her belly. She needed to create the next generation for the She'ehlarah. She was Yurelle, and a lot of people only trusted their own. If she couldn't conceive, her people, both the Yurelle and She'ehlarah, could think it was her fault. Her intentional fault. She needed to have a child for both colonies.

Fiare

Fiare paced her room with a letter in hand. "Every time you visit me, I am poring over some letter or notice," she said. She stopped pacing and looked over at Avena, who waited patiently for Fiare to tell her the contents of the letter or to say that it was private. She should say it was private. Looking at Avena, Fiare knew what she was going to tell her.

"You should come to my apartment one day. You'll see a stack of letters that pile taller than your pretty head," Avena said, poking Fiare on the nose.

"That's not my head, but my nose," Fiare said, crinkling her nose.

"You get so literal when you're thinking," Avena said with a laugh. "What's in the letter?"

Fiare sat down on the rug in the middle of the room, and Avena sat opposite her. She didn't ask again; she just waited, ever-patient. It made Fiare smile. Despite their many differences, they were quite similar.

"It's from my father. I don't quite know where to begin. The She'ehlarah received word from 'Kyra', queen of the Iewen, daughter of Farin. She's overthrown Methis and seeks an end to the hostility from her people against mine," Fiare said.

"Farin had a child?" Avena said.

Fiare didn't reply.

"Amaranthus Feth-ren's markings are well documented. If it's true, anyone could see in a moment," Avena said.

"It would be such a foolish thing to lie about," Fiare said.

"Then we go back to why or how she was hidden," Avena said.

"Maybe there's something wrong about her that the Iewen didn't accept," Fiare said.

"Such an awful thought," Avena said.

"It's so different here. You dethrone—I mean deseat—a person based on their performance. Not an aspect that you find unfitting," Fiare said.

"Sometimes it's one and the same. There was a senator when I was little who caused a lot of controversy. He fell off a beetle and hit his head and was never the same after. He made poor judgements and was deseated in the end. Ultimately, it's about what's best for all here. In the kingdoms, it's so often not like that; perhaps it was simply that she was born a girl," Avena said.

"Well, she did something to prove herself to be more than her gender if so, because my father wrote that her letter bore the official seal of Amaranthus," Fiare said, showing Avena the letter.

Avena read it carefully. She looked Fiare in the eyes, unblinking for a moment.

"Do we really have two queens on the thrones?" Avena said.

"Well, Syriel shares her throne with my cousin. But perhaps we are getting back to a point in history where we started at," Fiare said.

"I don't like that at all. It ended in murdered queens and their children," Avena said.

"Not for the Zrti. They're still ruled by a queen," Fiare said.

"Syriel and I talked a few times. Her father had told her a little about the Zrti, but it's so hard to understand without meeting them," Fiare said.

"You never met Syriel's father?" Avena said.

"I did once, but my family was talking to him about Syriel. We could talk to Olianna about him, if it's not too sad for her," Fiare said.

"You say we, like everyone, has your connections," Avena said, laughing.

"Well, that's the thing about connections: they connect. I never even thought of it before. Would you want to ever see my home?" Fiare said.

"How would they see me?" Avena said.

"As a friend I trust," Fiare said.

Avena handed the letter back to Fiare. "It sounds exciting, but I think I'm everything the She'ehlarah are not," she said.

"That's why I like you so much," Fiare said.

"Do you know what you'll do?" Avena said.

"About what?" Fiare said.

"The letter. Your father says it's safe to come home," Avena said.

"Nowhere is ever really safe," Fiare said.

"So you haven't decided," Avena said.

"I decided the moment I met you," Fiare said.

"Me?" Avena said, looking at Fiare wide-eyed.

"I want to be like you," Fiare said.

"You're going to stay," Avena said.

"I belong here, Avena," Fiare said. "All my life, I never knew it." Avena smiled.

"It seems like Malarmha wants me here, too," Fiare said.

"You're widely viewed as an oddity, but it doesn't seem like people are against you being here," Avena said.

"It's such a strange time. I think peace is an actual possibility," Fiare said.

"Most people still don't trust the She'ehlarah and they hate your plant, but I think we might finally coexist without anger. I'm not sure about the idea of peace," Avena said.

"Let a dreamer, dream, Senator," Fiare said.

"Forgive me, sweet fairy tale princess," Avena said.

"Oh, stop. It's not that bad, surely," Fiare said.

"You don't hear what people say when you're not around," Avena said.

"I know you find it fun to see me as a shiny new toy, but if I don't fit in here. You know I can't go home, right?" Fiare said.

Avena's face straightened at Fiare's serious tone. "You can always go home, Fiare," Avena said, sitting up properly.

"Imagine you found a world where you could finally be yourself, where you didn't have to pretend to be someone else. How could you ever return to the world that twisted and contorted you to being someone you never were?" Fiare said. Avena was silent. Fiare stood and put the letter on her desk.

"I didn't know it was like that," Avena said.

"The Yurelle are so free, you've worked so hard for that freedom. Many died for it, imagine your life without it," Fiare said.

"I can't," Avena said.

"I'm sorry," Fiare said, turning to face Avena. "I don't want you to ever know what that's like. You never have to hide who you are."

"If the Yurelle at large rejected you, I would live a life in hiding for you in Velwrith," Avena said.

"No. I wouldn't let you. I wouldn't give you the chance to throw away everything that you have. At least one of us would live the life they deserve," Fiare said.

"I don't know if I have the power to keep you free, but if there's anything I can do, you'd tell me, right?" Avena said.

"In a heartbeat. I want to be the person that I get to be here," Fiare said. "I want to keep living this dream."

Avena smiled. "I bet that Grand Chancellor Olianna would want you to keep that freedom, too. She cares for few things more than freedom for all," she said.

Fiare had never thought about it like that before. Everything she knew about Olianna was just that, and yet she'd given her daughter to the She'ehlarah when she was a baby. It didn't fit. Perhaps Syriel's father had wanted to see her in Velwrith. Avena was right that so many Yurelle, while they hated Cthessa, thought of the castle like a faraway storyland.

Fiare looked over the room that had once been Syriel's. She'd never felt closer to her, but from her room, Syriel seemed like a person she'd never met. Fiare looked at Avena, who was still staring at her.

"You're right," Fiare said, smiling slightly.

"I know. The Grand Chancellor seems to really like you, from all accounts," Avena said.

"Have you ever met her?" Fiare said.

"No," Avena said.

"I think you'd like her a lot. She is exactly how I see the Yurelle. Adventurous, self-aware, and surefooted enough to keep her self-identity," Fiare said.

"Is that how you see me?" Avena said, standing.

"Telling you how I see you is no fun at all. I would never spoil the ending of a good book for you," Fiare said.

"Am I the book?" Avena said.

"My picture of you is," Fiare said.

"Goodness, that's a big opinion," Avena said.

"It's a little book," Fiare said, her tone regaining its humour.

"Ah, then, never mind," Avena said with a smile.

"What can I say? I love the Yurelle," Fiare said.

"I want to hear your decision out loud," Avena said.

"I'm never leaving Malarmha. Nothing can take me away from here," Fiare said.

"Your wording is so intentional," Avena said with a smile.

Fiare smiled back. She knew what she meant, and she wouldn't change a word. Malarmha was home.

CHAPTER 7

THE LAST BLOOM

Kyra

Kyra had arrived hours early and sat straight-backed in what had once been her father's chair. On the rich wooden table before her was a large stack of papers. Kyra leaned on her elbows on the table, her hands interwoven. Incredible exhilaration and terror coursed through her.

She'd been the pet of a king her whole life—first her father, and then his murderer. She was free of that torment, her own person at last.

She leaned back into her family's seat at the head of the council table. She was finally where she belonged, where she'd been born to be. She remembered the moment in the throne room and the guidance of Reia. She had to make sure they all knew that this was her rightful place, lest some other opportunistic parasite try to take what was hers. She would never be her father. She couldn't.

She sat alone with such thoughts for hours before the door first opened. The first to arrive was an older male. He jumped slightly to see her sitting in the room before all others. He brought with him the scent of paper and ink along with a small stack of papers. He must have been her kingdom's treasurer.

"Alren, I expect," Kyra said, pulling her hands apart and resting her arms flat on the table.

"Of course, Your Most Radiant Highness," he said, bowing.

"Are you typically the first to arrive for meetings with your monarch?" she asked.

"Certainly, that is not to insult anyone of the King's … pardon me, Highness, the Queen's Council. It is simply that the most significant traits of my profession are planning and accuracy," he said, finding his assigned seat.

He opened his mouth to speak, but as he did the door opened again. An armour-clad male entered the room with the confidence of a trained soldier.

"Welcome, Kimure," Kyra said.

He looked at her and then at Alren. He smiled. "Good morning, Highness. Thank you for reinstating me on the council," he said, taking his seat.

Kyra nodded. She couldn't be too warm. She needed to make it known that she was not her father and that unlike Methis, she was a born leader. She had the blood of Amaranthus, after all.

The door opened again and the previously sole female member of the Council walked through. "Highness," she said, offering a deep bow.

"Good morning, Ha'ttri," Kyra said.

She found her seat as the door opened again. Two Iewen walked through it this time. One was dressed in priest's clothing and the second was dressed simply.

"Good morning, Eugh and Bain," Kyra said.

The both bowed, looking as wide-eyed as every other council member who'd seen their queen already seated at the council table.

"A pleasure to meet you, Highness," Bain said with his hand on his heart.

"Good morning, Highness," Eugh said, finding his seat.

Reia entered the room last. Her purple hair and She'ehlarah elegance was most foreign here. Never before had there been anyone but an Iewen on the council. Reia didn't react to the fact that every head was turned and every face was staring at her.

"Welcome, Reia," Kyra said.

"Thank you, Highness," she said, bowing. She sat in the spymaster's seat beside the king's chair.

As Reia entered the room, the council members looked to one another with furrowed brows and pursed lips. Kyra hadn't announced her spymaster to the council, so no doubt hers was a face they didn't know. As the council began to speak in whispers, Kyra interrupted them.

"The first issue I wish to discuss is our problematic relationship with our enemies," Kyra said, her voice confident and clear.

"A good and important topic, Highness. If we don't seem to repair things immediately, it's likely to get much worse," Ha'ttri said.

"Let it be worse. We've proved that the She'ehlarah Dragonriders can't even protect their own heir. If we were to strike now, Highness, we could cripple them," Kimure said.

"That certainly is an option, but they haven't retaliated after Methis assassinated their prince," Kyra said.

She measured the silence in the room. Reia had told her that the council knew that she knew about the assassination. What she wanted to learn was if they had been told she knew. By their silence, it seemed they were not aware. She had their attention now.

"I believe we could restore our shaky relationship and re-establish trade. I believe in that trade. I am no different than any other Iewen in hating their abomination. But I won't have our soldiers die in their castle maze to kill it. I've gone over our supplies and trades with them, and I think Alren would agree that we were in a bad place without them," Kyra said.

"That is true, Highness. Our farms have been working overtime since they stopped trade with us. We've had to ration food, and our armouries haven't had enough chitin since the Yurelle stopped trade. Our tool storage is problematic. If we wanted to destroy our enemies, we would first have to establish independence from them, but that takes time," Alren said.

"Or, we destroy them and take enough of their supplies to last until we have what we need to be free of them," Kimure said.

"That would certainly work for a time, maybe enough time to complete our goal. Defeating them is highly unlikely, though," Alren said.

"I know my craft, Alren. It is unlikely. The Dragonriders are incredibly skilled, and our understanding of their castle is limited, but they're vulnerable now," Kimure said.

"They're more skilled than we expected. They didn't see my sister when she killed their prince, but they still caught her," Reia said.

"We don't know that," Kimure said, his words rushed.

"I know my sister. She has been captured or killed. Trade ended immediately after with both the She'ehlarh and Yurelle, but trade between the two continued. It was a brave effort, but we couldn't stop their marriage. Now it's we who are in the weakest position in our history," Reia said.

"We were weakest when we were thrown out of Daltay, but we survived," Kimure said.

"We all know that moment in history. We all know what is cost us. Amaranthus barely survived, and my family and all of our ancestors nearly died then," Kyra said.

Kyra's words brought silence to the room for a moment. Her antennae twitched gently to feel a mixture of surprise and admiration in the air. It was subtle, but it was there.

"I think our queen is right, that re-establishing trade is by far our best option," Bain said.

"A necessity," Alren said.

"How do we go about achieving that?" Eugh asked.

"Contact with the king and queen of the She'ehlarah is our highest priority, I believe," Ha'ttri said.

"Agreed. I have already sent word of Methis's execution by exile and asked to meet with both of the other realms," Kyra said.

The room was silent again. Kyra looked at the faces of everyone in her meeting room, judging them carefully. She loved her father, but from everything she'd heard about him, he wasn't a confident king. For the two seasons of his reign and for the little time Methis ruled, there hadn't been a confident monarch. She could only hope the council desired a true child of Amaranthus, instead of the power they'd all been enjoying.

"Please pardon my praise, Highness, but well done. You acted immediately, and that will likely show your sincerity," Alren said.

"Agreed," Bain said.

Kyra didn't know them all well enough to tell if they were lying. With her limited understanding, they all seemed genuinely pleased, except her general, who still looked like he wanted to attack them all at once.

Tenro

An insistent knock sounded at Tenro's door. Confused at what would wake him in the middle of the night, he stepped out of his bed. Syriel woke beside him. He whipped a dressing gown over his shoulders and tied it in the front, then opened his door.

Yune, Lon, Bren, Saf, Acasia, and Hye stood at his door. They stood with stiff backs and sober faces. Upon seeing them in the middle of the night, their serious faces, and in full armour, he was immediately awake.

"Sire, the castle is about to be attacked. We need you and Queen Syriel to dress immediately," Yune said.

"We'll be one moment," Tenro said. He moved back into his room without closing the door. Syriel was already dressing. When the pair were clothed enough, they left.

"Lock it, please," Yune asked.

Tenro did as he was asked. Then he and Syriel were surrounded by protective soldiers as they walked the halls.

"Who's attacking us?" Tenro asked.

"We should speak about that later," Hye said.

Tenro wanted to ask more, but he knew there was a reason Hye wouldn't want to speak on it now. Tenro chose to trust his spymaster. They rounded a corner to find a small group of armoured She'ehlarah standing in the hall. Two bleeding Dragonriders lay on the stone ground.

"The king!" One of them called as she rushed forward.

Yune met her advance. Tenro wrapped his arm around Syriel as Lon stood between the royals and the attackers. Heavy blows of bone and chitin told of a deadly fight just beyond Lon's form. Heavy thuds and shouts finally ended the battle. When Lon stepped forward, she ran to collect Bren. He looked wounded but with Lon and Saf's help, he was able to stand.

They gathered themselves and then went onward, this time their pace quickening. Their footsteps echoed through the stone halls. The clash of bone and chitin came from what seemed like all around them. Voices and screams called desperately for help, pleading for rescue.

Tenro couldn't believe what was happening. The castle was being attacked not even a season after the glass crown had been put on his head. It was his fault. He should have refused to disregard of the line of succession. The stability of the She'ehlarah depended on tradition.

But he couldn't think of that now. He and Syriel would escape to safety, and when they returned, they would rebuild everything together. He couldn't think about who was attacking or the lives that would be lost tonight. There was no now for him, there was only their return and the kingdom's recovery. But that rested on his shoulders. He knew that nothing was more important than his and Syriel's lives.

Commander Yune led the group into the undercity, reeling back to break down the thick wooden doors. Before he could rush forward, the doors opened. Curling vines wrapped around them from within as they stood fully open. Cthessa's flowers glowed brighter than Tenro could ever remember.

"Quickly," Yune said. His tone of voice betrayed that he too was confused by the greeting from the typically distracted plant mind.

Yune ran through first, with Tenro and Syriel one step behind. As Acasia stepped through the undercity, the doors closed behind them. They all looked behind to see Cthessa's vines tangling together over the doors.

"I've never seen anything like that," Tenro whispered.

"Desperate times," Yune replied.

"I need to look at Bren's wound," Lon said.

She lifted his arm over her head as Saf did the same. They slowly lowered him to the ground.

"Come to me," a young female voice called.

Yune put his hand on his sword. "It's Leatti, an Aspect," he said.

Yune looked at Tenro as he put his sword back in its scabbard.

"Bring him deeper," Yune said, pointing into the undercity.

Lon nodded as she lifted Bren up, Saf assisting her again.

"We can't keep moving him," Lon said.

"Just a bit further," Tenro said.

Guided by Cthessa's luminous flowers, the small group walked through the narrow, vine-covered hallways to the main chamber. It was unusually dark. Cthessa's flowers were dim here; a small section of flowers grew dimly against a close wall. The lighting was too bright in parts and too dim in others. It felt wrong.

Lon and Saf lowered Bren to the ground, letting him support himself against the wall. Tenro looked to Yune, trying to mask his horror.

"We'll be just fine, Sire," Yune said, his words and tone showing Tenro that his fear was as obvious to Yune as it was to Tenro.

Tenro nodded back. He glanced behind him to see Syriel resting against a stone garden. He only looked at her for a moment, then he saw something that made him audibly gasp. The Aspect behind her turned her head turned towards Syriel.

Tenro could hardly believe it; they never turned their heads. As Tenro saw this, he looked around the dimly lit room to see that all the Aspects were facing Syriel. Tenro stood up as the flowers in the chamber grew bright, and in one horrible moment, he saw them all clearly.

Every Aspect in the room had their foggy, blind eyes open. Every pair of dead-looking eyes had fixed their full attention on Syriel. Their twisted mouths were all smiling.

"Get away from there," Tenro said.

As he spoke, Syriel stepped back, hands touching the stone behind her. It wasn't entirely stone. An Aspect's hand was waiting. As Syriel's hand touched the Aspect's behind her, she closed her eyes and fell to the ground.

"Syriel!" Tenro yelled, running toward her.

He shook his wife, calling her name, but she didn't respond. He looked up to see every smiling Aspect turning pale. The green from their plants drained as their skin turned grey, withering before his eyes, as if seasons had passed within a matter of minutes.

As the Aspects withered, so too did every flower and vine in the room. The dull sun disk above Cthessa's faded too. The undercity was plunged into a darkness that it hadn't seen since the bulb had been planted.

The last image Tenro saw before the light faded was one Aspect who hadn't withered: Leatti, who held Syriel's hand in hers.

"Sire?" Yune called.

"Here. Come to my voice. Syriel won't wake up," Tenro said.

"We have no light. Stay where you are, Sire," Lon said.

A gloved hand touched Tenro's boot, and he gasped.

"It's me, sire," Yune said.

"What do we do?" Tenro said, trying to control the hopelessness in his voice.

Before Yune could answer him, there was light in the room again. It was small at first but slowly gained brightness. Tenro glanced over at Lon, Bren, and Saf, who also stared at the bulb in disbelief.

Tenro looked back at Cthessa in the centre of the room as the light started to glow brighter. On the far wall, Leatti's hand was still holding Syriel's. Tenro ran to her.

Guiyn

A banging on his door awoke him. He rushed to open in, barely clothed. One of his spies stood, her face drained of colour and out of breath. She adjusted her posture as the door opened.

"He lied. It's now," she said, panting.

Guiyn had given his brother arms and armour to kill Amer before the wedding. His foolish brother had waited too long for it to not have been intentional. Laur surely wanted to kill Guiyn too.

"Siah, time to go!" Guiyn shouted with his head turned back into his room. "Get my children," he ordered.

The spy nodded and ran off immediately. Guiyn stepped out of his door to see that his guards were gone. The halls beyond were silent. He stepped back into his chamber, closed the door, and locked it. He ran from the entry to his bedroom. Siah was hastily dressing, and he did the same.

They were dressed in seconds. Guiyn had chosen his uniform, so he might look less threatening. Surely, they wouldn't kill a priest of the wild god.

"We're going to the children's room," Guiyn said, placing his hands on Siah's shoulders.

He wanted to stay there and hold her until the night was through. But he couldn't. Laur had planned this deception and his moronic brother would never get the best of him, not this night or any other. He released his shaking hands with a sigh and turned.

He opened the door slowly. The hall looked clear, so he entered it. He ran to his children's room. His line would not be undone; neither he nor his children would die this night. His heart pounded in his chest even faster than his footsteps fell.

Vira and Pame's room was close, so their run was short. A body lay in the hall, dressed in the clothing of the spy he'd sent to his children's room. Siah ran past him, jumping over the body to rush to her children. Guiyn, however, waited. In the few seconds that he stood there: the whole castle went dark.

He stood in the dark with shaking knees and one thought: he was the legacy of the crown, not Siah. His children were likely dead. He was not a fighter like his brother's army. In this moment, bravery was suicide. It was the sacrifice of the king's legacy. So he ran.

Natai

It was quiet at night. Sometimes when she was working late, Natai would hear Economist Craime talking to himself in the study beside hers. It was usually this time of night that she'd bring him a snack. It was always a good time to take a break. Her head throbbed. So many people needed help they weren't getting, and Natai could only advise the king in her position as advocate of the people. It was a difficult position, an advisory role only with limited impact if her advice wasn't heard.

She sighed, rose with a heavy heart, and left her study through the always-open door. It was always quiet at night, but this night something felt off. She couldn't put her finger on it. She walked to Craime's door next to hers. His door was often closed, as it was this night. She knocked quietly.

After a moment, the older man opened the door. Despite their differences in age and upbringing, Natai always admired Craime. He was working past when he should have retired. And somehow, despite the stress of his position and the incredible hours he worked, he looked younger than he was.

"Snack time?" Craime said, looking at her empty hands.

"I was about to go and get something from the kitchen, but it's weird tonight, isn't it?" Natai said.

Craime looked at her, unblinking.

"It seems quieter than usual," Natai said.

"You're working too hard. Advocates shouldn't work too hard, or they'll leave their positions early. I've told you that before," Craime said.

"I know you're busy, but can you come with me?" Natai said.

Craime furrowed his brow.

"The guards in the hall aren't even there, look," Natai said, pointing behind her.

Craime stepped out of his study to see. "I've never seen them not be there," he said, pocketing a scroll he held. "Perhaps we should stay here."

Natai furrowed her brow. She had no idea what they should do.

"But it is snack time," Craime said.

Natai smiled. Snack time was sacred. Natai nodded.

"Come on, then," Craime said, closing his study door.

Natai closed her study door also, and like Craime, she locked it. The two then walked down the silent hallway together.

"I was thinking I'd have some nectar and that leaf soup," Craime said.

"You always have soup," Natai said.

"Keeps you young," Craime said.

"I feel like that stuff ages me a season in a day. You should have the petal cookies," Natai said.

"I don't like sweets," Craime said.

"You always say that, and I always remind you nectar is sweet," Natai said.

"Nectar doesn't count. It's a She'ehlarah staple. If you don't drink orchids, I don't know what you're doing with your life," Craime said.

"Living life wrong, at least," Natai said.

"Shh," Craime said.

Natai went silent as Craime stopped walking. He tilted his head slightly as they both listened. It was a sound that Natai couldn't identify. And it was repeating.

"What is that?" Natai whispered.

"No idea. Let's find out," Craime said, changing direction to walk toward the sound.

The sound got louder as the pair walked toward it. They rounded a corner and saw something they'd never seen before.

Three armoured figures were fighting a Dragonrider. The sound they'd heard was chitin blade hitting armour. Both of them were frozen in place as the Dragonrider was killed before their eyes.

The three armoured figures looked over at them. "They're council members," one of them said.

"So that means they're dead, right?" another said.

"That's not the order," the first said. The second reluctantly sheathed her weapon.

"Damn shame," she said, turning away from them.

Craime took Natai's arm and pulled hard. They ran together back the way they'd come.

"They're not here for us. Our rooms will be safe," Craime said.

They ran back the way they came, and stopped short when they were met by another group of four unidentified soldiers. These did not seem to have the same restraints.

"Run," Craime whispered, letting go of Natai's arm.

The soldiers walked forward as Craime pushed Natai.

"Run, girl. Use that mind of yours," Craime said.

Natai shook her head. Craime sighed and then, taking her arm again, turned the corner with her hand in his. They ran together, the sound of heavy footsteps thundering behind them. Natai was faster than Craime, and before long it was her pulling him through the snaking castle hallways.

Every now and then, the sound of clashing blades and screams echoed distantly through the castle. It was impossible to tell from what hallway the fighting came from, so Natai ran blindly, her fingers around Craime's hand losing their feeling as she went.

From hall to hall she went, seeing soldiers and quickly changing course. She turned another corner to see two dead Dragonriders bleeding on the stones. She was lost. She'd had to change their direction too many times.

"Nowhere is safe. Just keep moving," Craime said.

Natai nodded and started running again. She went down another hall and pushed on every door. Finally, one opened. She closed the door behind her.

"They're in here," a voice beyond the door said.

"Hide," Craime whispered.

"Were they right behind us that whole way?" Natai whispered back.

"Just hide," Craime said.

They were in a bedroom. Craime took one dresser and Natai took the other. Just as the doors of the dressers closed, the room door opened. Natai looked through a crack in the dresser doors as four soldiers entered the room. They could have been the same ones they'd run into a moment before, or an entirely different set.

Now that Natai had a moment, she could clearly see that their hair was purple. Was this some elaborate joke? She'd never read anything in the petitions to the crown nor in any polls that talked about any sort of unhappiness like this.

This couldn't be real.

The soldiers laughed as they first looked under the bed. "They live well up here," one of them said, sitting on the bed.

"Not many of them will live tonight," another laughed.

One of them pointed at the dresser, and Natai's heart sank. She couldn't even imagine what they were going to do to them. What did they even want from two people who had spent their life serving the kingdom? Natai watched as they opened the doors of the dresser Craime was hiding in.

"I found the old one," a soldier said as he thrust his blade into Craime's gut.

Natai put her hands to her mouth, but it was too late. The other three soldiers looked at her dresser. Within a moment, one of them had opened the doors.

"I'm Advocate Natai," she said, her voice shaking.

"That must have been fun," the soldier said.

He grabbed the back of her head as Natai felt an extraordinary pain in her middle.

TEGAN ABBOTT

Shaking, she looked down to see a chitin blade sticking out of her. She could hardly believe what she saw.

"Help," she whispered.

The blade was pulled out, and she felt it pulling through her flesh again. She fell to the floor of the dresser as the soldiers left the room. She tried to speak, but now the words wouldn't come. Something hot came out of her mouth. She touched her chin and looked at her hand.

It was blood. She looked across to Craime who, like her, was struggling in his last minutes. She tried to speak, she wanted him to know she was sorry for taking him from his study, but it only got warmer in her mouth. Mercifully, the sight of Craime wasn't visible for long, as everything went dark. As if all lights in the castle faded.

The agony of the blade splintered through her as she slumped against the wooden dresser. A moment after, she fell forward, her head slamming against the stone floor.

Mayala

Mayala and Amer woke to screaming and fighting at their doorway.

"Get through the passage, now," Amer said.

"Not without you," she said quickly.

"I don't know who's at the door, but it's most likely they've come for me and our children. Get out, find them," Amer said, his tone deep and commanding.

She desperately wanted to argue, but she knew her partner. By the tone of his voice and the height of his antennae, she could not argue with him. She nodded and kissed the love of her life. She took up her dressing gown and then ran. The castle had numerous secrets; the hidden passages were chief among them.

Mayala moved a bookcase and then into the secret passage behind it. She pulled the bookcase closed as the little hallway illuminated at

170

her presence. She moved through the tunnel to behind the vine where it ended.

As she reached the end of the tunnel, the hallway went dark. She pushed on the section as Amer had taught her to, but nothing happened. She pushed harder. Then she panicked. She was trapped in an unlit secret passage. She could die in here with her children undefended.

She pushed and pushed, and finally the wall opened. Beyond the moving wall of the passage was more darkness. She was definitely out of the passage in what should have been a well-lit hallway, but it was dark. The flowers on the walls that were always glowing were absent now. Amer's instincts were right. Something was extremely wrong.

Mayala crouched in complete darkness. She was utterly terrified and was too old for any of this. Too old to crawl around in the dark, and definitely too old to be this scared. In that moment, she realised how pathetic she was in forgetting what mattered most: her daughters and her son. She moved into a higher crouch and felt for the wall. The passage only went one way, into a private study.

She needed to be strong. She'd just regained her courage and she couldn't lose it now. Amer could not protect them this time. Never again. It was all on her shoulders. She was the only one who could save her children. She didn't know who was attacking the castle, which is when she realised, she could not trust anyone. No maid, nurse, or any of her family.

"I'm coming, babies." she whispered to herself, almost inaudibly.

She needed to leave the city right away. She'd left her youngest in the royal nursery. She would get him first, as the nursery was closest. Maia would be down the hallway. She thought on the challenge of her task as she crawled along the floor. Every second or third step, she got stuck on her own frilled skirts. She cursed herself now for ever caring so much about such silly things.

Raishy would likely cry when he was lifted from his warm bed. She'd be carrying a crying baby through the city. As she crawled in the dark, she had to think if she would be able to save her daughter. Any moment now, the castle flowers would illuminate as they always did. She had to use the temporary darkness cleverly. As she thought this, she felt the heavy wooden nursery door.

She felt sick to her stomach. She took a deep breath and decided that even if she wasn't able to do so, she had to try. She could not choose to leave him. She pushed on the door, but like before, it seemed stuck.

She stood in the dark. She stepped on her dress again, however. She repositioned her feet a few times before she found herself standing on only stone. She then pushed the door open, far too hard without the use of her eyes. It thumped loudly on the wall behind it.

She stood in the doorway and realised there was no way of finding her son in the complete darkness. She felt her heart sink. Somewhere in this room was her boy. It was far too dark to see, though. Mayala felt around in the doorway with her antennae. She could not feel anything beyond her own terror. She needed to get it together and find her son. She pulled her shoulders back and walked blindly into the room. As she stepped into the room, she smelt blood thick in the air. Mercifully, she couldn't see its origin. She could only hope it didn't come from any of the cradles.

"Raishy?" she whispered.

Mayala moved deeper into the room, only to smash her leg against a low table. She let out a cry of pain and then instantly silenced herself. She looked to the darkness of the doorway behind her, but she had turned her feet too. She turned to face back into the room but realised that she didn't know where the doorway was. She felt for the table and found it. In her panic, however, she didn't know what side she'd found it from. She was utterly lost in the darkness.

"Raishy?" she whispered again, panicked.

No sound returned. For all she knew, she was searching for an already murdered child in the complete darkness of the hallway outside of the room. She felt herself whimper. She tried to stop, but nothing had ever been so terrifying. She remembered when Zona hatched. He had been so tiny! And she'd lost him so young, but at least she'd been able to see him grow to adulthood. What a good creature he was. She sniffed more and more. Before she knew it, she was on the floor in complete darkness, sobbing like a babe. But she had to find her son. She couldn't lose this one.

She was dead already. She knew it now. Her children were dead, so too was Amer, and soon she'd die too, murdered by Iewen invaders. Perhaps Yurelle. Maybe her own kind. She fought to stop herself from crying and tried to catch her breath. In a moment of quiet, she heard a tiny voice in the darkness. As she looked up through tear-blinded eyes, she saw light. She stood and looked right at her awakening son.

Raishy was in his cot, cuddled tight by blankets and stirring at his mother's crying. Within his cot was a little glowing ball. She knew what it was in an instant: Maia's toy.

In a moment of shock, she realised she had what she had come for and something to help her leave with him. She looked quickly at the doorway and saw only the outline of the door arch. A moment ago, she couldn't even see that. No one was there, that was what mattered. She ran, stumbling towards her son and picked him up roughly. Raishy woke and looked right at his mother. Mayala took the toy from the cot and turned.

The path to the door was still clear, so she closed the distance. She saw some figures down the hall and closed her hand around the plant ball. It wasn't bright; just enough to see. With her arms still cradling Raishy, Mayala turned her hand and opened it every now and then to glimpse the hall. The door to her daughter's room was open. She carefully moved to it and opened her hand for an instant. In that instant, all she saw was blood.

She felt utterly sick, but she had to see if they were alive. She moved into the room and opened her hand again. She saw the shine of eyes from one of the beds. Maia's tiny body was sprawled across her bed. She'd lost three children, but she couldn't let her thoughts stay on that. She turned to see that Alura's bed was empty, still made.

She turned to leave. Two bright discs shined out from under the bed. Mayala jumped. She then looked closer with her hand open again and saw her nephew Pame. She gasped and motioned for him to come over, but he didn't. Raishy wiggled in her arms. Mayala crouched to the ground and put her elbow out to him.

"Take my arm, come on," she said, gently.

He looked as terrified as she was, but he nodded and moved out of the corner, hugging her arm. He took her arm so tightly that he squished against Raishy, making him protest with a little cry. Mayala shushed him and then moved slowly out of the room, taking Pame with her. She stepped on her skirts a few times again but managed to stand.

"Where is your sister?" she asked quietly.

"With Alura," he said ."They went out, but I was too scared."

"We have to be quiet now, all right? And fast. Think of it like hide and seek," she said.

Pame nodded. Mayala then poked her head out of the room.

"Quickly now," she whispered.

She then moved out of the room through the hall as fast as she could. She had to get to Vira and Pame's room. They had to be there, as Mayala had instructed Alura and Maia's guards to not let them leave the castle when the doors opened.

Running through the halls, she heard other pattering feet. She went to close her hand, but got a glimpse of two tiny figures as they too saw her. She opened her hand again to see Alura and Vira.

"Girls," she said.

"Mother!" Alura said, running to her mother in the dim light. Vira ran with her. Both girls were dressed in their nightgowns, and both were splattered with blood.

"We couldn't go to our room. There was a dead lady there," Alura said.

"Don't think about any of that now. We have to run," Mayala said. Both the girls nodded.

"Stay close," she whispered, hugging them against her already full arms. She stood, and then they ran together. They hadn't run for long before Pame lost grip of her arm and fell. Mayala quickly bent down to help him up. He stared crying loudly.

"No, no, no, no, little one, shhh," she said gently. "Don't cry!" She said again, trying to calm him. "Please, little one!"

Nothing worked, and soon he was crying louder. Anyone near them would know where they were. Vira smacked her brother hard on the nose. Before Mayala could protest, the boy silenced himself.

"Stand up," Vira snapped.

Mayala was not appreciative of her method, but it worked, and right now his crying could get them all killed. She helped Pame up.

"Time for braveness," she said, her tone betraying her guilt.

Pame stood, and then the group pushed on. The four moved through the dark halls, with only moments of light to guide them. Mayala opened her hand every so often to make sure they were heading the right way. She was impressed that her daughter, niece, and nephew could follow behind her when she as an experienced adult was utterly terrified.

Seeking moonlight, Mayala guided the children to the castle roof. To her incredible surprise, she saw a mounted hawk. Three Iewen stood near it and approached as they saw her.

A male was dressed in simple but fine-looking clothing: the Iewen messenger who had been asked to wait. The two behind him were fully armoured Iewen guards. Beside his guards were two Dragonriders.

The messenger and his guards looked tired, like he'd been hastily woken. As she approached, the messenger had his wings pulled in behind his back, his guards and the Dragonriders close behind.

"It's Mayala," one of the Dragonriders said.

"Should we leave our posts? Why is the castle dark?" the other asked.

"The castle is under attack. Accompany me and the children with this messenger," Mayala said.

"Well, if there is an attack, I'm certainly leaving. I was asked to bring an emissary to my Queen. I'm sure my Queen would gladly shelter the She'ehlarahs' former queen and what looks like little nobles?" the messenger said.

Mayala nodded.

"If you would be so kind as to make haste, then?" the messenger said.

Mayala helped the children onto the hawk. The guards assisted her to carefully climb the ladder to the box on the box of the back of the giant bird with Raishy tightly clutched in one arm.

"Let's see you all to safety," the messenger said.

The guard tapped the bird's huge neck as it lifted into the air.

Mayala had never seen Daltay, and the reason for their flight had her knees still shaking, but she'd never been more grateful to put her life in the hands of an Iewen. She didn't know the new queen, the hidden daughter of Farin.

No one had met Kyra. There was no information on her. Hye had discovered she was wingless and young, but nothing else. She'd seen firsthand what could happen if she stayed in the castle. She could only hope an unknown was better than a highly probable death in the darkness. But it wasn't her life she was terrified for. She looked at the little boy in her arms, then her daughter, then to her niece and nephew. She hadn't found Meri, Tenro's sister.

The sight of Maia's body flashed into her mind again. She forced the thoughts away. She knew that it was only the start of battling those thoughts. Enough children had died. She would ensure these little ones lived.

Syriel

As Syriel's hand had touched the Aspect, she felt herself ripped into its twisted mind. She felt too many lives to count and saw images she didn't understand. She reached out toward a shining city, but when she touched the memory, it turned into a ruin. She felt her mind being invaded, but she felt a vulnerability as they pushed. She pushed through it, and the invading minds ran past her.

She saw what they hid, masses of vines and something else pulling into obscurity. As she reached for it, it felt like she was being pushed violently away. She pushed past them like pushing through a thick crowd with its own destination.

She saw something for the briefest of moments, a white stone city and a mass of fungus. Then it became what it really was: twisted patches of images. A ruin. Cthessa had rebuilt the image from pieces of memories. Who had ripped those memories apart? Who would do that?

She fell into a pool too deep to swim. It felt like she was being drawn under, and she pulled against it. Someone was ripping through her mind like lightning, causing extraordinary pain as is tore through her. It devoured her every memory at once. It happened in sequence, and yet it felt like it also happened at the same time. The harder she fought, the less control she had, as if her memories were being ripped away from her. She'd lost control of her own mind. She was forced to be an unwilling spectator.

She saw herself as a child: the life of a chancellor's daughter and her constant lessons. The first time she spoke up in class. She heard her voice as if she were an outsider, but also as herself in disjointed unison. She tried to conceal the feeling of excitement from the memory, but the lightning pain jolted through her mind and ravaged what little energy she had left.

She saw Wilf in the season she'd bloomed. She remembered her mother promising her to a foreign prince as she had her first kiss with Wilf. Then the argument with her mother, and the rift between them that had never healed. She remembered her first argument with her mother, about Wilf. She thought it was over then, but even now, her mother's venom at Syriel's choice still divided them.

She saw her first meeting with Zona and again was swept up in their world. She was flooded with the feeling of hope, that she could repair the rift she'd created with her mother. She felt again, a hopelessness in knowing that her mother was home and Syriel had made that home unsafe by falling in love with a Yurelle.

Then her thoughts were ripped toward lessons with her father. One of her most precious memories, it soothed her as she remembered. It was something she treasured deeply, and it was this memory that the invading presence focused on. Someone wanted this specific memory.

Syriel fought as hard as she could. The splitting pain of the lightning intensified. As she pushed against it, she finally saw it. So many faces were seeking this specific memory that she couldn't fight it as she felt her mind relent. Exhausted and in agony, she watched the precious memory unfold before her with no way to stop it.

Her father was teaching her to dream.

He told her to breathe deep, and then together they pushed into the plane of their ancestors. Her thoughts were locked in that feeling. She remembered it over and over, learning each success and failure.

Then she was in that deep water again. This time she wasn't struggling against it; she was floating upwards, but drowning slowly. She felt more alone she'd never been. She didn't try to hold her breath as she breathed in the water like air. Her lungs didn't burn, and the agony in her body melted away as she floated in a pool of emptiness.

She wasn't drowning, this was different. She merging with the water, melting ever so slowly into it. She then realised that her thoughts were her own. The lightning and all the faces looking at her were gone. Alone. She'd never known was it was to be alone until now. She breathed in the water that suspended her and turned over to see light above her. Utterly exhausted, she reached out to the light with energy she didn't have.

She was pulled into another dream. This was not the twisted mind of an Aspect, but the realm of her forefathers.

She was in Fasier.

"Daughter," Var called. "Do not fear."

She couldn't believe what she was seeing was real. She hadn't seen her father since he was murdered. Yet she had a childhood of memories fresh in her mind, as if she'd just lived them. The cave around her was always as she imagined it since she'd first walked with him in Fasier. It felt too real to be a memory, despite how clear her memories had been.

She could hardly move a moment ago, but here she was whole. Revitalised. It *was* Fasier. She looked at her father as her eyes watered to overfilling in a moment.

"Father. Can I dream at last?" Syriel said, desperate and lost. One moment ago, her mind felt wrecked and fractured, but here she bore no wounds.

"Do not fear, daughter. You have undone the last great mistake," he said.

Syriel tried to remember what had just happened in a place where her footing was secure. She felt the many minds within hers. Then she relived the memory of learning to dream. Did Cthessa want to enter Fasier? Had she just let her in?

"Calm, daughter. Breathe," Var said.

"Am I dead?" Syriel asked.

Her father smiled. "Zrti never die, daughter," he said, his tone gentle. As he spoke, however, his face faded.

Syriel's eyes opened. She looked up to see her husband cradling her.

"Syriel?" Tenro whispered.

"We should not have come here," Syriel whispered back.

Going from being under attack to stable and then back to her body was a shock she could scarcely understand. Her head pounded as if she'd been the victim of a brutal attack. She had been brutally attacked. She tried to focus her thoughts; something was important.

Focus, focus, focus, she heard in her mind. Was that her voice? What did her voice sound like? So many minds had just ripped through her head; she couldn't remember what her own thoughts sounded like.

The dream.

A strange sound emanated from all around them. Syriel looked across the room as all of the Aspects withered almost instantly. A moment ago, they'd been half plant and Ptery, but now they looked like old bark. There was nothing recognisable from their previous form to this, their faces completely gone. Then the light in the room went dark. Only the sun disk above Cthessa's bulb illuminated their surroundings.

Syriel sat up and looked at the bulb in the centre of the room. One of the leaves of the bulb moved. As it did, Syriel understood too much about their history to understand. The tattered memories that had been so clear in her mind a moment ago were gone. There was only one thing she knew for sure.

She knew what was going to happen next. History was repeating.

The curled tips of the leaves started to curl downward. The huge flower bud bloomed as Cthessa's bulb opened. A figure emerged from the sticky plant matter within.

Cthessa had needed the dream to unlock her prison. It *was* an attack.

Luminous flowers dotted her skin all over. She wore vines and leaves for clothes, but it looked like they were attached to her, part of her. Fine cracks all over her skin, like the markings of a Ptery glowed from light that seemed to come from within her.

She stepped out of the bulb, her pointed toe touching the withered roots of her garden. Sticky pieces of the inside of the Great Plant clung to her as she shook her head. She flicked her vibrant blue hair and expelled some of the viscous plant matter.

She wore Syriel's face. Syriel felt the need to vomit, but pushed the feeling down. Cthessa's wings were something Syriel had never seen. They were a combination of She'ehlarh and Zrti, as vibrant blue as her hair and eyes—in the shape of shattered glass, but with She'ehlarah patterning and vibrant colouring.

Cthessa stood for a moment only. She looked over everyone in the room, resting briefly on Hye. Then her attention rested on Syriel.

"I am a slave no longer," the creature said, her deep voice heavy with venom. Despite the anger in her voice, she smiled at Syriel.

Syriel understood everything and nothing all at once. She had freed Cthessa.

She had felt the twisted torment of a creature trapped for too many generations to count. Cthessa had used Syriel's mind to free herself, and in so doing had doomed Syriel She'ehlarah justice.

Cthessa ran. Yune got up to stop her, but she was impossibly fast.

As she went, so too did her light. The sun disk retained some light, but not much.

All within the room looked back at Syriel. Syriel's heart raced. They would kill her. They had to.

"I didn't do that, she did. She stole from my mind. The key to her prison was Fasier. I didn't give in, I fought her, but she took it," she said, her voice shaking.

Syriel, still sitting, shuffled away from Tenro and sat up.

"I didn't give in," Syriel said.

Yune put his hand on his sword and looked at Tenro. Acasia stepped closer to Syriel.

"We're still in danger. We're stronger together, and mostly unwounded," Acasia said, looking at Bren. The group turned to the wounded soldier.

"Bren?" Saf gasped, leaning back. Bren's head was rolled back, hie eyes staring at the stone ceiling.

"He's gone, we can't stay," Lon said, standing. She wiped some of the blood from her armour and then stood tall.

Syriel could hardly believe the solder's strength. Syriel didn't have the strength to stand, but Lon had just wiped her companion's blood off and was ready to move on. Inspired, she forced herself to stand with the help of the wall beside her. She blinked and shook her head. The feeling that she was going to vomit washed over her again. She shivered violently as she pushed against it. She didn't have time for this. They needed to go.

She wouldn't break twice in one day. She wouldn't think about the danger she was in. She'd just fought against numerous minds within hers, and though weakened, she would control her thoughts.

She walked toward the door where Cthessa had gone. Yune moved past her as the group moved on from the horrible aftermath of murdered Aspects in the dark castle behind them.

CHAPTER 8

CHAOS AND DARKNESS

Syriel

She followed the royal guard through the twisting tunnels until it opened into the dead of night. When the moonlight touched her skin, she breathed a heavy sigh. She didn't think she'd survive the castle, let alone escape with those around her. They thought she had intentionally killed their plant. She was sure of it. She would likely not survive the night. And she didn't blame any of them.

They were surrounded by houses. Syriel thought back to the twisting streets of Malarmha. An ambush likely awaited them among the sweet stone houses. She thought about that bitterly. She'd never seen the outer city, and yet she was likely to die here.

"We can't stay," Hye said.

"Come to the Painted Garden. There are many places to hide there," Yune said, driving the group onward.

The small group moved together, though disorderly. Yune led them forward with Lon behind them.

"Who attacked us?" Tenro asked.

"We're not safe yet, Sire," Lon said.

"I need to know now," Tenro said.

"You should rest first, Sire," Yune said.

The group continued running as the silence grew among them. Yune paused the charge for a moment, ducking behind a nearby building. He looked back for a moment of rest and then turned.

"Your father," Hye said. Yune scowled at Hye.

When Tenro heard this, he stopped walking. His tense posture went almost limp in an instant. Syriel had never seen him stand like that. In an instant, he went from king to child. When he stopped, so too did those around and behind him. Yune also then stopped and turned.

Tenro looked at Hye with his mouth wide. Syriel took his arm and he gave her his attention. But his furrowed brow discomforted her more than anything else. They hadn't been married long, but even still, Syriel hadn't seen him so visually shaken. Ever. She understood why.

"Sire, stopping is not an option," Yune said. Tenro didn't move, however.

"Sire, these outer houses aren't safe," Yune said, glancing at Hye.

"If we stay, we die. You now know the danger we face," Hye said flatly.

"Right," Tenro said, walking toward Yune at the head of the group. "Let's move."

Yune let out a sigh and then nodded. He confidently led the obedient group through the cobblestone streets.

Syriel could feel Tenro's pain in the air, and she did everything she could not to add her own. She thought that might be a futile wish, however, as she felt her own feelings around her even as they ran. Yune quickened his pace, and the group was forced to match it.

"I'm ashamed to have found out so late. We heard of the attack when it happened. I didn't have time to inform the city guard myself. I asked an agent of mine to inform the captain of the guard," Hye said.

"You think he wanted me dead?" Tenro asked.

"I'm sorry, Sire, but yes," Hye said.

"Thank you for telling me," Tenro said. His tone was flat.

Tenro was already regaining his strength and speed. He was incredible; Syriel was astonished. But it wounded her to hear her husband's hidden pain. Through everything, she knew how much she loved him.

The only thing she wanted was to be back home in Malarmha. She should have followed her instincts and never left. She wanted to have spent her life with Wilf instead of getting him killed. She shouldn't have trusted her mother and father. And she shouldn't have fallen in love with a She'ehlarah.

With her hand on his arm, she thought about her husband in torment and shared it. She hadn't intended to be a tool for his kingdom's ruin, but like his own father, she felt like she too had betrayed him.

"We'll rest and make a plan in the garden. Don't let it slow you, Sire," Yune said.

"Right," Tenro said.

The group arrived in the Painted Garden to see a gathering of Ptery looking towards the dark castle. The crowd divided for their king, queen, and their guard. They left the crowd quickly and followed Yune into a small building. Yune immediately closed all of the shutters, blocking out the night lights beyond them. The only light in the room was a small crystal jar on the table. Fluttering light bugs danced joyfully around in the jar.

"They've all seen us, and they'll have questions. We can't stay long," Yune said.

"We can try to get to Daltay," Hye suggested.

"They might shelter us, but would we make the journey?" Tenro said.

Syriel gulped. She didn't know if her own mother would shelter her. She didn't yet understand what her father had said, nor what he intended by it. She must have misheard him. Fasier wasn't telepathic, and miscommunications still occurred.

"Who was she?" Syriel said. All in the room went silent.

"Why did she look like me?" Syriel said.

"She looked like ancient Feularah, just as you do," Hye said.

"Why?" Syriel said.

"It's her original identity before so many generations of She'ehlarah were gifted to her," Hye said.

"But why do I look like her?" Syriel said.

"I don't know. No one in the castle did. We only knew it was important," Hye said.

Syriel glanced at Tenro and saw that he still didn't hold himself as he did before he'd learned that his own father wanted him dead.

"When you touched the Aspect, what did you see?" Hye asked.

Syriel turned back to Hye and picked carefully through the fragmented memories barraging her pained mind. It felt like memories of memories that even Cthessa didn't fully understand.

"It wasn't the Aspect's mind, but hers. I saw a city of white stone. I saw many faces, too many to count. It felt like I saw through ancient eyes, there was so much anger, it was hard to think. I saw a ruin, but it was like it was a memory from a dream, pieced together from legends. There was something that she tried to hide from me. The ruin was overgrown with fungus," Syriel said.

"Do you know how to find this city?" Hye asked, leaning toward her as he spoke.

"No," Syriel said.

"Do you think you can find it with time?" Hye asked.

"It might be possible," Syriel said, furrowing her brow as she looked at Hye.

She expected their anger, but it didn't come. She looked at Yune, but his face was too hard for her to read. Willingly or not, she'd brought downfall to their entire kingdom, her kingdom. She couldn't form the words to ask how and when she'd be punished.

"I think all She'ehlarah are in danger from her," Hye said.

"The kingdom is in danger too," Yune said.

"I think she's more dangerous. She knows our entire history and called herself a freed slave," Hye said.

"You think we should go after her and not abandon the castle?" Tenro asked.

"I think we need to stop her. But we should go to Malarmha and speak to the High Chancellor," Hye said.

"What if my mother planned all this?" Syriel said, her tone pained. She felt like she was betraying her family by questioning her mother's concern for her own daughter, but her first concern was her kingdom, which was by her mother's own design.

"That's why it would be good to go to her—to learn if this was her design, or by Cilessa's," Hye said. "But we could also try to go to Daltay and take a chance with the new queen. We'd have to find a way to make the flight up, as no Ptery wings can make it," Hye said.

"My beetle could make the distance," Acasia said. All eyes but Syriel's fell on Acasia. "We control the biggest realm. Yurelle are better scouts than any other. We train for distance, and our beetles are bred big enough that they can carry many. And they are exceptional climbers," Acasia said.

"All of our choices are risky," Tenro concluded. "We don't know who controls the castle, and we'll find out before we make any other choices. If it's my father, then probably he'll try to kill us again. In that event, we will go to Malarmha."

Tenro looked at Syriel as he finished speaking. Syriel faced him, her thoughts still muddled from connecting with all of She'ehlarah history.

"I think we should go to Daltay," Syriel said. She didn't say what she really wanted. She wanted to go to the city in the dream. She wanted to find the ruined white stone city overgrown with mushrooms. She closed her eyes and tried to picture it again, but it was distant now, already escaping her.

"We'll first decide if the castle is safe," Tenro said.

"We can't stay here long. A group already saw us entering here," Yune said.

"All right. We gather what we can, see who controls the city, and then leave immediately," Tenro said.

"Exactly. And wherever we go, we'll need your beetle," Hye said, looking at Acasia.

Syriel opened her eyes and looked at everyone in the room again. Her head was throbbing, but she needed to focus on the moment, as the dream was already gone.

"I don't think I should go alone. I'll need to saddle her, and it will take time," Acasia said.

"I'll go with you," Lon said.

"Hye could get some food while and Saf and I stay here with our queen and king," Yune said.

"Sounds like our best option," Tenro said.

"Yes, Sire. I'll leave now, then," Hye said, leaving the building.

"And us?" Acasia said.

"The less time we spend here, the better. But the beetle will draw attention, so we should retrieve it as we leave," Yune said, looking at Tenro.

Tenro nodded.

Versai

Versai walked carefully through the dark castle, her unit of twelve close behind her. Her home stank of blood, rage, and insurmountable fear. She knew the castle better than most, but not in the dark. She preferred to have let her senses guide her, but the violence overwhelmed her.

"Keep together. Find light. Protect the castle," Versai said again. It was almost a chant now. Every time the footsteps slowed; she repeated it. The sun should be coming up soon, but the castle had so few windows to light their way. They needed light.

The group rounded another corner and slowed their steps when they saw the promise of light coming from a doorway just ahead. Versai moved forward, her steps careful and quiet. Every armoured step she took was intentional.

It was a study with two desks, two chairs, and a couch against the wall. On one of the desks stood a small crystal jar, a number of captured glowing bugs within. Versai quickly collected the jar and inspected it briefly before looking down at her armour.

Every part of her armour was splattered or covered in blood in multiple states of drying. It had been a long night, the hardest night of her life. She left the study with the light.

"You and you, take your flask and put a glow bug within. Split into three groups, we need to cover more ground, find anyone who can still be saved," she said.

Both soldiers took their crystal flasks and carefully collected a bug. The unit split, leaving her with four soldiers as she then quickened her pace.

"Anyone alive?" she called, moving quickly down the hall. She stopped when she heard crying.

"I am Versai, Captain of the Castle Guard. Come to my voice," she called.

"Captain!" a female voice exclaimed.

The voice sounded familiar, but the single word from a sore throat was hard to identify. It sounded like it was coming from the nursery.

"Come toward the light in the hall," Versai said.

An older female stood in the doorway; the hem of her nightdress was bloodied. Her dress wasn't otherwise bloodied or ripped. Wyma was lucky.

"Wyma, have you seen Vira or Pame?" Versai asked.

"No, captain, the children in here are …" Her words trailed off.

"They shouldn't have been in the nursery," Versai said.

"They weren't in their rooms," Wyma said.

"We'll find them. Stay with us," Versai said.

"Where are we going?" Wyma asked.

"The throne room. it's bright and big," Versai said.

The small group moved through the hall. Light had made Versai more alert but had also shaken her somewhat. The light splashed against walls, making monsters that she'd never before imagined. Like all those who lived in the castle, she'd lived her whole life in light. She'd never seen how imposing shadows could look against the stone walls.

The light showed the blood and occasional body around them, exposing the extent of the damage. It shouldn't have been possible to cause such harm to the castle of the incredible legacy of the Dragonriders, and yet Versai wore the blood of an invading army.

They arrived at the throne room, lit by a number of luminous sources as always. It was tradition to keep it bright since before the Cthessa had grown enough to brighten the room. The cold stone walls were almost brought to life with the patterns of light splattered on the walls from hanging jars.

It was only here in the proper light that Versai could see the dead vines on every wall. It was a more harrowing sign than even the light against the walls of the castle. For the first time in her life, Versai felt genuine concern. She swallowed that feeling hard, and then focused her attention where her kingdom needed it to be.

The throne room wasn't only well lit, but it was also where one of her groups stood. A number of people had already been found in the darkness, Guiyn and Laur among them. Laur stood beside his shaking partner, Siah, who was holding their daughter, Meri.

"Captain, have you found Tenro?" Siah asked.

"I'm sorry, we haven't," Versai replied.

"Guiyn," Wyma said, running to her husband.

Guiyn embraced his partner, whispering to her as she pressed her face into his shoulder. It was a good sight. Some of the royal family had survived. Versai again focused on her task and turned to the smaller group who'd arrived before her.

"Keep searching, we'll stand guard. Keep together. Find light. Protect the castle," Versai said, handing the crystal jar to the leader of the smaller group.

"Immediately, General," the leader said as she took the jar and left the throne room.

Versai walked up to Guiyn and opened a pouch on her hip. "I'm sorry for all of your losses, but they need you," she said, producing the fragile glass crown.

"That's mine, brother," Laur yelled from across the room. Guiyn looked at his brother as he took the crown and put it on his head.

"Thank you," Guiyn said.

Versai nodded. "I'm sorry about your brother," she said.

Guiyn bowed his head as Wyma hugged him.

Versai stepped away from the grieving couple. She had a great deal of work to do.

Syriel

Syriel looked at Tenro in the house of the Painted One. They had only just changed out of their night clothing. Their guards still had their backs turned.

"I'm so sorry about your father," Syriel said.

"Thank you. He's always been hard on me, but I never expected this. At least now I know why he didn't want to get to know you. I'm sorry," Tenro said.

"No. You didn't choose this. We've only just gotten married …" Syriel said, trailing off.

"Amer told me it would be challenging, and if I had known this would happen, I never would have. Forgive me. I'm being unfair," Tenro said.

Syriel glanced at Yune and Saf, whose attention was fixed on the door and a closed window. "You regret marrying me," she said in a whisper.

A part of her deeply regretted it, too. She'd glimpsed a life of happiness she'd never known, but it had been ripped from her. Her happiness harmed her own colony. She was her mother's only heir. She was a fool; it was never really hers. Not happiness, not the seat of the Grand Chancellor, not the She'ehlarah throne. Nothing was truly hers.

"No. I can't regret something I didn't know about. We're out of there. I'm glad my wife is safe and with me," Tenro said.

Syriel smiled, but she sensed something new in the air between them. It was an uncomfortable scent, one she'd never felt from him. It was almost like guilt, but ever so faint. Syriel furrowed her brow as her antennae tasted it in the air.

Tenro glanced over at her, and then the scent was gone, replaced with the same affection she'd felt before. It was diluted, however. It was true that he still cared about her; it was in the air between them, unmistakable. She could only hope it was pain that made the scent so scant.

Syriel forced herself to smile. Tenro smiled back, but with the emptiness in the air between them, it felt like a lie. Just like her smile. She couldn't find a single warm phrase to comfort her husband, not with what she'd just felt in the air between them. Her focus was on what was between them, trying to understand what she'd felt for a moment. Trying to find the reason for it.

She searched for the words to heal the rift she'd felt between her and her husband, but in vain. Perhaps she should have talked about the Zrti belief that all things are already set in motion, that all choice is an illusion, but she herself didn't understand that. And she didn't believe it. She'd tried to do the best she could, but even then, it would mean nothing. She said nothing and felt the divide between them grow in the excruciating silence.

Her mind swirled with the incomprehensible belief of the Zrti as she tried to find the words to comfort him. And she still tried to discover the last whispered feeling lingering between them, the feeling Tenro had tried to hide.

Hye

Hye stepped back into the small building that housed the King and Queen of Velwrith. A scout entered with him. When he closed the door, the light he brought with him was shut out, but the scout remained. Yune jumped up immediately.

"This is scout Payon," Hye said immediately, his eyes flicking briefly to Yune before returning to his king and queen. Payon bowed to his king and queen.

"You were sent for food, but you retrieved a scout," Yune said, more dryly than usual.

"I also brought food," Hye said, placing a number of bundles on the table and nodding at Yune, who returned the gesture. He then turned to his silent king and queen.

"Payon is an experienced scout who's spent almost more time in the tangle than the city. I've told him our plan: we have to hide until it's safe to return here," Hye said, choosing his words carefully.

He needed all within the room to know that Payon didn't know about Cthessa. He could only hope they thought as he did: the more people who knew, the higher the chance of chaos, instability, and panic.

"Majesties, I don't know if I can find the way to Malarmha or Daltay, as there are no paths to ether anymore. But the best chance to get through the tangle is with someone who knows the dangers firsthand," Payon said.

There was silence for a time. Hye looked at Syriel and Tenro. Nothing remained in the air, but they were not huddled together as Hye expected. Trouble can divide, but it needed to unite them now.

"We'd be grateful for your help," Tenro said.

"I am honoured," Payon said, bowing again. "Forgive me for being direct, but it sounds like you'll need me. I was told you travel with a Yurelle beetle," Payon said, glancing at Hye.

"That's right," Tenro said.

"I don't know how they interact with scout geckos. I do know they all get on well with dragonflies," Payon said.

Tenro looked at Yune. From Tenro's frown, Hye could almost read his mind. Retrieving the dragonflies would be even more helpful to assist a scout. Hye had wanted to suggest this, but leaving the king and queen with only a single guard could have been problematic.

"We'll pass by the dragonfly roost on our way out of the city," Yune said.

"Can we make another stop when we leave the city?" Tenro said.

"Retrieving the dragonflies could be too dangerous. The pools are closer to the castle," Lon said.

"Every choice we make is dangerous. The city isn't safe, but the riskiest prospect of all is being on foot in the tangle," Payon said.

"Should it be a question of who is opposed to it?" Tenro asked.

"We will need to get the beetle and Payon's gecko," Hye said.

"Pardon my phrasing, but are you a confident beetle rider, Syriel?" Yune asked.

Syriel was silent. Her frown made Hye believe she was thinking, but it shouldn't have been a hard question.

"We've done a lot of training through Malarmha," Acasia said, looking at Syriel. "The Grand Chancellor requested that Syriel be trained to ride on the underside of the city's bridges. I myself have been riding beetles since I was small. We'll be able to keep up with dragonflies as long as there are enough branches nearby."

"Good. Dragonflies bond with their riders and can only seat a single rider. Hye, are you a competent gecko rider?" Yune said.

"Yes. I've been trained to ride geckos and beetles in dangerous situations," Hye said.

"Hye and I have worked together before," Payon said.

"Then we'll leave you all in the care of Acasia while we retrieve our dragonflies," Yune said, looking at Acasia.

Acasia nodded.

"I never imagined I'd be in this position, but I'm prepared. If we ever need to split up, I'll always stay with my queen and my king," Acasia said.

"Thank you," Tenro said.

"That will be ideal. My team and I work well together. We can fight or distract anything you can't outrun," Yune said.

"Yurelle beetles can comfortably mount four on the round saddle mine has, plus a driver. Should one of you Dragonriders stay with us?" Acasia said.

"We're more powerful in the air above you," Lon said.

"My team will retrieve our dragonflies, Payon his gecko. Hye will get Acasia's beetle so she can stay with us," Yune said.

"That's a lot of splitting up, and saddling the beetle by myself will take time. We'll be most vulnerable when we split up," Hye said.

"We could go to each place together, but it extends the time when we'll be exposed," Yune said.

"It's best to split up and meet at the eastern farm gate," Tenro said.

"Pardon, Majesty, but the northern gate is closer," Payon said.

"Northern gate it is, then," Tenro said.

"Are we ready to leave the city?" Hye asked.

"Yes," Tenro said, picking out some dried flowers from one of the food bundles and putting them into his mouth.

The group gathered the bundles of food. Hye surveyed Syriel. Her silence spoke volumes, and her face looked far darker than when he'd left. He must have missed something. With morale so low, the King and Queen needed to keep their spirits as high as they could. He'd have to watch over them more carefully, especially his queen.

Hye handed Syriel a hood. After a time, she looked up and took the hood from him.

"We can't cover those mesmerising wings, but your unique hair can at least be covered," Hye said.

Syriel nodded. She didn't acknowledge his compliment. She'd always reacted favourably in the past to compliments.

She put on the hood, tucking her hair up. Hye took another moment to look her over. Hye hadn't known her long, but he'd been watching her, as Amer instructed. She hadn't even been this dejected after Zona's or her father's death.

It could have been from the trauma they'd all just been through, but she'd run through the castle with far more energy. Even after she'd touched the Aspect. she'd had more spirit than this. Something didn't add up. It was something Hye would have to figure out later. For now, he could only hope that the horrible events of the night had caught up to her.

"We have one chance to get out of the city. Stay together, move quickly," Yune said. Hye opened the door and led the way from the room. Sunrise was only a matter of hours away, and the morning was a busy time. They had to rush.

Mayala

Mayala carefully dismounted from the hawk's box and climbed down with Raishy still in her arms. Despite dawn just now approaching, the hawk port was well lit. A number of Iewen guards stood silently at their posts.

"Arriving with an emissary from Velwrith and news for the Queen," the messenger said.

"Go right ahead," another voice replied.

Mayala helped the children dismount as the messenger came around the bird beside her. The two She'ehlarah port guards helped Alura down last.

"Stay close to me, please. This city is quite different from Velwrith," the messenger said.

He guided them to an edge and stopped. Mayala looked down into the hollow tree. Numerous lights dotted the wall of the hollow tree as far as she could see, but the centre was incredibly dark. "It's a short flight but a long drop. Perhaps the guards should hold the little ones," the messenger said.

Mayala crouched down to Alura.

"This guard is going to carry you, and I'll hear no arguments about it. Same for you, Pame," Mayala said.

Neither complained, as they too had stared into the depths of the city only moments ago. Pame was fully grown, but only just, as he'd spent most of his time in the castle as a backup royal. His immaturity was typical of a noble in his position. He'd spent his Bloom locked in the castle, which would stunt any Ptery's growth. None of that suited the situation. Mayala could only hope he'd behave long enough to ensure their safety. "Lead the way," she said, standing upright again.

The messenger said nothing as he turned and dove off the platform. Mayala did the same and turned to see the three-season old Vira flying behind her. Vira had never needed much guidance; Mayala had always thought she was determination itself.

The She'ehlarah guards flew behind Vira with Pame and Alura in their arms, the messenger's guards following after. The flight was short, as the messenger had said. They landed on a squishy fungus disk as Alura took Mayala's hand.

"We're just fine," Mayala whispered.

"I'll have to retrieve the Queen. If you'd be so kind to wait in the throne room," the messenger said and gestured to his guards.

Mayala walked quickly into the throne room. It was smaller than that of Velwrith and incredibly different. The She'ehlarah and Iewen were as different as two colonies could be. That had never so clear as now, when Mayala stood in the alien throne room. Instead of the security and strength of cold stone, they were enveloped by soft fungus walls. The floor on her naked feet was mushy, but it wasn't comforting; it made her stomach lurch. She was in the depths of enemy territory, and it was likely the safest place she could be. That alone was nauseating. Glowing mosses had been splattered over the walls as if by some deranged painter, illuminating the entire chamber.

Her eyes stopped on the most dominant figure in the room: the so-called Gnarled Throne. In Velwrith, the throne room was a statement of strength, defiance, and devotion, but this royal room of governance was utterly disturbing. The throne was gaudy and twisted, like a crooked agonised remnant of something that once could have been beautiful. On the most terrible day of her life, Mayala stared wordlessly at the Gnarled Throne and could only think of what the Iewen could have been if they hadn't contorted their view of the world—warped like their throne.

The Iewen world was so unlike hers that Mayala had to remind herself it wasn't a nightmare. If only the events leading up to this moment had simply been a bad dream. If only. Amidst her torment, her mind snapped to the memory of the children beside her. She remembered seeing their tiny faces in the dark, twisted in terror and desperately seeking guidance.

Mayala looked at Raishy in her arms. His silence was as chilling as both why they were here and where they stood. He stared wide-eyed at her. Mayala chose not to question why he wasn't crying as she looked around for Alura, Vira, and Pame.

There were no guards in the room. Vira sat on the floor with Alura next to her. Pame was touching the moss on the wall. "Don't touch that," Mayala said. "You two, stand up please."

"But Mother, it's soft," Alura said.

"This is not a bedroom; it's the throne room. Stand up," Mayala said.

Alura looked exhausted. Her red eyes stared up at Mayala, begging her to change her mind. Alura's nightgown was hemmed in blood. Vira's clothing was ripped, dishevelled, and also stained with blood.

Vira stood when she was scolded. She looked at Pame, who quickly removed his hand from the wall. "This night has been more to bear than any person should, but we need help, so we need to act properly," Mayala said.

"Yes, Mother," Alura said. For the first time, her voice was as small as she was.

That was enough to break Mayala's heart, but a heart can't break if it's already broken. She thought about Zona. Nothing could break her like that had. This night would soon be behind her, behind them all—if they survived it.

"Chin up. We get to be the first to meet the new queen," Mayala said, tapping Alura on her chin. Alura nodded.

She looked at Pame as he straightened his nightclothes, then looking at her own. Her nightgown was ripped and bloodied from the hem to almost her knee. She looked behind her to see her bloody footprints; she hadn't even realised how bloody she was. Had she crawled through the blood of her daughter when she'd found Pame?

As she thought about that moment, the image of her daughter's body flashed into her mind, and like that of Zona's body, it wouldn't leave. Raishy fussed in her arms. As she pushed against the last image of her little girl, Raishy cried. Mayala shushed him, but it was no help. She bounced him gently, but his crying only escalated.

"Raishy, please," Mayala whispered, her words swallowed up by his screaming. As his cries reached a volume Malaya had never heard, a side door of the throne room opened.

A wingless young female stepped through, with three guards behind her.

The female wore simple clothing and a twisted wooden crown on her head. She had the longest ruling family of any realm, and the markings of her line were legendary—clearly the markings of Amaranthus on her skin.

She walked with confidence, despite the late hour and her famous reign. This was most historic, and not for her gender alone: no female had ever ruled the Iewen. But her winglessness was more incredible. Seeing her confidence despite her position unnerved Mayala even more. She stood as tall as she could through the fatigue, the torment, and still with the image of her children's bodies bombarding her mind. And the screaming of Raishy.

Kyra seated herself on the twisted wooden throne. Two of her guards flanked her as she pointed at Raishy, and the last guard took him from her arms. Mayala didn't try to stop him from taking her baby. She couldn't have if she wanted to, and she needed to trust those she was about to ask to save their lives. The guards took her baby Raishy out of the room. Mayala was equal parts terrified and grateful.

"Welcome to Daltay, Mayala. I am Queen Kyra." Her voice sounded musical and gentle.

Mayala bowed deeply, and Alura, Pame, and Vira copied her. She was grateful that even in their distress, they knew the significance of showing respect to the foreign queen. When Mayala stood upright again, the Queen looked her up and down and frowned.

"Thank you for seeing us, Your Highness. Please forgive the state of our dress," Mayala said.

"Of course. I'm sorry for what you've been through. My messenger informed me that Velwrith was attacked," Kyra said.

"Yes, Highness. I don't know by whom," Mayala said.

"I've arranged a room for you together. I'll see to it that clean clothes, water, and food are brought to you all as soon as possible," Kyra said.

"We can't thank you enough, Highness," Mayala said, bowing again.

"I realise this is an awful time, but I'd like to ask you three some questions. It's best to talk when things are fresh in your mind. You might know something of value that you don't even realise you know," Kyra said.

"Of course," Mayala said, bowing her head.

It was strange that Kyra was asking about this now. All four stood in their nightclothes, most covered in blood, and one was a child. Even if her questions were tactful, it was still a deeply traumatic event.

"I don't know much. They were skilled She'ehlarah attackers who didn't identify themselves," Mayala said.

"They were looking for my uncle, and ..." Vira looked at Mayala when her words stopped.

"Go ahead. Anything you know could help us identify them faster," Kyra said.

"We heard them in the hallway. They wanted to kill my uncle's family," Vira said.

"They said they needed to go to the nursery to find my brother," Alura said.

Mayala couldn't believe where she was. She couldn't believe what she was hearing. All of it was beyond unreal. She just wanted to wash her daughter's blood from her skin.

A wretched thought hit her, a historic fact: there was time when this was normal. When females last sat the throne, princes killed queens and their children. And now two females sat the thrones again. That thought circled in her mind over and over again.

"I can't imagine going through what all of you have. Thank you for your help. Anything can help us learn who attacked Velwrith," Kyra said.

"I don't know anything else, Highness," Mayala said, her voice shaking.

"We were posted at the hawk port, so we saw nothing," one of the Dragonriders said.

"Thank you," Kyra said, gesturing to her guard. "She will show you to your room. I would ask you and your guards to please stay in the room. I'd like to keep your presence here a secret for now. Until we know who attacked, we'd like to be cautious," Kyra said.

Mayala was grateful. Kyra seemed to be taking this as seriously as she should be. It seemed callous to question them as they stood bloodied in their nightclothes, especially with little Alura in the room, but Mayala understood the danger. She'd seen it firsthand.

Mayala saw the first light of the sun colouring the sky through the huge glass window behind Kyra. It started to paint the room in warm shades. Kyra leaned to whisper to a guard beside her.

"Follow me, please," the guard said as Kyra left the throne room. Mayala bowed her head and looked back into the throne room for a final look at the wingless Iewen queen. If Mayala died in the night, she could be grateful to have seen Kyra with her own eyes. When she thought that, another thought invaded her mind. She wished she would die in the night, that the nightmare of her existence since the death of her son would finally be over.

The worst part of this was that the Dairsen children needed her; they needed a strength that she didn't possess. She would never be the mother she once was, never be the person she'd been. She'd brought them here. It was all she could do. It was enough.

Syriel

None of them knew who was attacking the castle, but a part of Syriel wanted to surrender to them. She didn't have the will to run or fight. The gaping chasm inside of her was all-consuming, and she had nothing left to fill it. She sought pieces to throw into it. But they were all gone with no evidence they existed.

She reached back into her mind for the memory of the first time she'd met Tenro, the joy they'd shared and the vulnerable nature of their private conversation. Then the memory turned on her as if it were a living thing. The humiliation of being drunk her first night in the castle. The horrible reason she was even there. The death of Zona.

And then it hit her like a dart: the memory of the night her father was murdered in her place.

"Syriel," Tenro said loudly. "We have to move."

There was light in his eyes when he looked at her again. He wanted her to live. His eyes promised her that. Whatever would happen later, she needed this moment. He wanted her to live. It didn't matter why. He wanted her to live.

She stood and with a burst of energy she didn't know she still had; she ran on bare feet over uneven cobblestones through a city she didn't know. The outer city was like a different colony than the castle.

It wasn't the She'ehlarah realm she knew. It wasn't like Malarmha, it was like nothing she knew. This was the realm she ruled, and it was so foreign to her that it wasn't hers. Nothing here was. Nothing was.

Tenro pulled her behind a wall. Acasia put a finger to her lips as she looked around the wall. In a brief moment of forced clarity, Syriel heard the clattering of a cart's wheels. She looked up to the leaf-covered sky to see stars past the canopy of the forest. There was a slight colour in the sky. Just a hint. It felt like a warning, a threat. They needed to move faster. They needed to get out of the city.

Morning was coming, and their window was closing. She felt Tenro squeeze her hand as another pang of torment and delight washed over her. Heartbreak, she realised. She remembered this feeling. She'd tried to forget it. But amidst all the other complicated feelings swirling in her head, she felt the heartbreak of losing the love of her husband.

That was something she knew, and something she could fix, so she held it. She felt the excruciating pain of her heart tearing in two, and she held it. She squeezed Tenro's hand back. He was right there. She could fix it, but she needed to get out of the city first.

She couldn't fix all the people inside the castle who had died. Couldn't save her father. Or Wilf. Couldn't stop the plant she'd freed. But she could feel his hand in hers. It was real. And a world existed where she could fix it. He had loved her before, and he could love her again.

Tenro pulled her from their hiding place as Acasia ran into the street. She ran with them, now no longer pulled along by Tenro, but running with him.

The three ran over the cobbled streets all the way to a gate flanked by two guards, who looked from Acasia in her full Yurelle beetle armour to Tenro and Syriel. They scratched their heads. "Let them pass in secret," Yune said.

Syriel looked up to see the surviving king's guard riding their dragonflies above them. The guards did as they were commanded and opened the gates. "The castle is under attack. Keep your post, and make sure no one knows the King and Queen came this way," Yune said.

"Under attack by whom?" one of the guards said.

"Unknown," Yune said.

"We'll keep to our posts," the other guard said.

"And this secret," the first said.

It was only a moment until Hye arrived on the beetle. It was an incredible relief. He was far faster than predicted. Syriel, Tenro and Acasia climbed quickly onto the flat, oval saddle. It didn't have specific seats as much as it had corners. Oval saddles were comfortable, but didn't let those seated look out without sticking their legs over the raised edge.

They needed the saddle, but it would be uncomfortable for long distances. That's why they had the Dragonriders, Syriel reminded herself. They had what they needed; if only Syriel felt that way inside.

"Let's go," Yune said, flying over the gate.

Acasia drove the beetle from the city with Payon beside them. Syriel gulped as they left the safety of the outer city walls for the depths of the everchanging tangle.

Kyra

Kyra sat on the gnarled throne as she watched the She'ehlarah ex-queen taken to her room.

"Vujet," she said, her voice quiet. Vujet stepped closer to her.

"Make sure no one knows of their presence here," Kyra said.

"I've already done so, my queen. I prepared a room close to the throne room," Vujet said.

"I'd like you to personally oversee their security and secrecy. I want you to look after the prince in particular," Kyra said.

Vujet was silent for a moment. "He seems more like a child," Vujet said.

"So did I," Kyra said, looking at Vujet. Vujet nodded. "You know better than most that there is nothing I won't do for my queen," he said.

Kyra smiled, looked over at him, and turned her hand over. Vujet put his hand in hers.

"It's best to think ahead and be prepared than being caught off guard. I need to not be my father, in all ways," Kyra said.

"I wholeheartedly agree, Highness," Vujet said.

Kyra kept looking at him for a moment. The most critical thing to remember was that she was queen. She couldn't ever forget the weight of the crown. She loved Vujet more than the crown, but she needed to put the crown first for her realm to remain stable.

The crown was first her prison, and then it had become her freedom. Each day that followed, it changed. She knew the weight on her shoulders better than any ruler alive, but she struggled to see her best choices. Perhaps her imprisonment had made her even weaker than her father. Perhaps overthrowing Methis had been a mistake.

She worried that her legacy was too far from Amaranthus. Vujet, however, was exactly as he should have been. Having a child with him would safeguard all of their futures, and perhaps no one would ever know what she lacked.

A child with a She'ehlarah prince, however, could be the weapon that would finally end them. Kyra needed to already have had a child. She shook these impossible thoughts from her head and stood, his hand still in hers. "I wouldn't be half the person I was if I hadn't met you," she said.

"You're more responsible for your fate than you realise," Vujet said.

Kyra let go of his hand and turned to face him directly. "We need to be ready to make a show of them if they're found here," she said.

"I'm always ready to end any She'ehlarah," Vujet said.

"All but Pame," Kyra said.

"We can hide him. We should separate them early," Vujet said.

"Can you inform Reia of my intentions? I expect her purple hair and She'ehlarah wings will be a welcome sight," Kyra said.

"I'll do so immediately," Vujet said.

Kyra nodded and turned. As long as she had Vujet and Reia to guide her, no one would know that Amaranthus's legacy was weak. She left her throne room, Vujet walking behind her. As always, his presence was ever-empowering, always comforting.

CHAPTER 9

A CHANGED WORLD

Cthessa

The awakening light barely touched the forest floor, and yet Cthessa squinted. Sharp pain splintered through her broken mind, like a lightning strike through the very centre of a tree. Her eyes were not just blinded by her first sight of light, but by tears that she couldn't stop. It felt like she was going to rip in half. Her skin shivered like a fever every time the agony in her mind reached a crescendo.

Something was wrong, it had to be. Ptery were not born in pain. This was not her first birth, she reminded herself. She'd been flesh before she'd become the second seed. But she was more than she had ever been.

She ran through the tangle without pause, her naked feet pattering across the earth, branch, stone, and leaf. Every step she took added percussion to the agonising symphony in her mind. Lightning and thunder dominated her mind. Countless voices screamed in combined torment, all calling for the pain to stop. Her own voice was lost in the chaos.

She had opened her mouth when she'd been born, but she didn't know if any words had come out, nor if she'd been replied to. All she heard was the screaming within her as her mind tore itself apart over and over. Each mind within hers fought for dominance, but it was hers. It was her mind and she would fight to keep it.

Her shaking legs had been running all night. She barely felt their fatigue through the torture of her mind as she fell. She put her arms out to stop herself, but felt her head hit the earth as they too failed her. She tried to lift herself with shaking arms, but they were too weak to comply. Her limbs were vines when they should have been branches.

Through her bombarded senses, she smelled water. She crawled toward the scent until she saw a sparkle of light against the surface. She drank greedily and then brought two shaking, cupped hands of water to her face. She let out a pained cry as her feverish shivering reached its peak.

She closed her eyes tightly as her stomach convulsed. She pushed the feeling down and breathed through the incredible discomfort. The second time, however, the convulsion brought something up. She vomited, a shudder driving through her like a spike. She breathed between the convulsions as another came over her. After the second time, she breathed easier.

She opened her eyes, expecting to see something that would make her feel even more ill. She didn't see disgusting things in the pond. She saw nothing. The screams in her head had calmed enough for her to hear her own thoughts.

She brought another two handfuls of water to her face, but before it reached her, she heard something in the water. She opened her hands immediately, spreading her fingers to hear the voices go silent. She didn't understand, but she knew that some of her gifted Ptery were somehow already in the pool.

She had pulled every link to her through her vines before she'd been born. But this was not of her choosing, it was theirs. Somehow, they'd found their own freedom. Her broken mind could not contain them. She sought a particular voice in her mind.

"I remain," Leatti said.

Cthessa sighed, deeply.

"We are stronger without them," Leatti said.

Cthessa tried to stand and found truth in her words. Together, the strongest of the She'ehlarah history stood. Cthessa breathed easier. One of her personalities caught sight of two strange creatures across the pond. One was in the tree above, the other on the ground.

They were hard to see, covered as they were with green fur. When they realised they had been seen, they were gone in an instant. She'd had only a glance of them and couldn't be sure of what she saw.

"What was that?" Cthessa asked aloud.

"They looked like wingless Ptery, but with fur," an ancient voice said within her mind.

"We should follow them," another old She'ehlarah voice said internally.

"We have a goal," Cthessa said, a slight edge to her voice.

"Nothing is more important," Leatti echoed.

Cthessa smiled. The storm within her head was distant now. She took another heavy breath. It felt strange to feel her chest expand. She'd forgotten what the sensations of living had felt like. It felt incredible. She willed her legs to walk, and shortly after they did.

Her shared mind saw images of a city of white stone.

"Follow the flowers," Leatti said.

Cthessa saw the flowers in her mind as Leatti spoke of them. The tiny five-pointed blue flowers.

"Follow the flowers," Cthessa repeated quietly.

She then began to run. Her naked feet again pattering across the earth, stone, and vegetation. The sensation was extraordinary, like a memory from a dream, but it was real. She was free at last.

Olianna

Olianna sharply tapped the back of her index finger against the wooden door. The sun had only just risen, but still she tapped her foot on the stone apartment walkway. She looked behind at her guard, who shrugged. After a minute or two she'd received no answer, so she knocked again.

"Fiare, sorry to bother you so early, but I have news from Velwrith," Olianna said.

After a moment and a few small sounds from within, the door opened a crack. Fiare looked uncustomarily dishevelled, so much so that it took Olianna aback. Her hair was hastily smoothed over, and she'd dressed in a mismatching skirt and loose shirt.

"Apologies, Grand Chancellor," Fiare said.

Regaining her purpose, Olianna furrowed her brow. "Please, I told you to call me Olianna," she said. Fiare smiled. "I have a letter for you from the General of Velwrith. The messenger said it was urgent," Olianna said.

Fiare opened the door all the way to receive the letter. Her sitting room was a mess. Two glasses sat atop the stone table with a carafe between them. Olianna looked around the room as Fiare gasped, her eyes wide. Olianna's confused attention snapped back to Fiare in her doorway. Olianna seldom felt anything from Fiare, but just then her antennae felt a wave of horror emanate from the foreign princess.

"Do you know what this says?" Fiare asked.

"I do not," Olianna said.

"Velwrith was attacked last night," Fiare said.

Olianna gasped this time. "Who by? Was anyone hurt?"

"It's unknown who attacked. The Velwrith general is Versai. She says that Syriel and Tenro are missing. The bodies of my father and youngest sister have been found. My mother, middle sister, new baby brother, niece and nephew have not been found, but the tunnel in my father and mother's room was open," Fiare said.

Olianna realised her jaw was open and closed it. She wrapped her arms around Fiare as she felt her little body start jolting with tears. "I'm so sorry," she whispered.

Fiare nodded, her face darkening.

Olianna could not even imagine what Fiare was going through. When she lost her husband, her world had nearly ended. She chose to believe that Syriel was safe. She was the ruling queen; they would have had an escape plan for her. They had to. She was safe, she promised herself.

The fate of Fiare's mother, siblings, and the children of her uncles was concerning. There were few policies or concerns for the safety of lower senators. She was certain it was the same for ex-queens and backup princes and princesses.

Further within Fiare's room, Olianna saw movement.

"Are you alone?" Olianna said, looking again at the two glasses.

"No," Fiare whispered.

Olianna sighed in relief as Fiare pulled away from her. A barely clothed female peered from the bedroom doorway.

"I'm sorry, I heard," the female said.

Fiare walked into the room as the female held her arms out in response. Fiare hugged the female in return. In one moment, Olianna realised why Fiare had never coupled or had children. "I'm sorry to have interrupted. If you need me, you know where I am," she said.

"Thank you, Olianna," Fiare muttered into the female's shoulder.

"You should know that here in Malarmha, we don't punish people for being themselves. You don't have to hide anything from anyone," Olianna said.

"Unless it gets back to my people," Fiare said, stepping away from the female.

"That depends on who you see as your people," Olianna said, frowning. She turned to leave.

"Forgive my bluntness and poor timing, but I'm Senator Avena," the female said.

Olianna nodded. She knew why Avena had introduced herself. It wasn't politeness but forthrightness. Olianna was going to check up on the stranger staying with her foreign guest, and they both knew it. Avena had just made it easier. "Thank you," Olianna said, turning to leave the room.

First, she would send a guard to Velwrith to help her daughter. She turned back to the room. "You are Yurelle, Fiare. You have a home here as long as you want it," Olianna said.

Fiare looked back at her in silence.

Olianna closed the door and sighed deeply. She would find her daughter safe; she was sure of it. Velwrith was older than any of the three cities, it had stood the test of time and would continue to do so. She needed to understand more about the turmoil of her allied city immediately. She was sure she'd get a letter about the specifics when Tenro and Syriel again sat on their thrones.

She would have to complain to the She'ehlarah that she hadn't personally been told about the attack. They had an agreement, and she'd upheld her end.

Pame

It was early. Pame woke in a silent room. The bed felt too soft and too warm. It was strange. He must have still been half-dreaming, perhaps confused. He sat up. Luminous moss on the walls around him revealed that the nightmare of the previous night had been real.

One bed sat against the wall beside his, with two others against the opposite wall. There was a crib in the corner. Pame wanted to cry, but he didn't have the energy. And if he did, Vira would hit him again. He got out of bed and looked down at himself. He vaguely remembered bathing and changing into the Iewen night clothing. He walked quietly to each bed until he came to Mayala's face, blankets up to her neck.

"Aunt, are you awake yet?" he asked. He took her hand. It was cold. He waited.

"Aunt Mayala," he said, slightly louder. Vira sat up in her bed.

"Go back to sleep," Vira said. Pame looked at her with a frown. In the small room, he knew Vira would feel his defiance and irritation in the air. She always told him what to do. He turned his attention back to Mayala and shook her hand.

"Pame, it's too early," Vira said, getting out of bed. "You'll wake everyone." She closed the distance between them and all colour drained from her face. Pame looked at her, tilting his head slightly as he did.

"You're talking louder than me, you'll wake everyone," he whispered. As if on que, Raishy started fussing. Pame went to Raishy as Vira pushed on the door.

"It's locked," she said. Pame looked over Raishy as he wiggled in his bed.

"We're locked in," Vira said.

"She said we'd be safe here, Vira," Pame whispered, looking over his shoulder at her.

"What's happening?" Alura said, rubbing her eyes as she sat up.

"Alura, I need you to come over here," Vira said, walking back to Mayala's bed.

"Why?" Alura said.

"You have to say goodbye," Vira said.

"Where am I going?" Alura said.

"Nowhere. Come here ,please," Vira said. Alura climbed out of bed and walked over to Vira. As Pame realised through his tiredness what was going on, Raishy fussed more.

The room was silent but for Raishy, who now started to cry. Pame didn't know what to do now. Mayala had taken them here. Perhaps he wouldn't have to do anything, Vira was the oldest.

The door creaking as it swung open broke the silence of all in the room but the baby. A She'ehlarah in nursemaid's clothing entered the room with bundles of cloth in her arms.

"Do you need any help?" she said.

Vira pointed at Mayala.

"I see," the nursemaid said. She gestured behind her as two guards entered the room. "The guards will take you to the baths; we'll see to the baby and clean the room," she said.

"What do you mean 'clean the room'?" Vira snapped.

"We'll take care of her," the nursemaid said.

"Can I stay with her?" Alura's tiny voice asked.

"We'll take her away and you can see her later," the nursemaid said.

"I want to stay with her," Alura said.

The nursemaid walked up to Alura, crouched down next to her, and whispered something in her ear. Alura hugged her. Pame looked down at Raishy, whose crying was getting louder.

Alura walked toward Vira. "Come on, little Highness. We'll see you reach the male bath quickly," the nursemaid said.

Pame didn't understand what was happening, but Vira wasn't shouting, and Alura was already walking out of the room. He was scared but too tired to fight all these strangers, so he too left the room. As he did, he glanced back at his aunt, whose death was still too much of a shock for anyone to react to.

She looked so peaceful. She was with Zona, at least. And the clean god would protect them now.

Syriel

Syriel saw sunshine. The first rays had finally reached the undergrowth. She clung to the beetle so hard that her hands had lost their colour. The thundering of its many strong legs had been her rhythm for too many hours to count.

She'd gone past the point of nearly falling asleep numerous times already. She felt so nauseated and dizzy that her only goal was holding onto the saddle and keeping upright.

The beetle stopped slowing and turned toward a tree. She was so delirious in fatigue that she worried she'd fallen asleep.

The beetle climbed up into a massive hole in the tree where Payon already stood, his gecko resting on a ledge above.

"This is abandoned we can rest here for a while," Payon said.

Hye jumped down from the beetle and put his head between his knees. Tenro then climbed off the beetle's saddle with Acasia right behind him.

Syriel sat for a moment and unclenched her hands. She still couldn't feel her hands, even as the colour rushed back into them. She looked her hands over as she tried to focus on anything else but how ill she felt.

A hand came into view. "You should come down, Majesty," Yune said, holding out his hand to her.

Syriel had thought it would have been Tenro's hand. She pushed the surprise from her mind and accepted Yune's help getting off the tall beetle. Tenro was leaning against the wall of the hollow, looking as awful as she felt. It made her feel slightly better.

"We'll need our rest," Yune said.

Syriel didn't understand why he didn't look tired. She couldn't see the other Dragonriders.

"Are the others all right?" she managed.

"They're above," Yune said, pointing out of the hollow.

"I can join them," Payon said, leaving the hollow.

"Can I speak to you?" she whispered.

"Of course," Acasia said, leading her into the massive hollow.

"We talked once about your son," Syriel said. Acasia nodded.

"How did you know when you were with child?" Syriel said.

Acasia looked her over.

"Can I presume?" Acasia started. Syriel nodded.

"Might I, majesty?" Acasia said, placing a hand above Syriel's belly. Syriel nodded again. Acasia pressed gently on her belly. "My mother always said when you think you're with child, it's already time. I was going to go to the physician this morning," Syriel said.

"As always, your mother is astute," Acasia said.

"What do I do?" Syriel said.

"We'll have to stay here for a few days at most," Acasia said. "We need to inform the others."

Syriel nodded.

"The egg is unlikely to harden out here," Acasia said.

Syriel's head was already swimming. She'd never felt so exhausted and ill. She was overwhelmed when she'd woken up in the middle of the night. She didn't even know what she was now.

Acasia gestured for Syriel to follow as she walked towards the others. Acasia looked back at Syriel and then at Tenro.

Tenro looked up at Acasia and Syriel.

"Is something wrong?" Tenro said. He looked tired and slightly slumped, but he still held his shoulders back more than he had when he'd found out his father tried to have him killed.

Syriel was in awe of him, as ever. Yesterday she was too excited to tell him the news she needed to, and now she was terrified. One day she was too happy to tell him, and now she was too afraid. Acasia looked at her, and Syriel felt undone.

She had to tell Tenro. She knew it.

"Acasia suggested we wait here for a day or so," Syriel said.

"You're with child?" Tenro said.

"My stomach is hard, following weakness and fatigue," Syriel said.

"When did you know?" Tenro said, immediately closing the distance between them.

"Yesterday night, but we had the council meeting. I was going to go to the physician this morning to confirm it before I told you," Syriel said.

"Can I," Tenro said, his hand above her tummy. Syriel nodded. Tenro touched her tummy and pushed a little. She felt the pressure of his fingers and the hardness underneath.

"It has to be," Tenro said, smiling.

Syriel felt his happiness in the air around her and smiled. Then they both realised where they were again. Syriel didn't truly forget, but for a moment they were in union together. She felt Tenro's happiness dissipate quickly.

"It won't harden here. We have to take it home," Tenro said.

"Yes," Syriel whispered back.

"We'll have to find a way to keep it safe until the Eclosure," Tenro said.

"I can't go with you," Syriel said.

Tenro stepped back, his eyes wide and eyebrows raised. She knew he'd be confused. She didn't have to feel it in the air or see it on his face to know. She looked up to ensure Payon wasn't able to hear them as they whispered.

"I created a problem that I have to fix," Syriel whispered. "Besides," she said, speaking normally, "I can't hide amongst the She'ehlarah like you. I'd give you away. You know I'd have the egg destroyed." Tenro said nothing.

"I can't think at the moment. I'm so tired that I could barely sit, so standing and talking about this is …" Syriel said.

"We both need sleep, but you especially," Tenro said, putting his hand on her stomach again. "We'll plan later." Syriel nodded.

"I'll tell Yune we have to stay here," Tenro said.

"Why?" Syriel said.

"I have to. Sleep. We'll talk about it later," Tenro said.

Syriel could feel hurt and anger in the air as the distance and the lingering feelings that separated them. He had to know she was right, beyond fatigued as she was. She found a soft place to rest, and just like Yune said, she fell asleep once she sat.

Kyra

The midday light warmed the council chamber just enough to make Kyra want to go back to her warm bed. She'd come to deeply hate interrupted sleep.

Reia entered the room and bowed to her queen as she seated herself opposite Kyra and Vujet.

"Good afternoon, highness. Mayala died in her sleep. I separated Pame from the females as I sent them to separate bathrooms," Reia said.

Kyra's eyes went wide. This was ideal. She'd planned to seduce Pame away from his family, but Mayala's death would be a perfect reason to justify splitting them up for their own safety.

"We should keep them separated," Kyra said.

"Most certainly," Reia said. "I served the Dragonriders some breakfast and poisoned them and disposed of their bodies. One of the Dragonriders was female. I could have the armour adjusted to wear if needed."

"Good work. And you're sure our guards won't talk?" Kyra said.

"When Vujet told me what the messenger had said, I handpicked them. They won't say a word about our … guests," Reia said.

"Thank you. What should we do with the female nobles?" Kyra said.

"I suggest keeping them together. I've also separated the baby from the others. We need to find out who attacked Velwrith. If it was the Yurelle, they are doubly valuable prisoners. I have an agent in the castle now," Reia said.

"What's their name?" Kyra asked.

"Because of the depth of their position, I promised them I would keep their identity a secret. With deep apologies, Highness, but I promised to not speak it to even my queen," Reia said. Her eyes flicked to Vujet as she bowed her head low.

Kyra didn't understand spy work. She felt foolish for asking their name. She should have met with her advisors after she'd gotten more sleep. She needed Reia's respect, but more than that, she feared her talents.

Reia had already betrayed her former spymaster and king for the crown. Kyra had to be a queen worthy of her, or Reia might betray Kyra if she thought Amaranthus's line had already been broken. It must have been far more comfortable for Reia to not have to explain such simple things to her king.

"The moment they uncover any information, you will know of it, I assure you," Reia said.

"Very good," Kyra said. "So we can only wait for now?"

"We should prepare our defences, for if it was the Yurelle who attacked Velwrith, it's possible they could attack us," Reia said.

"Indeed. Attacking Daltay has numerous problems for the ground-dwelling Yurelle. But we should be prepared," Vujet said.

"Who else could have attacked?" Kyra said.

"It's possible it was an internal struggle. They appointed a king out of turn and accepted a foreigner as queen, bonded by marriage, even. If it was internal, they could target us next," Vujet said.

"If it was internal, they could be weakened, but we shouldn't rely on that without more information," Reia said.

"It's possible, though most unlikely, that an outside group is responsible. Such as a private army or a rebel colony," Vujet said.

"It would be almost impossible for a private army to successfully attack Velwrith while the Dragonriders defend it," Reia said. Vujet nodded.

"My messenger said the castle went dark," Kyra said.

"I was consulting about this all night, Highness. I believe the monstrosity turned the castle dark to protect itself. There is no record of Velwrith being attacked with such a successful force, but we expect the abomination would protect itself," Reia said.

"Most interesting," Kyra said.

"I will learn more when my agent contacts me," Reia said.

"Thank you, Reia, for your hard work through the night," Kyra said.

"It is my great honour, Highness," Reia said, bowing again.

"We should act like we know nothing until the contact reaches out," Vujet said.

Kyra had an economy meeting in the afternoon. She wanted few things more than to return to sleep, and she hated economy meetings, but Vujet was right. She needed to give no one any reason that anything was different.

"I can do that," Kyra said. "Is there nothing else we can do now?"

"We can only wait, Highness," Reia said.

"Thank you, Reia. And Vujet. I would never say this outside of the privacy of the two of you, but I don't know what I would do without you," Kyra said.

"You'd do far better than you think. We often echo your own thoughts, Highness," Vujet said, standing.

"I couldn't agree more, Vujet. We exist to serve Daltay, Highness," Reia said as she too stood.

"There are fewer eyes on Vujet than on yourself, Highness, so I will inform him the moment I know anything," Reia said.

"Thank you," Kyra said as she stood last. Reia left the room.

"I have a lot to do this morning, but I will be by your side again soon," Vujet said.

Kyra smiled.

"Don't fall asleep in the economy meeting," Vujet said.

"That's harder than you realise," Kyra said, with a laugh.

Vujet bowed deeply and then left. Kyra watched them both leave with a sigh. She needed them deeply. She could only hope that she would be worthy enough of them that their guidance made her worthy of her people.

Remin

Remin knocked softly on her door two times fast and one time slow. It opened almost immediately.

"Remin," Leisa said.

Her musical voice soothed the aches in his body almost instantly. The fatigue of working a long day was almost completely gone when she said his name. She made everything worth it.

She stepped back from her doorway to let him enter her home.

"I am convinced your voice has magical powers," Remin said, walking through the doorway.

"Is that so?" Leisa said.

"You're better than a hot bath at the end of a long day," Remin said.

"Why choose one when you can have both?" Leisa said.

Remin smiled. "Thank you."

"You shouldn't thank me. I enjoy your company as much as you enjoy mine," Leisa said.

"I find that hard to believe," Remin said.

Leisa laughed. It was so genuine and light. Living in Daltay he questioned everyone he knew. But she was effortlessly herself. She was so free and sincere. He never knew it was precisely what he'd been needing his whole life.

"Your day wasn't too long, was it?" Leisa said.

"My days are getting longer. I don't think I have what it takes to be a healer. I heard more about life in Daltay, though," Remin said.

"You're an outlier now. You don't have to be anything," Leisa said, getting two cups from her countertop.

"But I have to be something," Remin said.

"Someone searching for what they want is something," Leisa said.

Remin smiled without joy. He seated himself at her table as she placed the two wooden cups and a bottle on the table. Remin sniffed. "Is this fermented?" Remin asked.

"Have a cup," Leisa said, filling his cup.

Remin smelt the drink; it seemed alcoholic. He drank appreciatively and leaned back in his chair.

Leisa sat down at the table and poured herself a cup. She took a big gulp.

"What's all this for?" Remin asked. "Is there a festival I didn't know about?"

"Another healer told Tsune that there is an exile you'd both have an interest in," Leisa said.

Remin raised his eyebrows.

"I would have liked you to rest first, but I found out today and I wanted to tell you. He's on the other side of the city. I thought you could visit him tomorrow. But I don't think you'll wait," Leisa said.

"Who?" Remin said, leaning on the table.

"Methis was exiled, as he said, 'by Kyra'," Leisa said. Remin stood up. He looked at her in silence, unmoving.

"Can I help?" Leisa asked.

"Please. Can you come with me?" Remin asked.

Leisa took his hand.

"Anywhere you need me," she said.

"Can you come with me now?" Remin said.

"Empty your cup," Leisa said.

Remin looked at the table in front of him. It was surreal. Too many distant thoughts circled for him to form a single cohesive thought. He picked up the cup and downed it. Leisa did the same and then took his hand.

They left her home, and as they walked through Hald Remin still couldn't think. It could be a lie. But if it wasn't, what could it possibly mean?

She was alive. It was true.

The blood of Amaranthus was unbroken. The Iewen could survive. And she was alive. Kyra was alive. His daughter wasn't dead. He couldn't imagine what she'd been through, but she was alive. She'd exiled Methis? It couldn't be her doing.

"Leisa," Remin said.

Leisa kept up a fast pace as she walked through the city.

"Are you okay?" she said.

"Yes. Fine. I ... did you say that Kyra exiled him?" Remin said.

"I heard it from Tsune, who heard it from someone else," Leisa said.

"It's not a thing you mishear," Remin said.

"They might have misunderstood," Leisa said.

"My daughter's name wasn't known," Remin said.

"We'll only know it all when we see him," Leisa said.

"It's best to hear it from his mouth," Remin agreed.

Leisa picked up her pace. He could feel her energy in the air between them. He'd never been more appreciative for how honest she was. She was excited but also scared, likely scared he'd get hurt.

With his hand in hers, almost pulling him through the streets of the Sprawl, he realised something. He was flooded with emotion, and not just for his daughter. He'd never been more grateful to anyone. It was late at night, and they might not even be able to see Methis, but still she took him to see him.

He loved her.

He squeezed her hand. She glanced at him. She didn't ask if he was okay this time. She saw his expression and sensed his feelings in the air. As they pushed through the city, she wordlessly returned his feelings. He drank in her affection from the air.

He didn't know what Methis would say or if he could be believed, but he was in love with the person who held his hand. He focused on that as he pulled his shoulders back. He was ready for whatever Methis could do to him. He'd survived him once, and he could do it again.

Leisa led Remin to a healer's building on the other far side of the Sprawl. She spoke to the healer and then they walked again. Remin couldn't feel the ache in his muscles now; he was too energetic. Leisa took his hand again and walked to another healer's building. After another short conversation, she gestured for him to come over.

She stepped into the doorway, blocking his entrance.

"You can't hurt him, no matter what he said," Leisa said.

"Okay," Remin said.

"Rem, really. If you hurt him, you'll be charged for attacking an exile and inciting violence," Leisa said.

Remin looked at her unblinking. He hadn't thought about the time he'd been hit since it had happened. He pushed the thoughts from his head and nodded.

"I won't do anything that would take me from you," Remin said.

Leisa stepped out of the doorway, allowing him entrance into the building. "Middle left," she said.

He stepped over the threshold of the newly built, forever wet building. Memories flooded his head from when he'd woken up in such a building as he pulled open the curtain of the middle-left room. He looked into the eyes of the spymaster who'd betrayed him. Methis sat up, a cup of water in his hand.

"Methis," he said.

"Farin," Methis said, as he stared wide-eyed.

"It's Remin now," Remin said.

"I was told I should be Ulyss now, but I refused, I was Methis there, and I am Methis here. My name is who I am," Methis said, placing the cup on the small table beside him.

Remin leaned against the wall. A drip from the roof tapped on his shoulder, but he remained.

"So you've seen me. What now?" Methis said.

"Is she alive?" Remin said.

"She was when I left. The castle guards betrayed me just like they did you. Does that make you happy?" Methis said, his tone dripping with bitterness and malice.

"Yes," Remin said. "I'm glad she's alive and on the throne where she belongs. How did she do it?"

"I changed the law to let the wingless live with us," Methis said. Remin laughed and Methis scowled.

"Sorry," Remin said.

"If you're going to kill me, just do it. I'd rather that than this conversation," Methis said.

"Unfortunate. I'm not here for that. I just want to know about my daughter," Remin said.

Methis sat up further and stared wordlessly at Remin.

"I wish you'd died in your fall. But I'm glad you lived to tell me about Kyra," Remin said.

"What happened to you?" Methis said.

"The same thing that will happen to you. The gift of a grounded perspective. Resurrection has a humbling effect. How did she turn your own guards against you?" Remin said.

Methis scoffed. "She turned my spymaster."

Remin laughed.

"That's beautiful," Remin said.

"Amazing," Methis said, his tone flat.

Remin never thought he'd enjoy a conversation with his spymaster. He couldn't believe what he was hearing. It couldn't be true. Remin stood upright again and tipped an imaginary hat.

"Whatever brought you here, it was poetic. Enjoy your new life in this soggy paradise," Remin said. He left the healer's hut to see Leisa waiting for him. She held out her hand.

"He spent his whole life in deceit. I expect he's unable to become honest now," Remin said.

"I heard," Leisa said. "It's still possible she's alive."

"At least I can dream she is," Remin said.

"Am I going to have to carry you home?" Leisa said.

Remin laughed. "I think I'll make it. Let's walk a little slower, though," he said.

Leisa started guiding him through the city. "If we walk too slow, we might meet sunrise," she said.

"I like watching the sunrise with you," Remin said.

Leisa laughed, but it was laboured, showing her tiredness. It was quite late.

"Thank you for coming with me," Remin said.

"I couldn't let you do this alone," Leisa said.

"The sincerity of your kindness is something I've never known," Remin said.

"How good does it feel to see the man who tried to kill you down here?" Leisa said.

"I can't articulate it," Remin said, smiling. Even if he hadn't worked a full day of labour, he wouldn't have found the words to describe his delight, and to have Methis lie so poorly added to his satisfaction.

"I thought he'd rule until he died," Remin said.

"You might find out one day how he got here," Leisa said.

"I'm surprised, but I don't care who exiled him," Remin said. "I'm just glad he's here."

It was bitter that the blood of Amaranthus was still broken. But a part of him didn't care about the Iewen at all now. He was an outlier without a calling, but he had the time to find it, and he could do so at Leisa's. He couldn't return to Daltay, and his daughter would never make it to him.

Remin needed to focus on what mattered most. His life going forward. And Leisa.

Versai

Temporary lights of luminescent animals and plants had been placed all around the castle. It still felt utterly alien, but walking the halls, Versai could see clearly. The undercity hadn't been fully checked yet. With light in hand, she led a group of soldiers to the hallowed underground.

She walked into Cthessa's chamber, gesturing to her right and left as her soldiers circled the Cthessa's garden. She walked slowly to the raised stone section where the Cthessa sat. The aftermath of Cthessa's death was immediately apparent.

"This must have been what they came for," Versai said. She looked across the garden bed to her soldiers on the other side. Like her, they stared wide-eyed and open jawed at the open bulb that had once been the Cthessa.

"Why would She'ehlarah do this?" one of her soldiers said.

"Unclear, but we've seen it firsthand," Versai said.

There was silence for a time until Versai re-established her priorities. She looked around the room to see all of the Aspects withered like husks. One of the King's Guard sat unmoving against the wall. She ran to him and checked what she already knew: Bren was dead.

The far door was open, leading to the tunnels and then out of the undercity. She thought the tunnels had been sealed. There were no footprints leading in or out, which meant they'd most likely come in from there. It was unlikely that anyone leaving through the bloodied halls would leave no footprints.

"You two, with me," she said, pointing at two of her soldiers. "And you four, continue to clear the undercity. Light it up and check every corner." She then turned and left the undercity with haste. It was sickening to see their Cthessa murdered. She couldn't even speculate on why a She'ehlarah would betray the Cthessa.

Versai knew the castle better than most. She pushed on a wall and took a far shorter route. She needed to get to the throne room immediately.

"I didn't know about that one," one of her soldiers said.

"You still don't," Versai said, looking behind her. Both soldiers nodded.

Versai stopped walking when she reached the throne room. Numerous mattresses had been brought in, and small curtains had been set up around them. It was a disturbing sight to see the room go from a place of power to one of hiding.

She walked right up to Guiyn, the oldest surviving brother, and bowed. He stopped his conversation and turned. He shooed the person he was speaking with away so that only he and Laur a short distance away could hear their conversation.

"Sire, forgive my interruption," Versai said.

Guiyn gestured for her to speak.

"My soldiers are searching the undercity now. There are still no signs of Tenro, Syriel, Mayala, Vira, Pame, Alura, or Raishy," she said.

"They why have you stopped searching?" Laur snapped, stepping forward.

"Silence, brother," Guiyn said, his tone calm.

"Cthessa is destroyed. The leaves of the bulb look like they've been torn open. We shouldn't make this information public," Versai said.

"That's why we're in darkness," Guiyn said.

"Yes, Sire," Versai said.

"I don't know what it means that the bulb was open," Guiyn said.

Versai remained silent. She could only guess what had happened. It seemed that someone had intentionally destroyed it, which confused her, as all of the attackers they'd killed had purple hair. It was beyond her understanding as to why She'ehlarah would destroy their greatest asset.

"Where is my spymaster?" Guiyn said.

"Missing," Versai said. "His second-in-command was found dead."

"Is there anywhere yet to search?" Guiyn said.

"Only the undercity. My soldiers have searched the city beyond the castle but have found none of the missing people. Bren was found dead in the undercity; it's possible he was alone there. Sire, the door to the seed chamber was open," Versai said.

Guiyn looked sideways at his brother and then stepped closer to Versai.

"How likely is it that they came for Cthessa?" Guiyn whispered.

"I wouldn't expect any She'ehlarah to attack Cthessa, but it looks like that was one of their goals," Versai said.

"Do you think the missing people could have been captured?" Guiyn whispered.

"I could not guess, Sire. Bloody footsteps are everywhere in the city," Versai whispered.

"Is it possible they escaped?" Guiyn whispered.

"Given the bloody state of the castle. I think that's most unlikely. No one in the city saw them pass through," Versai whispered.

"At least no one admits it," Guiyn whispered.

"Yes, Sire," Versai whispered.

"You said one of the King's Guard was in the undercity?" Guiyn whispered.

"Yes, he died there, Sire," Versai whispered.

"Have someone check the dragonfly roost and look for the Yurelle beetle. If was Tenro and Syriel escaped, they couldn't have gone on foot," Guiyn whispered.

"I will have someone check. But Sire, even if they're not on foot, their survival is most unlikely in the tangle. I wouldn't imagine they'd go into the wild," Versai whispered.

"I agree," Guiyn said.

"There is often more than one Yurelle beetle in the outer city, but the dragonflies should tell us a lot," Versai said.

"See to it now," Guiyn said.

"At once, Sire. Is there anything else you need of me?" Versai said.

"No, thank you, General," Guiyn said.

Versai bowed and then left the throne room to do as she had been instructed. She would go herself. If no one in the outer city had seen Tenro and Syriel, then people loyal to their king and queen would likely keep the secret.

Fiare

Fiare sat at the back of the Senate playing with the strings on the front of her otherwise simple shirt. She brushed down her pants with a half skirt and looked across the room to Avena, and then looked at Olianna in the literally and politically highest seat in the room.

Only one in this room had a bigger stake in this conversation than Fiare, but she was just grateful to have been invited to a private Senate meeting. Fiare sat between her guards Oryza and Sativa, but she didn't feel safe. Olianna was about to tell the Malarmha senate that Velwrith had been attacked.

"Silence, please," Olianna said. The room's low chatter ended immediately. "We're here to discuss some chilling news of an attack on the Velwrith three days ago."

Her words were met with gasps and shouts. "We could be next," someone near Fiare shouted. Numerous eyes landed on Fiare as they soon looked around the room and then eventually back to Olianna when she spoke again.

"We have been informed by King Guiyn that this was an attempted coup. King Tenro and Queen Syriel are missing. King Guiyn has assured us that our agreements will all remain in force," Olianna said.

Fiare thought about her beloved cousin who'd been like a brother to her. And Syriel, who she'd only just met, but admired greatly. She looked around the room at all the angry, scared faces.

"How do we know it wasn't Guiyn who attacked to kill Syriel?" someone said.

"Malarmha will not be jumping to any conclusions. That is not our way," Chancellor Echi said.

"King Guiyn asked for us to send a diplomat to Velwrith to discuss the situation," Olianna said.

"We should cut all ties. Their danger is their own doing," someone said.

"Anyone you send won't come back," someone else said.

"Send the She'ehlarah princess," someone else said.

Fiare looked at them directly. Like the others, they looked scared. They were more similar than they realised. The She'ehlarah and Yurelle ultimately wanted security. They saw each other as a threat because their goals were so different, but their goals didn't differ as much as they all thought. If only they knew that.

In that chaotic and loud moment as others spoke their fears aloud, Fiare thought that even the Iewen in their brutality just wanted to be safe. That's why the Fanatic Prince had murdered so many, after all. They all just wanted to live. It should have been obvious to all, but living so separated, Fiare had never seen how hard the Yurelle fought to live.

She'd never thought that what the Iewen had done was for the same reason instead of, as most She'ehlarah thought, because the Fanatic Prince was crazed. Or perhaps her imagination was getting carried away.

She was so disconnected from Velwrith that none of this seemed real. Her father and sister were dead and she'd probably never go to their funeral. Her waking nightmare was likely the delight of people in this room. She couldn't think like that. They just didn't know how similar they were. She reminded herself of how many conclusions she'd jumped to before she'd come here.

"We need to maintain our agreements with the She'ehlarah at all costs. We rely on their trade," someone said.

"She's right! The Iewen were crippled when their trade agreements broke down after Prince Zona was killed," someone else said.

Fiare grimaced. She'd known it was going to be difficult, but she had no idea how unprepared she was for this meeting. She went to stand to leave.

"Wait, please, Princess," Oryza said.

Fiare looked at her guard with wide eyes.

"Forgive me, but I'd like to know what they decide," Oryza said.

Fiare stayed in her seat, but she, alike Oryza acted inappropriate as Fiare took his hand. She realised how inappropriate it was when she did it and let his hand go again. But Oryza took her hand, and Sativa took her other hand. Fiare looked at Sativa with as much shock as she had at Oryza.

"We're not in Velwrith anymore. The social rules are different here," Sativa said, her voice calm.

Fiare looked from one to the other again. "They're going to vote to send me to Velwrith," she said.

"We'll be with you," Oryza said.

"I don't know if I can go back," Fiare said.

"You'll never forgive yourself if you don't attend your father's funeral," Sativa said.

She could hardly believe how her guards were acting. They were all regarded as exceptional Dragonriders, yet they were talking like Yurelle citizens.

"The Yurelle have rubbed off on the both of you," Fiare said.

"I'm proud of it," Oryza said.

"Sometimes you need to experience something to understand it," Sativa said.

Fiare was utterly baffled, but she smiled. They were right. She had to go home, no matter if she was sent on diplomatic business or not. Despite the danger, she needed to see her father buried. The death of her father wasn't real. It didn't seem possible.

He'd been such a monument in her life. They'd been close, but it was more than that. Amer was a constant force that kept her together. She wanted to avoid his funeral so she could pretend he wasn't dead, but he was, and she needed to see him buried. She needed to bury her past.

She looked across the chamber to Avena. Avena was looking back at her. She had no idea if Avena would go with her, but she wanted to come to Velwrith. And she didn't care who knew they were together anymore. *Everything* was different now, and there was no turning back.

CHAPTER 10

THE WEIGHT OF A GLASS SYMBOL

Vujet

Reia's house was small and wooden. It seemed bizarre for one of the most powerful people in the kingdom to have such a disappointing home. She likely had another, but even still it seemed cruel. Reia would prefer it that way, he was sure. It was incredibly dark at the bottom of the tree, but more so when the day's light had departed.

The bottom of the tree was like another world. If there were secrets down below, Vujet would not be surprised. He leaned against a wall of the house. The last few days had been some of the best of his life. Kyra had leaned on him more than before, and she'd been grateful for his help and his voice. He'd never been so important to his kingdom. He hoped the foreign crisis would continue for many reasons, but above all because Kyra needed him. The kingdom needed him.

Reia flew to her house far later than she'd promised.

"Sorry, Vujet," she said.

"Unnecessary," Vujet said.

"Even still," Reia said.

"You have far more work to do than me at the moment," Vujet said.

"Come inside," Reia said, walking past him into her house.

Vujet followed her inside. Reia went from room to room, checking to make sure it was empty. Vujet seated himself at her small dining table. After a moment, Reia reappeared and sat at the table with him.

"My house is unguarded, but has no hiding places. I searched the house a moment ago, and I wanted to ensure we were alone in here," Reia said.

"I'm grateful you're so thorough; I too circled outside the house. Always a pleasure to see a fellow professional at work," Vujet said.

"Both of us work in secret at times, but we are very different professionals," Reia said with a smile. Vujet gestured to her, as if pointing to her statement.

"I have some exciting news for you to tell our queen," Reia said.

Vujet smiled.

"Velwrith was attacked from within," Reia said.

Vujet was seldom shocked, but today was an exception. It was the most likely probability, but it was so beneficial for the Iewen that it felt too good to be true. It was poetic. Embracing another colony to get stronger had only weakened them. That's why the Iewen were strong: Iewen trusted only Iewen. It was a bizarre thought to have while looking at Reia. Her purple hair and wings didn't define her loyalties, though. She was an exception. She was Iewen.

"We should advise our queen to attack," Vujet said.

"Agreed," Reia said, letting slip a rare smile. Vujet smiled too.

There was a genuine possibility of destroying their biggest competition and most bitter enemy in their lifetime. They might even finally obliterate the abomination that twisted its tendrils throughout the entire wretched castle, and finally turn the nightmare into a dream.

There was silence as Vujet was sure Reia was enjoying the same thoughts. "You discovered it. You should tell her," he said.

Reia shook her head. "We all have parts to play, and you are a bigger influence on her. She's most likely to agree if you say it to her," she said.

Vujet respected Reia deeply, but even he was taken aback by her words. Her dedication to the Iewen might even rival his own, and he was willing to sacrifice even his legacy for his colony.

Vujet gave Reia a shallow bow. "You are a master of many things," he said.

Reia returned the gesture. "None of this would be possible if you hadn't saved and strengthened Kyra when no one else saw her as a queen," she said.

For the first time, Vujet felt Reia's feelings in the air between them. Her admiration and respect mixed with his.

"You shouldn't tell our queen immediately," Reia said.

"Right," Vujet said, standing. "It's an honour to work with you, Reia. Forgive my opinion of your predecessors, but Methis and Lyren have nothing near the strength of your legacy."

As he went to leave, he felt something strange in the air. He turned to face her again as the feeling departed. It was almost like Reia seemed to mourn them. Vujet wasn't sure which of them the feeling came from, but it was almost like family mourning a relative. But the moment he'd felt it, it was gone. Perhaps she'd intentionally shared that with him, or perhaps it was an accident from her guard being down.

Regardless of why Reia had shared it with him, or what connection she had with Methis or Lyren, Vujet had work to do. Vujet left Reia's house quickly. His queen would likely be concerned about war, so he had to be flawless in her delivery of the incredible news.

Fiare

Clad in practical Yurelle fashion, Fiare stood at the Yurelle hawk port early in the morning. She was so accustomed to short skirts with pants and loose shirts that she hadn't even thought to wear the far more feminine and oppressive She'ehlarah clothing collecting dust in her apartment. She was Yurelle, and she needed to look the part. She ran her hand over her neck to feel the end of her now-short hair.

"Stop fussing, you look incredible," Avena said.

Fiare looked over at her and softened her tense face. She knew they would send her, and they had. She didn't want to go. She desperately wanted to stay here.

"Hair grows back anyway," Avena said.

Fiare stopped worrying and focused on her girlfriend. "Are you sure you're ready to meet my uncle?" she asked.

"I was ready to meet your family when I first saw you in the market," Avena said.

Fiare sighed deeply. Avena was as good with her words as she was with her hands, but even Fiare hadn't expected such smoothness on such a rough day.

"Sorry, Senator Petal," Avena said.

"Petal?" Fiare said.

"You're from the orchid kingdom, and you're the one that got away. Like an autumn leaf. It was only a matter of time until you left. And because, you're a senator now," Avena said.

Fiare had resolved not to enjoy the day, yet she couldn't stop from smirking. Avena's lips curled as she looked away from Fiare. Fiare sighed. "Some people get all the natural talent," she said.

"Legacy of smooth talkers," Avena said.

"It shows," Fiare said.

It felt utterly bizarre to be a senator. It wasn't official just yet.

Olianna promised a big party when it was. Of course, that meant she needed to get through this day first, one step at a time. Even if she didn't get to be a senator, she was a Yurelle now.

"Princess Fiare, Senator Avena, this way, please," a hawk guard said, gesturing to a doorway that led outside of the great rock that housed Malarmha.

Fiare looked behind to see Sativa and Oryza behind her. Fiare hadn't openly flirted with Avena before, but she was confident both her guards had seen enough of Fiare and Avena together to have worked it out. Fiare was confident they knew that in the first moment she'd seen Avena. She had to remind herself that she wasn't She'ehlarah anymore. She wasn't subject to their outdated customs, and she didn't have to hide.

As she thought about home, her obligations and the pressure of the day returned to her. As they did, the turmoil of losing her father was pushed below the weight of the day that was to come. That was a mercy. It was easier to think of momentary discomfort than the loss of a father she hadn't gotten to properly say goodbye to.

The four travellers followed their guide into the open hawk port. One hawk, saddled, piloted, and calmed, waited at the port. Fiare gulped. She embarked first, followed by Avena and her two guards.

"Hold on. Take-off will be a bit rough," the pilot said.

He didn't give Fiare much time to react as the bird lifted quickly. He was not joking; the ascent was far shallower than the port in Velwrith. In what felt like an instant, the cracked, glass-sectioned rock of Malarmha left their view along with what felt like her stomach. Despite how badly she hadn't wanted to leave, she didn't feel sick; she felt excited. It would be good to close a chapter as long as she didn't think about her father and sister. It was a last visit so she would never have to return.

The only thing in Fiare's vision over the wing of the mighty hawk was green, too many different shades to count. Massive moss-covered trees towered over them like mountains. It was impossible not to marvel at the profoundly awe-inspiring world that they hid from. It was surreal that this forest was their home when they saw so little of it behind such thick walls.

Fiare looked over at Avena. If Fiare could capture any moment on canvas, it would be Avena's face in this moment. Avena's eyes were dotted with sparkles. She looked like an utter cliché, but she was so perfect that she simultaneously overcame a stereotype. Her delight was too extreme to be real, too magical to be fantasy. It filled Fiare's heart so much that it almost hurt. The surrounding verdancy was a blurred mess. All Fiare could see was Avena.

"Hold tight, landing coming," the pilot said.

His words snapped Fiare out of her stupor as reality flooded back instantly. She focused her attention forward and started making lists of her obligations. Firstly, she needed to establish that she was Yurelle now, to ensure she wasn't a threat if the violence had been a coup. Secondly, she needed to learn everything they knew about the attack. Thirdly, she needed to ensure she would attend the funeral for her family and others. The list went on even as the hawk landed at the Velwrith port.

"Thank you," Fiare said as she departed first. She heard Avena and then her two guards behind her. She didn't look behind her. All silliness and joy needed to be crushed. She had a vital obligation that she would fulfil flawlessly. Clad in masculine Yurelle fashion, with short hair, Princess Fiare walked, escorted by her two Dragonriders.

She walked down the stairs of the hawk port to see the halls lit with jars of luminous fluid. It was horrifying to see the castle so dark, but she reminded herself of her obligation. She walked the long halls she knew well, taking the most direct route to the throne room where her uncle now ruled.

Tenro

Tenro woke in Hye's clothing on what was expected to be another soggy day in the abandoned hollow. He was grateful for the discomfort because he was alive to feel it. He sat upright and looked around. An empty section of dented moss was beside him.

His sleepy casual morning turned serious in an instant. He stood and saw the back of Lon and Payon on watch at the entrance to the hollow and the other Dragonriders at rest. Hye slept a small distance from where Acasia was sleeping. No Syriel.

Tenro walked around a little and saw her on the other side of the Yurelle beetle. He saw part of her naked, half-covered body as she jolted. He rushed to her.

Between her legs was their emerging egg.

Tenro touched her shoulder gently, startling her. "Hi, love," he whispered. She looked at him wordlessly for a moment, and then back to the egg.

"I'm okay," she whispered. "It's not painful."

Tenro sighed in relief. "Don't rush it," he whispered, taking her hand. She squeezed his hand back as she continued to push their egg into the world.

"It's nearly here," she whispered.

Almost as she said that, the bottom of the egg appeared, and the pressure of her hand released.

"I'm fortunate it didn't hurt, but that was so horribly uncomfortable," she whispered, wiping the sweat from her brow.

"I can't imagine," Tenro said, sitting down next to her and staring at the egg.

"Do we have any spare cloth?" Syriel whispered.

Tenro got up immediately and took some rags from the beetle pouches. She pushed a little more, her body jolting in near convulsions until the egg was free of her.

He handed the cloth to her as he touched the still-wet egg. He'd never touched such a new egg. The protective coating was watery. He thought it would have been sticky. That was a fact that most males would never learn, as the egg was quickly washed by an attendant. Syriel wiped herself as she pulled her clothes back on.

"I was concerned it would hurt you, since I know it can if it's late," Tenro said. Syriel nodded weakly.

"Do you need to go back to sleep?" Tenro said.

"I couldn't," she said, picking up the soft egg.

It was so strange to see a soft egg when it was so vulnerable. Already it had started to harden so quickly it surprised him. It wouldn't harden enough for their child to hatch out here. It was far too wet. It would be more so in the Bloom.

Tenro cuddled her as they held their child together. Syriel looked utterly exhausted, but she looked at him with a smile as she leaned her weight on him.

"I hope he has your hair," Syriel said.

"I hope she has your wings," Tenro replied. As their voices started to rise, Tenro heard movement in the hollow. Hye stood over them, his eyes wide.

"It's a perfectly sized, unbroken egg," Tenro said.

"A little small, I think," Syriel said, her voice only a little louder than a whisper.

"Perhaps they'll be as short as you," Tenro said, with a slight laugh.

"No, I want your height," Syriel said.

Hye left as Syriel started humming to her child. Tenro knew he'd have to take the egg from her. A part of him wished that having the egg in her arms would make her change her mind, but he knew that the egg needed to be safe, and like she'd said, her hair and wings would give her away in Velwrith. He also knew that someone needed to stop Cthessa.

"When will you leave?" Syriel said.

Tenro exhaled. She must have read his mind. "Syriel …" he started.

"I need to think about it now. I've had my only moment. We need them to hatch more than anything, and we both know it. Their life is most important—more so than me being able to see them hatch," Syriel said.

She'd read his mind again. "I don't want to leave you," Tenro said.

"I don't want you to leave either, but you know we both have to do what we must. Let me fall asleep with them in my arms first. I don't think I could let you leave if I were awake," Syriel said.

"Syriel…" Tenro started.

"Please," Syriel said, looking directly at him. "Promise."

Tenro nodded. For one of the first times in his life, his eyes were clouded by tears.

"Don't. Don't cry, this moment is ours. The last time we might ever be together," Syriel said.

Tenro couldn't oblige that. He turned his face away from her. While still holding her he turned enough that she couldn't see his tears. He knew his reign would be difficult, but nothing had prepared him for this.

"I want to name them after my father," Syriel said, her voice barely audible.

"Then our baby will be called Var," Tenro said, keeping his broken voice as steady as possible.

Guiyn

Guiyn sat on the stone throne in the newly established light of the throne room. The light was patchy. There was no comparison to the light Cthessa had given them before her death, but it was something. He adjusted the crown on his head as Fiare entered the throne room.

She looked so unlike herself that he hardly recognised her. She wore a short skirt and pants. Guiyn had never seen a female wear such clothing save for the day the Yurelle family walked the castle halls, the day he'd told his brother they needed to break their arrangement with the Yurelle. She walked with a Yurelle female that Guiyn had never met. What a meeting this was about to be.

She was one of many who filled the throne room this day. He'd sent a letter to her requesting her attendance, but like to all in the room, he hadn't told them why, not honestly. In his letters and messages, he'd said it was for his coronation.

Fiare was here so the Yurelle could hear from a firsthand witness of what had happened today. There were a few more guests whom Guiyn needed to wait on, so he leaned over to his partner who sat in the chair beside the throne.

"You're sure we're making the right decision?" he whispered.

"We already made the choice when we made the deal with him," Wyma said.

"You've practiced to run?" Guiyn said.

"Love, I was ready well before he changed the day," Wyma said.

Guiyn sat upright in his throne again. He was nervous. He was within his rights for all that was before him, but even he knew things could get out of hand quickly. His children hadn't been found, and nor had Tenro or Syriel. There was a beetle in the outer city, but all the dragonflies had been released. Every one of them was missing.

By Amer's ruling, both Tenro and Syriel had a more legitimate claim to the throne than his, and it was possible that he had no heir. His choice could undermine the already fragile security of the kingdom, but it needed to be done for him to ever be safe. He knew that. The throne room was full enough. He stood.

"I asked you all here on false pretences. You were all asked here for different reasons, but none of them were true," Guiyn said.

The guests in the throne room reacted loudly, but he'd expected that. Guards silencing the crowd with gestures and quiet words. Guiyn took a patch from his pouch and threw it into the middle of the throne room floor.

"For anyone who wants to look, this is my family crest. Guards, seize Laur and Siah," Guiyn said.

There was silence following his order, but after a time, a shouting Laur and his terrified partner were brought before him.

"Some of the commanders of the army wore this symbol on their arm as they slaughtered the innocent people in this very castle and killed Cthessa. These soldiers were the private army of my own brother," Guiyn said.

He looked at his shouting brother, who looked at him with a scowl that was more aggressive than Guiyn had ever seen. "You armed them!" Laur yelled.

"Bitter words," Guiyn said. "It was well known where he kept his army, and yet those tents are empty now. And with this crest on the ground, found on your soldiers, your foolish choices have guided you here," Guiyn said.

"You did this!" Laur yelled.

"Gag him," Guiyn said calmly. He watched as the gathered guests started getting louder and louder.

"He didn't give anyone in this castle a chance of survival, so I give all of you the choice. Should we kill or spare him? He whose order slaughtered those behind these walls of the castle? Whose order killed

Cthessa?" Guiyn asked. He was grateful that his guards couldn't silence the crowd, as their shouts had already answered the question.

"Then let it be decided, for the first and last betrayal of a She'ehlarah royal of his own family. General," Guiyn said, gesturing to Versai.

As the crowd's shouting grew louder, Versai didn't move. Guiyn looked over the crowd to see that their anger was still firmly fixed on Laur. Fiare looked even more out of place, as unlike the others, she wasn't shouting. Good. Hopefully she would stay gone.

Guiyn opened his mouth to issue the command again, but he didn't need to. The guards holding Laur drew their weapons and ended his life in the middle of the throne room. The guards holding Siah abruptly ended her life also. That was a welcome surprise. Guiyn smiled and seated himself on his throne.

"We see justice for all our fallen today," Guiyn said.

He looked at Wyma. She sat up in her chair and looked like the proper queen she was. She looked less mad that he'd left her now. She wanted to see them dead almost more than he had, and he'd given their deaths to her.

"We will bury all of our fallen this night and move on from this, our most brutal moment in history. And together, we'll move toward a long and peaceful future," Guiyn said.

The crowd cheered as the bodies of Laur and Siah were dragged from the throne room.

Remin

Hald's central dais was half-enclosed by a vined roof. The quality of construction was nothing like that of the rest of the city. It looked like a city within a city. Phelendra sat on her flowered throne as she listened to the charges of the accused.

"Are you sure you want to be here for this?" Leisa said.

"I need to know," Remin said.

Remin's attention wavered as a guard spoke about the young, wingless, green-haired female kneeling before the queen. Remin knew the charges; she'd attacked someone in the city. He looked around the gathered crown for Gerathen, as he hadn't seen him in a while. His eyes stopped when he saw Lshar. They looked back at Remin.

Remin had wanted to wave, but there was great darkness in Lshar's face. He'd never seen them with anything but a bright disposition. Remin knew that the accused was about to die, but she'd broken their most fundamental rules. So why did Lshar look so troubled?

Lshar turned their attention back to the dais, and Remin continued to attempt solving the puzzle of their disposition. Remin knew a lot of people disagreed with laws of their own city. But the accused had acted knowing the law. And then it hit him: perhaps he knew the accused.

Remin looked back to the accused and tried to remember. If he'd been the one to exile her, then the exchange he'd just had with Lshar would have been far more awful than he realised. Remin didn't recognise her. He turned to Leisa.

"Who exiled her?" Remin said.

"Methis," Leisa said.

"Why?" Remin said.

"You know Methis. Do you want to know why?" Leisa said.

"Please," Remin said.

"She was one of his consorts. I don't want to say more," Leisa said.

Remin could only imagine what small thing she'd done to get sentenced to exile. It's possible she hadn't even come to him willingly. Perhaps she didn't have desire for him, or perhaps she'd given a cracked egg. He knew this would be tough, but this was even worse than he thought.

"Stay if you want to. I'll meet you at home," Remin said, turning.

"Wait," Leisa said, following him. They walked away from the centre of the city together.

"I was only there because I knew you'd need support," Leisa said. "But from what Methis did to you, I think he should have been an exception to our law."

Behind them the crowd roared. "Not executed?" someone near the couple yelled.

Remin turned and rushed back through the crowd. The female was sobbing, kissing the feet of the queen.

Leisa pushed up next to him.

"There has never been anything but execution for attacking an exile in all of our history," Leisa said.

Queen Phelendra locked eyes with Remin for a moment, as she then stood and helped the female to her feet. Remin's jaw dropped.

"Why this one?" Leisa said, looking at members of the crowd.

"What's the punishment?" Remin said.

"A life of service," someone close said.

Remin took Leisa's hand and pulled her back though the crowd.

"Again? Come on, exile!" someone complained as he pushed past them for a third time.

"You're hurting me," Leisa said.

"I'm so sorry," Remin said, releasing her wrist. "I didn't want to be in a crowd. If the punishment is lowered, do you think I could be attacked again?"

Leisa looked at him with wide eyes. In her expression he saw it was possible.

"Why her?" Remin said.

Leisa shook her head.

"Oh, exiled by not a king," someone in the crowd said.

"So anyone the spymaster exiled has different rules?" another said.

"New era new rules," someone else said.

"Well, there's a wingless queen on the throne," someone else said.

Remin tapped the yellow-haired Ptery on the arm.

"Did you say wingless queen?" Remin asked.

"I don't know all of it, but that's what my friend said the Iewen she exiled said," they replied.

Remin and Leisa looked at each other.

"Back to the healing huts?" Leisa said. Remin moved away from the crowd as to no longer hear them.

"Do you think Methis was telling the truth?" Leisa said.

"Yes, but it doesn't matter. I'm down here," Remin said.

He didn't know how to feel about Methis being honest, but he was grateful his daughter was alive. He wouldn't wish to see her because that would mean she'd end up here. But she lived. The legacy of Amaranthus was unbroken. He'd gone back and forth so many times that he didn't know how to feel about that now, but he knew how he felt about his daughter being alive. He breathed a sigh of relief.

"Remin, are you okay?" Leisa said.

"I am. I can't do anything about it," Remin said.

"But you're allowed to feel," Leisa.

"I do. I'm glad. I'm so glad. But I'll never see her again. She's effectively dead to me. I just never knew it until I realised she was alive," Remin said.

"You might feel differently about it in a few days," Leisa said.

"Maybe. Only time will tell. Right now, I don' know what to feel," Remin said.

"That's okay, too," Leisa said, smiling.

Remin smiled back, but even he felt that his eyes didn't smile. She was right. He needed time to work out how he felt about it.

Fiare

"I'm sorry I dragged you here," Fiare whispered, pushing out of the throne room.

The pair rounded the corner with Fiare's guards right behind. Fiare opened the door to a study she hoped was empty. It was. Her guards followed her in.

"It's not safe here today," Oryza said.

"This isn't your fault," Avena said. "In everything I know and you described about your people, this is …"

"These aren't my people," Fiare said. "Not even the people I left."

"I know I encouraged you to be at your father and sister's funeral, but it might not be safe to stay," Avena said.

Fiare nodded. "Can we leave?" she asked.

"We should. We can come back when things calm down," Sativa said.

"I don't want to come back," Fiare said.

"We don't have to. You're our charge, and we stay with you, wherever that is," Oryza said.

"Malarmha," Fiare said.

Both of her guards nodded as they led the way out of the small room to the hawk port. They passed enough guards that it would be obvious that they left.

Fiare was glad she had somewhere else to go. She felt horrible for her cousins; seeing the darkened castle was too much to bear. She couldn't imagine Velwrith without Cthessa. They should have told her everything. Had they done so, she most likely wouldn't have come, but she deserved to know.

It was all an incredible nightmare. She didn't even know everyone who had been killed or lost in the fight. She hadn't seen her sisters. She pushed it from her mind. She'd said it already: these were not her people. And most important, she couldn't save them.

Tenro

She slept like someone without any concern for the future. Tenro knew better than her face showed. They'd known each other for such a short time, but he knew her so well. The doubt he felt about her involvement in the freeing of Cthessa didn't matter.

So little mattered but her and the egg in her arms. He gently lifted her arms from around the egg, and for the first time he held the egg himself. He only saw it for a moment before Lon helped him cover it in cloth. She strapped it gently to his chest. Tenro then wordlessly left the hollow.

He climbed onto the back of a snaking gecko with his three Dragonriders in the sky above him, holding his egg securely, but gently. He couldn't imagine his future, let alone the next few days. He tore his thoughts from the exhausted face of his wife as he left her sleeping in the hollow where she'd given him what was likely to be his only child.

He looked back into the hollow as the gecko moved silently forward. He needed to endure. He needed to survive. His kingdom and the next generation in his arms needed him to survive for her and for the tiny cloth-wrapped egg in his arms.

A growing discomfort rose in him. He remembered speaking with Leatti, who'd said something about an egg. He was too irritated to remember. He wished he hadn't thought her words to be rambling. What else did she say? Something about leaving.

"When she comes to me…" Leatti had said.

Was she rambling? It seemed too accurate. Cthessa had seen this. Had she planned it? Tenro shuffled in his seat. He couldn't lose sight of what mattered most. Var, the egg. His child needed him, and he couldn't abandon them. He had no choice.

Reia

Since Kyra had been queen, no one had idly stumbled into the council room; each member of the queen's council was on time or early. Reia watched as the room filled up quickly. Vujet sat beside Kyra here as he did in life.

"Thank you as always for coming," Kyra said, standing.

She hadn't stood before. That was a nice touch. Some of the councillors started to stand.

"Please, stay seated," Kyra said, gesturing for them to sit back down, which they did.

"I stand because of the weight of what I am about to say. I want this moment in history to be delivered while standing. Velwrith was attacked—not by us, but from within. I want to spend these next hours planning an attack against them, with Vujet as general leading our forces," Kyra said.

The council was silent. Reia breathed in the feeling in the air. At first there was confusion, but matched to the energy of Kyra's confidence came excitement, and then anger. A crescendo of rage flooded the small room.

It was perfume to Reia.

She shared their rage. At last She'ehlarah would feel it too, not just read about the bloody path cut by Amaranthus.

"War at last?" Ha'ttri said, standing.

"We need to ask our citizens if they are prepared for this, Highness," Eugh said.

"We don't need to waste a second asking. We all know the answer. We all want that abomination obliterated. But Highness, are we ready to face the full might of the She'ehlarah and the Yurelle?" Bain said.

"If things get too dangerous, we ensure that the She'ehlarah are crippled and then withdraw to the safety of Daltay," Kimure said.

"Their alliance was of trade. We should wait for a moment to see if they leave the She'eh to their demise or if they send troops to help them," Ha'ttri said, sitting down again.

"We need time to train and outfit our army. Without the Yurelle chitin trade, we'll have to make their armour from bone. The loss of trade has put us on a backfoot, but likely far less so than a castle that was attacked," Alren said.

"How long do we need to wait?" Kyra said, sitting back in the small throne.

"We'll take whatever time the armouring takes to gather more information on the situation," Reia said.

Kyra smiled at Reia.

"Give us only weeks," Alren said.

"Which is not long enough for the Yurelle beetles to reinforce the castle. They can't fly them; they'd have to cut a path," Kimure said.

Kyra put her hands together. "Well then, let's sort out the details," she said.

Reia watched her with pride. She and Vujet had helped make her, and her confidence was perfect. She wasn't as true an Iewen as Methis, but unlike him, she'd serve the crown. She looked at Vujet, who mirrored Reia's expression. The dream of a future without the She'ehlarah was looking more and more possible.

Syriel

She woke up to a much emptier hollow, and with empty arms. She had thought it would make it easier, but every fibre in her being wanted to run after them. She couldn't even if she'd wanted to. It felt like many seasons of her life had been ripped out of her, just as roughly as her egg had been torn from the shelter of her arms. She felt hollow, cut open.

She screamed in silence as her eyes flooded with tears, hidden away in a soggy hollow, deep into the deadly tangle. She felt lesser, but she knew a part of her would live on.

Syriel felt armoured arms wrap around her. She turned to see a forlorn-looking Acasia holding her. Syriel cried against her armoured chest, finally making her pain audible.

Hye touched his hand to her arm. "We'll make it worth it, my queen," he said.

She was surprised to see him. "I thought you'd leave," Syriel whispered.

"To the end, Majesty. Acasia, you and I," Hye said.

"You'll see your child again," Acasia said. "In a safer era that you will create with Tenro."

Syriel wanted to believe them, but all that she felt was absence. She needed to stop the Great Plant. She needed to already be travelling through the deadly tangle, but all she wanted was to say goodbye to Tenro. It was almost impossibly hard to handle having him leave without saying goodbye. She was wrong. She was wrong about her whole life, and the extent of her error echoed through every event that had brought her here. After a time, Hye joined the little huddle.

"We *will* make it worth it," Hye said.